DRAXTON: CHILDREN OF ANZULLA, PART ONE

FINDING LOVE IN THE WORLD OF TITANS

CHILDREN OF ANZULLA
BOOK ONE

KASHEL CHAR

Title: Draxton: Children of Anzulla, Part One. Finding Love in the World of Titans.

Amazon Large Print Paperback: ISBN: 979-8-272744-98-2

Amazon Hardcover: ISBN: 979-8-242018-18-1

D2D Electronic ISBN: 978-1-998713-20-2

D2D Paperback ISBN: 978-1-998713-21-9

Publisher: Koda Calmz Publishing

Editors: Teresa Fornoff, Anita Ford

CONTENTS

DEAR READER/LISTENER

I HOPE YOU ENJOY THE TUMBLE WITH Draxton and Kellan, but before you do, I suggest reading or listening to my New Beginnings Trilogy to enjoy Draxton and Kellan's story fully.

You can find my suggested reading order on my website at https://kashelchar.com/timeline

My books and audiobooks are available at all the major outlets, including libraries.

THANK YOU FOR YOUR SUPPORT AND REVIEWS.

LOVE TO ALL CREATURES.
Kashel Char.

WARNING

control or assume responsibility for author or third-party websites, blogs, critiques, or their content.

This story contains speculative, twisted versions of history, rescue missions, explicit graphic depictions, and crude language unsuitable for young or sensitive readers or anyone offended by gay sex.

One of the main characters is on the autism spectrum, and people sensitive to this character type may find certain situations triggering.

REFERENCE MAPS
THE RISING STAR CAVE SYSTEM
IN THE CRADLE OF MANKIND

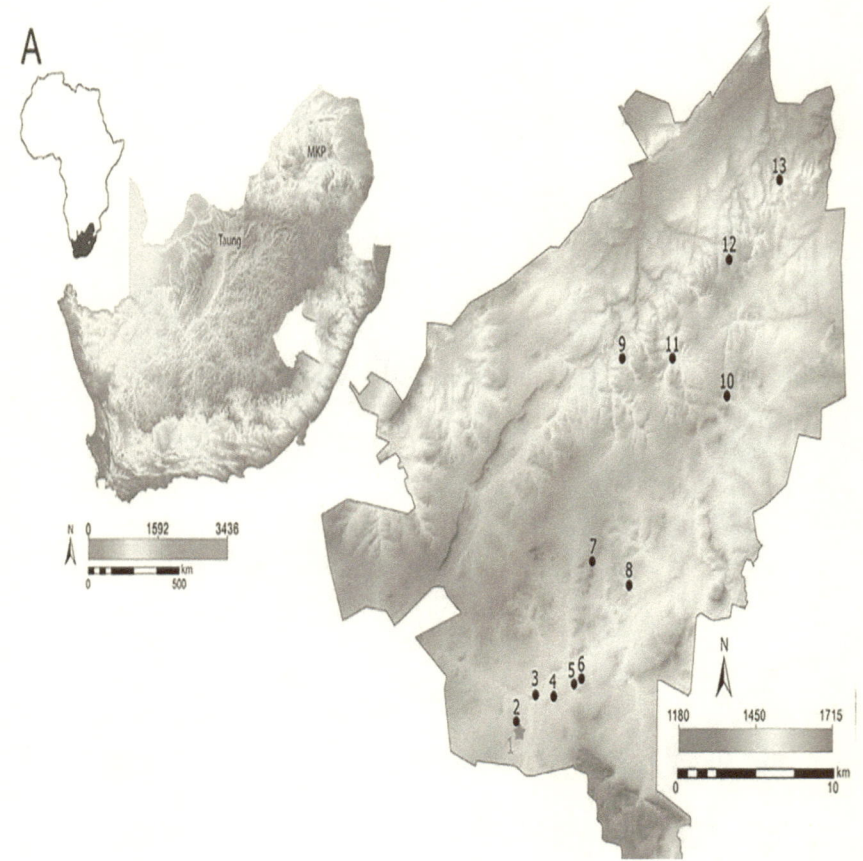

A) Map of South Africa showing the location of the Cradle and two satellite sites of Makapansgat Lime-works (MKP) and Taung. B) Inset showing the key fossil-bearing sites in the Cradle: 1) Bolt's Farm 2) Rising Star 3) Swartkrans 4) Sterkfontein 5) Cooper's 6) Kromdraai 7) Drimolen 8) Plover's Lake 9) Gladysvale 10) Malapa 11) Motsetse 12) Haasgat and 13) Gondolin. Elevation data made available from

Jarvis et al. 2008, figure adapted from Edwards et al. (2019)

Source: Reconstructing the depositional history and age of fossil-bearing palaeokarst: A multidisciplinary example from the terminal Pliocene Aves Cave Complex, Bolt's farm, South Africa - Scientific Figure on ResearchGate. Available from: https://www.researchgate.net/figure/A-Map-of-South-Africa-showing-location-of-the-Cradle-and-two-satellite-sites-of_fig1_347783213 [accessed 2 Jan 2025]

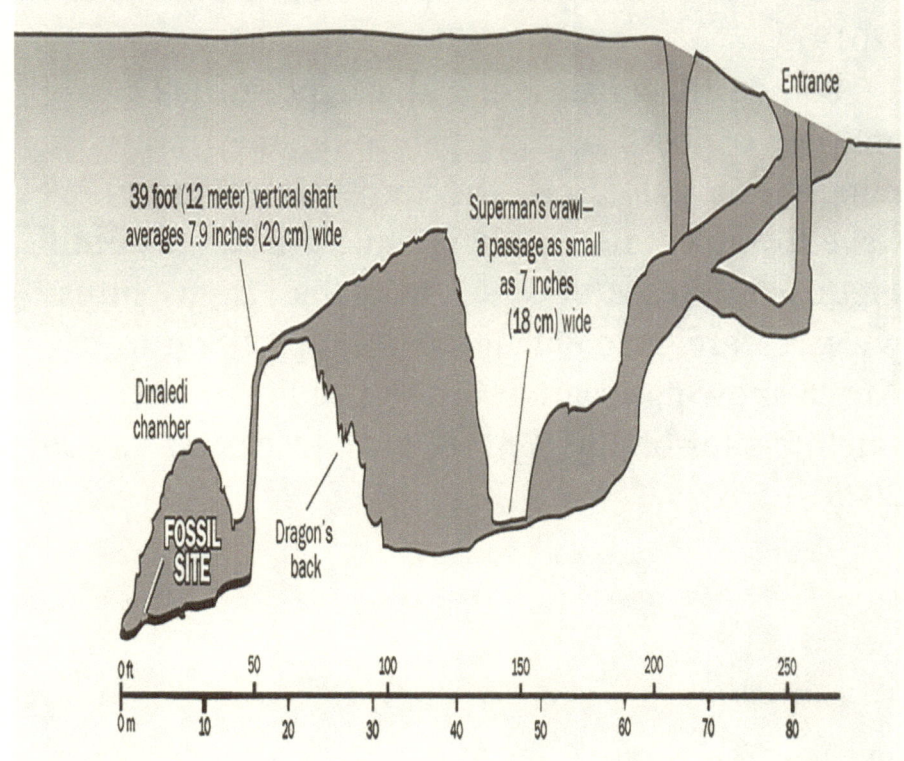

The Rising Star Cave System, showing access to the Dinaledi chamber.
Credit: Illustration by Pat Linse, based on image by National Graphic.)

The Rising Star Cave System in the Cradle of Mankind, showing access to the Dinaledi Chamber. (Credit: Illustration by Pat Linse, based on image by *National Geographic*.)

Source: Big news on Homo naledi: more fossils and a surprising young age by Nathan H. Lents, Ph.D.

CHAPTER 1
DRAXTON
THE CRADLE OF MANKIND

PRESENT DAY
South Africa

With a disorienting jolt, the *neeb-neeb-neeb* of my alarm ripped me from my dreams. *Holy shit!* I startled awake and jumped to get ready. "The door!" *I must find the door or lose all my grandfather's credibility.* "Today's our last day," I groaned out loud.

Tobias reprimanded me last night. He told me to stop searching and start packing up today. So, I set my alarm extra early to sneak back inside the caves. It was now two hours after midnight, still dark outside, and the stifling hot January night air had just cooled down before the sun began to bake the caravan into a furnace once more.

The summer chorus of insects that usually

soothed me pushed me to move faster. Each irritating, repetitive *krrrrr-krrrrr-krrrrr* the insects produced outside sounded like a persistent *tick-tick-tick* as I rushed to beat the clock. It grated on my nerves, so I threw my favorite long-sleeve shirt over my head, popped my earbuds in, and pressed play on my phone. The rhythmic *thump-thump-thump* of Armin van Buuren's latest song started and instantly lowered my anxiety while lifting my mood. I switched on the small gas stove to boil some water, then got dressed, brushed my teeth, skipped shaving, and put on my boots. For breakfast, I made myself an extra sweet cup of coffee, grabbed a cold vetkoek, smeared it thick with Marmite, and left to greet my day. We had run out of time, with the thunderstorms bringing six hundred and fifty millimeters of rain that halted my operation last week. So, yes, I wanted to go inside one last time.

No camp lights in sight. No one was up yet. Good. When I reached the entrance to the cave, I gulped the last of my coffee, shoved the whole vetkoek into my mouth, and started to put on my Gonzo Guano seat harness. My denim shorts were still damp in the crotch. Typically, they dry overnight, but I'd only managed two hours of sleep. A little chafing and heat rash in the groin were the least of my concerns today. We'd been digging in this area for two years with no results. Sweet blue fuck all. Sure, there were plenty of skulls and bones from what they claimed was a graveyard, but not what we were searching for. First of all, I was a speleologist, a cave archaeologist, but my field of interest has taken a detour I didn't like to brag about. Those who knew what I was looking for believed me, and those who don't…Well, I knew they would laugh, and that was why I would never trust or share my secrets with them. Let them be content with their three hundred fifty-five-thousand-year-old Homo naledi. The species name, naledi in Sesotho, meant star, hence the Rising Star Cave system.

It was also where the *Stardoor* was, according to my grandfather's map. I believed the door opened into another time or reality. It had to be there!

I'd also discovered evidence of a massive global fire that scorched the Earth's surface around twenty thousand years ago. This fire was likely triggered by an EMP storm, leading to worldwide lightning storms that devastated the grasslands and transformed the crust into rivers of molten rock, shaping the surface into what we see it today. We know there are ancient civilizations that date back much further than Homo naledi. Tobias and I had scanned this belt of fifteen cave systems that form the Cradle of Mankind. Surely the entrance they used should be there as well. If I could find that entrance, I could demonstrate that modern humans and other ancient advanced species, like winged creatures, occupied that area for centuries before Homo naledi left their sick there. I believed that was not a burial place but rather the threshold to the home of advanced races. They brought their sick and dying because they knew someone on the other side could heal them or, better yet, transport them to another world or time. All I needed to do was find that damned door.

I traced my fingers over the geometric shapes discovered in 2023. They matched the cuneiform wall etchings my great-grandfather transcribed in 1922, over a century ago. Those patterns of squares, triangles, crosses, and ladder shapes were also found deeper within this cave system.

Shaking my head, I clucked my tongue and scanned the wall by moving from side to side as I slowly descended into the tight space. The low hum of a male voice and flickering light caught my attention, prompting me to look up. Someone was waving a torch down the shaft. I removed my earbuds and, yes, damn it, Tobias was calling me from above.

"Draxton, do you want to take a break? You've been gnashing your teeth and talking to yourself for the past hour, and I'm sick of listening to you."

"Fuck off!" I shouted, but he didn't respond. I

couldn't see him, but I could tell from the volume of his voice how far above me he was. "So, you've decided to get up early, too?"

"Yes, I knew you would pull a trick like this. It's our last day. Our approval expires at midnight."

Our voices echoed up and down the tunnels. I had to wait a moment for it to die down before speaking again. "I know! Now kindly fuck off and go get us that extension." I adjusted myself so I could slide back and look up. The familiar warm feeling of seeing my best friend made me smile.

He waved his hands and pointed. "I'm not going back into Johannesburg. I've been to the geosciences offices every bloody day for the last week. The potholes alone are enough of a deterrent. Accept it, the permit will not get renewed. It's a waste of time. I'd rather use the time to take as many scans as possible. You might get lucky. Why don't you go?"

Frustration ignited that short fuse in me. "Damn it, Tobias!" I lifted my arms and then slipped my whole body out of the narrow crack. "Okay, okay! I'm not wasting time arguing. Come down and make yourself useful. I will fucking go!" I said, irritated. "It took those wannabe archeologists months to remove those bones, and now that we have access, our permit is expiring—their precious skeletons and stupid red tape. I know the door is here. I fucking know it!" I murmured to myself, not to Tobias, because he'd heard it all before. Several times a day. I waved my arm up and down, our signal for "stand ready, I'm coming up."

"If it were here, we would have found it by now. We may have overlooked it and need to start over from the beginning." Tobias stood with his hands on his hips, waiting for me.

"How can we do that if we're not allowed to search?" I reattached another cable I had used earlier to descend, then swung back, found my footing, and wiped my brow with the back of my hand. Tobias cranked the wheel to hoist me up. My back was killing me, and Tobias was right. We needed a miracle. I've been saying that for two years, and nothing has changed. I'd found one clue on the map with hidden text that pinpointed the Cradle of Mankind, in South Africa.

"I can feel it. We are close. So, so very close." When I stepped out of the chamber, Tobias pushed me to the side so I could stand next to him. He handed me the remote. I pressed the button to shorten the cable, then unclipped it. Tobias stood there, arms folded, shaking his head at me. I made sure the light from my helmet blinded him because I was spiteful and passive-aggressive like that. Once I'd climbed out of my harness, I tossed it and the tools still attached to it onto our worktable, removed my shirt to wring out the sweat, and walked over to a trough of fresh rainwater where I scooped a cup and drank the refreshing liquid. After drinking three more cups, I tipped one over my head to wash the dust and sweat off my body. The muscles in my back rippled and contracted as I cooled, and I let out a cry of frustration.

"I'm going to pack up," Tobias said.

"Absolutely not. I'll go and demand an extension myself. Please work the chimney at level WU1485. Push a camera down that groove we identified in the photos last night. It's not just a crack. I'm telling you, it's too perfectly long to be merely a crack. Break it open if you need to. Please, do that for me. If I'm denied today, at least we'll have those photos to work with until we can get permission to go back inside."

"Draxton, we've worked that chamber many times before, and I assure you it's only a crack. It's too narrow for anything except maybe an ant or a spider carrying an ant in there. I'm one hundred percent sure the door isn't there, not the house-sized one you described," Tobias said, and I grunted a warning not to patronize me today.

He sighed. "I will indulge you. I'll go deeper and take more lateral scans. National Geographic withdrew its funding, and the university instructed its researchers to cease excavating the site. They are also packing today. I'll ask them to leave the cameras so I can do the scans until you return."

I pointed deeper into the cave. "That's all I ask. The cables are still in place." I made air quotes. "They like you. Beg them to forget about them, at least until the day after tomorrow, for us. Tell them there's a chance we might get an extension and that I'm personally going into the city. Tell them to come pick up their brushes and toothpicks, but to please leave the oxygen and the three-mile fiber optic cable for us."

I pointed in the direction of the camp. "Those one thousand five hundred fifty bones, which they call a treasure trove, have now suddenly made this a graveyard and a holy place. This is about money. The government and university claim ownership, and entrance is now granted by renewal of permits. Since they found what they found, they don't even want to leave the scraps for us. No, they want money. That's the only language these officials understand. I'm not concerned with bones, Tobias."

"You need to explain to them why we're here and that we're seeking much more than bones or fossils. Describe why the bones are here, why this appears to be a graveyard, and why we assert that it is not. Naledi and the sapien primitives knew that this door opened to another plane," Tobias said.

A feeling of frustration clawed and gnawed at my insides. I sighed. "Alright, I'll tell them about the tomb discovered in 1922, along with the cuneiform inscriptions my great-grandfather found, which serve as the first tangible evidence of an ancient kingdom thought to have existed thousands of years ago. I'll bring my great-grandfather's map to show them. I'm willing to share all my family's research if we can keep working in this cave system. They will see the texts and schematics revealing evidence of an ancient race, the naledi, utilizing the door to another world."

"Yes, tell them to look closer at the rock carvings."

"I will." I scratched my head. "They could argue that divine beings enter through a door in the sky." I chewed the inside of my lip.

"No, they won't. I promise you, one look at your map and they'll be speechless. Go to Professor Kilroy first. He's gay."

"Oh my God, Tobias! You want me to sell myself out!"

"Yup, he'll either eat it up or toss you out."

"You mean eat me out." I laughed, and Tobias chimed in.

Chuckling, he pointed a finger at me. "Yes, that too. But I agree, if you had a suitcase full of gold, it would quickly change their minds."

I shook my head slyly. "I don't have a suitcase of gold, but I have my family's research. If I show the university just a glimpse, they'll be all over this. The risk is that they might grant us digging rights, or will they boot us out and continue the search themselves."

"I told you, there's at least one gay man. I know how much you like a man in a suit. Start with Professor Kilroy. Use everything in your arsenal to sway him, and then the others will be falling over themselves to extend our excavations."

Waving my finger and smiling, I said, "Tobias, you may have a point. I'll do that if I think they're interested." I adjusted my shorts, which had been riding up my backside while I sat in the harness.

Tobias shook his head at me. "I will take pictures from every angle of that crack in the rock," he retorted while climbing into his gear. I couldn't let that opening slip by.

"You could take pictures of my crack, too, but I don't have time." Fist high for the victory of the winning last word, I shouted, "I'll be back in four hours, with the extension. I will. I promise."

Tobias laughed and said over his shoulder, "I love you!"

"Love you too!" I shouted. I didn't romantically love Tobias. He was becoming my best friend, even though he was just a business partner and mouth-piece for me.

CHAPTER 2
KELLAN

TOBIAS

Hey, how are you, brother?

KELLAN

Fine, wazzup?

TOBIAS

Guess😈

KELLAN

Don't have time, on my way to work.

TOBIAS

Tweety's coming.

KELLAN

Tweety who?

TOBIAS

Tweety, your canary.

KELLAN

What?

TOBIAS

Your birdie.

KELLAN

Dude, I have no clue what you're talking about.

Text later, getting into the car.

TOBIAS

Bring catnip.

KELLAN

Starting car.

WTF??????

Catnip?

TOBIAS

Draxton is on his way. Wear your gray suit and that car cologne—catnip.

KELLAN

Today?

TOBIAS

Yes. Now! Don't fuck this up.

Listen, agree, and be cool.

KELLAN

Fuck!

Getting out of the car.

Shit!

What car cologne?

TOBIAS

The Ford cologne.

KELLAN

Ah, Tom Ford.

TOBIAS

Yup.

KELLAN

Thanks…have to go.

BTW birds don't like catnip.

And don't call him Tweety!

TOBIAS

Whatever.

Good luck.

KELLAN

Thank you…bye.

TOBIAS

Be a cool kitty cat

KELLAN

LOL

Thanks.

Will do 😇

CHAPTER 3
DRAXTON

I SKIDDED OVER THE LOOSE PEBBLES AS I exited the cave entrance and changed direction to sprint toward my caravan. The sun was rising, and I estimated it was just after five. Scattered lights from inside the other campers flickered on. George's noisy electricity generator was already running. It was probably him waking everyone else up so early. After I unlocked the caravan door with my fingerprint scanner, I grabbed my toiletries bag and stuffed it under my arm, then stumbled out the door, slamming it shut behind me.

Darting to the clothesline, I snatched a fresh pair of shorts and a t-shirt from the wire I'd tied between two thorn trees, then headed to the communal bush shower. No one else was using the facilities, so I quickly showered and shaved, then hastily put on a clean outfit, swapping my boots for a pair of Nike flip-flops. This outfit was dry—thank the Gods. There's nothing worse than trying to navigate Johannesburg traffic with itchy balls and pulling on my shorts to make room while holding onto the steering wheel. To make matters worse, South Africa was an English colony until a hundred years ago, so I was also driving on the wrong side of the road. I didn't particularly appreciate driving in foreign countries, especially amidst trucks, taxis, and potholes. I checked my toenails—they were clipped neat and clean. Combing my unruly black curls, I winked at myself in the small rusty mirror and donned my black wide-brimmed hat. "Draxton Dubois, you can do it. You go get that extension," I told myself.

A thrill ran through me. I was as gay as they come, but in my line of work, there weren't many sexual social interactions at the camp unless I was lucky, which I rarely was. As my grandfather used to say, I walked around with flaps covering my eyes like a racehorse, only focusing on what interested me at that moment. I never had time to go clubbing or made it my mission to find someone looking for a quick in-and-out while standing ass up for me in the washrooms. I was also not fooling around in the camp where National Geographic could walk past my home and see the thing sway as I rocked into a willing body. The moans and groans would echo off the horseshoe cliffs of the Magalies mountain range surrounding us. Tobias's remark earlier wasn't a bad idea. Hitting two ostriches with one shotgun kind of thing. The thought of hooking up today energized me, giving me a buzz—a feeling that things were finally going to go my way for a change.

I darted back to the clothesline to hang my wet clothes that I had just washed in the shower, and by the time I dove into the caravan, I was a jittery ball of plans, pumped full of adrenaline. I dropped to my knees to remove the carpet I'd used to conceal the trapdoor hiding the safe I had built into the floor. Once I entered the code and unlocked the ratchet wheel, I pulled out a rolled-up map dating back to 1922. I placed it inside a map tube to transport without damaging it. That piece alone was worth millions in South African rand, and with the information on it, unspeakable numbers.

I've scanned, photographed, and even X-rayed it for more clues, so handing it over won't hinder my work. In any case, I've memorized it too. If I gave it to them and signed over the credits for finding the door, they could either agree to extend my permit or refuse. I still had one extra layer to seal the deal—the family's secret to decode the map, locked inside my mind. Yeah, I wasn't reckless enough to give them the entire map on a fifty-fifty gamble. My grandfather wouldn't object to me using this map as a last-minute backup barter, as long as I didn't reveal my family's secret.

I grabbed the keys, rushed to the Mitsubishi Triton "bakkie," which was what they called pickup trucks in South Africa, and then drove off. Halfway up the dirt road, George came running from the opposite side. I rolled down the window and slowed the bakkie. "You selfish jerk, your generator is running, and you're not even home! For crying out loud!" He stopped running, arms at his sides, mouth open, heaving clouds of dust into his lungs. First, he looked at me as if I were crazy, which I am, then he began coughing. I rolled my window back up, pressed the gas pedal flat, and pulled the handbrake to spin the wheels and smother him further. Then I released the brake, leaving him in a cloud of dust while I laughed until tears streamed down my face as he vanished from my rearview mirror. Gods, that felt great. I shifted in my seat and rolled the window back down for fresh air, chuckling as the bakkie shot onto the main road.

As usual, at the first four-way stop at a red traffic light, men panhandling and selling various items swarmed the vehicles that were coming to a halt.

"Hey," I called to the guy selling warm corn on the cob, boiled and salted. It's early in the day, so they should be good. "Are those fresh? They won't give me the shits?"

"No, sir! I just took them out of the pot. You want one?"

"Yes, and please peel, butter, and salt it for me." He turned and stripped the leaves. My empty stomach gurgled. That vetkoek from 2 a.m. was long forgotten. My mouth watered as I watched him toss the leaves onto the ground, revealing the delicious white corn native to this country. My gaze caught that of a little boy, probably around ten years old, selling bottles of soft drinks on ice from an old cooler hanging from a yellow nylon rope around his neck. Man, that must be heavy. "Five rand for a Coke?" I asked, and the others made way for him to hand me an ice-cold one after he popped the cap, which tumbled to join the corn leaves on the road. Next, the "mielie," as they called corn in South Africa, was handed to me, and I paid him with a five-rand coin. Others selling fruit, toys, and art saw I wasn't interested and turned away to sell to and panhandle the other cars behind me. As soon as the light turned green, I sped away to try to beat the morning traffic in Johannesburg.

An hour and a half later, I slammed my foot on

the brakes, bringing the bakkie to a screeching halt in front of the security boom gates at the entrance of the University of the Witwatersrand. I sighed as I watched the security guard get up and saunter over to check my credentials. "Come on," I mumbled, "a pregnant sloth moves faster than you." The man frowned deeply, he must have heard, but wasn't processing the insult. He handed me a visitor sign-up board and stepped back to read the logo I had attached to the side of the bakkie. "Behind the door... um. Spel-spel-l-e-o-speleologist?"

"Yes," I nodded. "I am a cave explorer."

He chuckled. "Oh, wow. That's a big word."

Suddenly, I liked the man. I labeled him innocent and then put him in the Jack and the Beanstalk box of my mind, but he wasn't Jack. No, this dude was the giant. But a friendly one. A humble one too.

"Yes, it is. I like caves and big things," I said, turning on the charm to one hundred percent.

I noticed the gears turning behind his narrowed eyes as they widened, revealing naughty twinkles. "Yoh-yoh!" he exclaimed in surprise, catching my innuendo.

Smiling, I scribbled my name and handed him my company's temporary University Faculty pass, which I kept behind the sun visor.

He took longer than usual to read the information.

"Has it expired?" I asked, tapping the steering wheel while waiting for him to hand it back to me.

"No, everything is fine. Thank you, Mr. Dubois." He returned my card with a twinkle in his eye. The big man was making a pass at me, but I didn't have time for that now.

"Thank you kindly," I said with a smile as I shifted the stick into first gear, allowing the bakkie to roll forward a bit, hinting to him that I was in a hurry. Luckily, he went ahead and pushed the gate open for me.

I waved, saying another, "Thank you!" and then drove onto the gigantic campus grounds to find visitor parking in front of the administration offices. It was still early, and students were arriving by taxi-buses and worn, rusted old cars. Two young female students hurriedly approached just as I opened the door to enter the building. I held the door for them. Engrossed in conversation, they barely made eye contact and walked inside without even saying thank you. "My pleasure," I muttered, but they didn't hear me.

At the front desk, an eager-looking receptionist with a big afro looked up at me.

I greeted her with a warm smile. "Good morning."

"Yes, good morning," she responded, sitting up straight. I was an attractive man, and I knew exactly how to use my looks to get what I wanted. I removed my dusty hat and held it respectfully before me, like a well-mannered explorer.

I glanced at her I.D. badge. "Sylvia, would you please contact the head of the Geoscience faculty? I believe it's Professor Kilroy?"

Batting her long false eyelashes, she said in a sweet, condescending voice, accentuating her s's, "Sorry, sir, do you have an appointment?" She rolled her head from side to side, looking me up and down while nervously starting to chew on her pen, seconds from swooning.

Gods, I felt like vomiting, but I smiled, leaning forward on the counter. "My colleague, Tobias Benson, visited a few times without results, so I'm here to bring your professor a gift he can't refuse. Will you ring him for me and let him know I have something for him? If he doesn't want it, I'm more than happy to give it to National Geographic." I waved the black map tube at her. She must chew on the germ-covered pen often, as it was stained reddish-brown with her lipstick and chewed flat. I stifled a shiver. This was why I hated interacting with the public. They were disgusting.

"Okay, give me a second," she said, tossing the pen aside and reaching for the desk phone. I should have felt nervous, but instead, I was irritated and wanted to return to the caves, where it was cool, quiet, and free from annoying people. "Morning, sir." She shifted in her seat, and I imagined he greeted her curtly. "Yes, I know you start working at nine, but there is a Mister..." She covered the mouthpiece and glanced at me questioningly.

"Uh-hm." I cleared my throat. "Draxton, Draxton Dubois."

"Mr. Dubois." She checked the university visitor pass I showed her. "Oh, it's another archaeologist from 'Behind the Door,' sir. He has something that he claims would interest you, but if you're not interested, he can always give it to National Geographic."

"Or any other university interested in the 1922 treasure of the tomb of King Solomon," I added, leaning in closer so he could hear me.

"Yes, Professor." She ended the call. "Down the hall. Last door on your right." She pointed with her red-painted finger.

"Thank you, Sylvia," I replied.

"It's my pleasure, Mr. Dubois," she said with an unflattering nervous giggle.

I turned, and my flip-flops clicked, clacked, and squeaked down the long, dimly lit hallway that smelled of floor polish and old books. My gaze shifted to the name plaques and door numbers as I passed the offices. Most doors were closed, but I focused on the last door on the right, which was ajar, judging by the light spilling into the hallway. His office door featured an unusually customized, polished copper bear-head knocker. I craned my neck to peer inside and tapped the knocker, enjoying the dull reverberation from the solid acacia wood. Amused, I peeked inside, eager to meet this man.

"Come in." I heard a smooth baritone voice say as he opened the door wider for me to enter.

I stepped into the office and was welcomed by a warm smile from Professor Kilroy. I'd always left negotiations to Tobias and suddenly wished I hadn't. This man, with his impeccably tailored gray suit and clean-shaven head, was a perfect ten. Swiftly, I tucked the tube under my left arm to free up my right hand. The nauseating aversion I had felt earlier for Sylvia turned into absolute attraction as our palms touched in a handshake. His grip was firm, and his Tom Ford cologne made me zoom in on all his attractive features. His friendly, intelligent eyes met mine, and he carried a self-assurance that I found irresistibly attractive.

I was fortunate to have Tobias as both my best friend and business partner, who helped me navigate and negotiate South Africa's complex culture. Tobias mentioned that this man was gay, and judging by the glint in the professor's eyes, I believed Tobias was correct in his assumption. I wasn't leaving without that extension, and bending this attractive man over his antique French desk would be no chore.

"Please come in and sit," he said, and his voice rolled through me and settled in my groin. Moving aside graciously, I gave him room and watched as he closed the door.

"Thank you." I turned on my charm and raked him up and down appreciatively, signaling my interest, before handing him the tube containing the map and sitting down. His eyes sparkled with delighted interest. He cleared his throat and sat casually with one leg draped over the corner of his desk, watching me. I tipped my chin up, hinting for him to have a look, and waited. He opened the lid but didn't glance inside. Instead, he sniffed it, not breaking our stare, eye fucking me with those beautiful, dark brown orbs.

"It smells authentic. Very old. No hint of vinegar. Maybe a small amount of baking soda," he said, closing his eyes as he continued to inhale its scent. Though he couldn't see me, I studied his face, noting his full lips, sharp, high cheekbones, and broad African nose. The mix of his appearance and the way he casually suggested that he's the most intelligent man in the room truly captivated me. I've always been drawn to well-groomed men, not the rugged, bad-boy mafia types or the fumbling, awkward professors with bow ties. No, I'm attracted to the refined, bald, intellectual types. I was attracted to the best of men, those who know they are a step above the rest because they can survive and adapt to any situation, leading others behind them. Yup, if I ever questioned my sapiosexuality, this man would prove me wrong. I was infatuated with brilliant individuals, to the extent that I considered it the most essential trait in choosing a partner.

His nostrils flared as big as quarters as he inhaled the scent of the map inside the cartridge. "Something smells sour, someone used milk for invisible ink," he remarked with a sly smile tugging at one corner of his mouth, interrupting my train of thought. *Damn it, I should have known.* This exotic beauty had brains, too.

"Um, yes, please take the map out and see why."

He positioned the map tube beside him and entwined his fingers over the leg draped across the corner of the desk. "No, first tell me what you want, Mr. Dubois. Why are you bringing me gifts?"

"Call me Draxton, please." I leaned back in my chair, resting my right foot on my left knee as I relaxed, invitingly, while covering my groin with my hat. The office was thick with the scents of leather-bound books and our mingling colognes. Clearing his throat, he flared his nostrils, soundlessly sniffing the air. He tilted his head to the side, sizing me up. Waiting. The silence felt like a challenge. He got up and moved to sit behind his desk. I wondered if he was hiding his arousal, just as I was concealing mine.

In his maroon leather executive desk chair, he mirrored my posture, waiting patiently. He seemed comfortable, even amid the uncomfortable silence. I almost didn't want to ask for an extension. Setting up camp in this man's office to explore his cave might be more adventurous. I smiled at the thought. He raised his eyebrows, still waiting for my response.

I cleared my throat. It was time to talk business. "So," I said, pointing to the map, "that map is worth millions of rands." He reached for his drawer, but I raised a hand to stop him. "No need for gloves," I interjected. "I have preserved and waterproofed it."

"Smart man," he remarked as he carefully took the map from the protective tube and began unrolling it. He reached for a carved wooden box decorated with elephants, lifted the lid, and removed four paperweights. I stood up, placed my hat back on my head, and moved my chair closer to help him by placing weights at the two corners nearest to me. Together, we examined the large, faded cream map covered with smudged charcoal etchings, that nearly filled his entire desk. Each time I looked at it, the drawings, cuneiform translations, and various symbols called to me. The silence and awe seemed to affect him as well.

I sat down. "This is a replica of the northern wall of the king's tomb before it crumbled. My great-grandfather sketched this in 1922 A.D. while the French and English bickered over who discovered the tomb of King Solomon first. He gave it to my grandfather, who then passed it on to me. Now, it's yours," I whispered.

"Hm," he grunted.

"I'm begging you to extend our permit to search those caves, and I'm also offering you the chance to take all the credit when I find what that map says must be there." I looked up at him, doing my best to give him puppy eyes.

Looking up at me and tilting his head to one

side, he asked, "What do you think is there, Mr. Dubois?"

Taking a deep breath, I blurted, "I believe it's a door. Those caves match the drawings of the Ziggurat structure from the tomb of King Solomon, which resembles the Gate of Judgment."

"Gate of Judgment? Are you saying you're searching for the door to Heaven?" He chuckled in disbelief at me.

"No, of course not. Maybe. I don't know what lies beyond that door, but I'm one hundred percent sure it is there. Those tunnels are ancient passageways. Your naledi made the same symbols as the ones found in the tomb of King Solomon. It's not called the Rising Star Caves by coincidence. The locals have referred to it that way for eons." I pointed to the symbols on the map. He knew exactly what the drawings in the caves looked like. He was doing his best not to appear surprised, or perhaps this was old news to him. I wondered what else this professor knew. "Why does it seem like you already knew this?"

"I see you are an intelligent man. I'm not sure it's accurate to call them ancient passageways."

Ah, so he knew something already. "Why not? They are part of a labyrinth. I've compared them to the Cradle of Mankind, and to all those caves in that area from above." I moved to the edge of my seat. "Fold the map in half, then fold those flaps back again." I cleared the paperweights on my side to assist him. The more I folded the map, the more his eyebrows scrunched together. "Yes, just like a paper airplane." He shook his head, looking from the map back to me in astonishment. "See, it's a massive, complex structure leading to the center, to the door."

He sat back, crossing his arms. "A door for pixies, maybe? I've seen those tunnels. There's no room for any door or structure down there, Mr. Dubois," he said with a serious expression. I couldn't tell if he was joking or not. I broke our stare and let my eyes wander over the bookshelves, which were stacked from the floor to the ceiling. Behind him was a tall glass showcase filled with various artifacts. A small, glimmering white marble carved into a polar bear caught my attention. I pointed to it with an open hand.

"This map isn't something you would save there. It needs to go into a place with better security."

His eyes flicked to mine. "You know, Mr. Dubois, I call bullshit. You didn't preserve it. You were hiding something." He was correct. I hid my great-grandfather's code that he had written with milk on the side of the map.

I waved off the statement. "Look, the passages

on the map turn left upon entry and pass in front of the chimney, but then it turns sharply down and to the right. We need more time because we've been scanning that wall repeatedly. We can't go right. We need time. Here, Tobias and I found a fine line. I call it a line, but he insists it's a crack. It's unusually straight and long. No human could have scraped that with a piece of rock. It's not rock carvings. Look, the door has to be there, somewhere in this exact spot, either up or down. You know the rock carvings look just like these." I pointed to ladders, triangles, and squares. "I know the door is there. All I need is time, Professor. Once I find the door, all the credit goes to you and your faculty. You won't have to spend a cent. All you have to do is say yes. Let National Geographic pull out, as they planned to today. I need space to work without any interference or distractions. Give me three months. That's all I ask. If there's no sign other than what we've found up until today, I will gladly pack up and call it quits. I'll go home and start my research all over again. Because then I'm wrong. So wrong."

I tipped my head down to catch my breath and waited. Usually, people hated it if I stayed quiet for so long, it made them uncomfortable. My grandfather told me it's not my fault if people got impatient and thought I was rude. The silence in the office finally doused my echoing words. When I looked back up, he sat patiently waiting for me with a smile. *This man was really at the top of the food chain.*

He pointed a finger at me. I wanted to sink to my knees for him. Not to beg, but to crawl closer and smell him like a dog. I bet he smelled like soap and tasted sweat. "I will give you three months, but I will be visiting and checking on your progress. No one else goes into those caves but you and Tobias. You work for me now. Without pay, of course. Anything new—be it the door, any bones, or anything, I don't care if it's just a hair. It belongs to the Wits, to my department."

A broad smile spread across my face. "Thank you." I stood up weak in the knees, to shake his hand. "You just made the best deal of your career. I won't disappoint you."

"Famous last words, Mr. Dubois." He unfolded his new map, then rolled it back up and slipped it back into the protective tube.

"Famous indeed, as you'll see. You are about to become very famous." I chuckled. "I was about to flirt with you and persuade you with my body." I laughed, awaiting a reaction.

"No need for that. We'll see more of each other, Mr. Dubois."

"Please, I asked you earlier to call me Draxton."

"Only if you call me by my name, Kellan." He looked like a Kellan. I liked the alliteration of the k's.

"Professor Kellan Kilroy, I look forward to working with you." We shook hands longer than necessary. His long, slender fingers were surprisingly callused for a man who spends his days in an office. I shivered at the thought of those rough calluses scraping against my skin down my spine on their way to separate my butt cheeks.

Gods, I have to stop gazing into his all-knowing eyes. I can't...I can't look away.

He beamed at me knowingly, and we paused for a moment. In that instant, for the first time ever, my entire world went silent as I made eye contact. It didn't make me nervous—no buzzing noises urging me to find silence—just a profound and unexpected comfort that settled deep within my bones. All the usual frantic chatter in my mind faded, replaced by a singular, unwavering focus as we shared the understanding of mutual attraction.

"We'll see each other again the day after tomorrow. Please tell Tobias I said hello." He patted my arm, and my skin prickled where he had touched me.

Swirls of heat detonated inside me. "I...I will, until then," I said hurriedly, opening the office door, flustered and eager to resume my trek through the Johannesburg traffic—with a victorious grin.

CHAPTER 4
KELLAN

OUR FAMILY WASN'T THE CONVENTIONAL South African black family. We've been guarding a secret for a few hundred years.

My father had passed away just after I finished my final year of professorship. He had guessed that he was about nine hundred years old.

Even before the English and Dutch set foot beyond the Drakensberg Mountains, my father had waited here for someone, anyone, to join him or at least come get him.

He wasn't from around here originally. He knew our history because he'd witnessed it firsthand. Earth's true name was Anzulla, and back around 1600 A.D., he had arrived here, when he'd escaped death during a war that erupted in a time and place hidden somewhere behind a door, exactly where Draxton had been searching.

Our old stone house, which had stood for hundreds of years, sat on the outskirts of Diepmeadow, Soweto. It was along my route, and I had been stopping by my mama's house for coffee either in the mornings before or in the afternoons after visiting the Rising Star Caves.

She enjoyed hearing about my adventures, but lately, there had been little adventuring, as I had mostly been stuck in my office, shuffling paperwork and piecing together funding for my department. As her only biological child, telling her about my meeting with Draxton, after Tobias arranged it, ignited her curiosity about my love life.

"You be good to that white boy of yours now," my mama pointed her crooked, arthritic finger at me. I smiled warmly at her. She was much shorter than I was.

On our way out the door, we found someone had dropped more groceries for my mother and clothes for the children, which always seem to arrive at her doorstep, so I helped her carry the stuff inside before leaving.

I gently grasped her bony shoulders and pulled her closer for a hug. "Drive safely," she murmured into my chest, while I bent my neck to rest my chin atop her head.

"I will, Mama." I chuckled. She wrapped her arms around my middle, squeezing as hard as she could, which wasn't much, but the familiar feeling of overwhelming warmth and love enriched me. Her faith in me, regardless of what her neighbors and nearly everyone else who thought they knew better were saying, motivated me every moment to improve.

I had been brought up in a very unorthodox manner. They'd taught me to be a role model for the younger generation. Instead of responding with hate and violence, absorbing negativity, I would cleanse it and return the opposite to the world. I'd always aimed to turn hate into love and kindness, staying true to my values. It was how I was brought up by a father over nine hundred years old and a mama, though small, shielding me and instilling in me the strength to face judgment while remaining proud and motivated to keep my head held high. I wanted to prove to those who doubted me that I was the better person, despite our differences in sexual orientation. My parents taught me to love people for who they are, and to disregard things like race, gender, wealth, possessions, or social status.

Guarding the caves was a team effort. Aside from

my mother, Tobias knew about our family secret. He worked in the field, excavating and mapping the caves nestled in the Cradle of Mankind, keeping an eye on Draxton and National Geographic, as I could not be everywhere. It had been my mother's idea, after my father had passed away, to entrust Tobias, who had been the second eldest of our weird family. She probably thought the two of us would eventually hook up and fall in love, but Tobias had only been a sidekick, a friend, and not a lover. I wasn't his type anyway. He liked dainty twinks, which was a good thing, because Draxton was none of those things. No, he was a beautiful, untamable beast, and that's why I had concocted a plan with Tobias to make an offer Draxton couldn't refuse.

Tobias had suggested approaching and teaming up as business partners with Draxton, not only because he could help him excavate and search, but also navigate South Africa safely. That was especially beneficial, as Tobias would assist with the talking and dealings, given his familiarity with me, and thus be my inside man. Together, Draxton could avoid the red tape while they were spelunking for the very door we've been hiding and guarding all my life.

So far, no one had seen a door, not even my father. I was more worried about someone coming through from the other side. Perhaps searching for my father, who thought, and I tended to agree, that the door couldn't be opened from our side. As an extra precaution, I had infrared cameras situated at the cave's entrance and surrounding areas. While I monitored from afar, Tobias would have to intercept and contact me if someone out of the ordinary suddenly appeared or exited the cave.

For the last two years, they've been in and out of the caves, and still nothing except for my growing obsession with meeting Draxton.

My parents guarded the secret until I was old enough to understand what they shared with me. After I turned nineteen and left home for university, our house had become a haven, a revolving door for all kinds of ages and backgrounds of queer children. Tobias was the first gay kid who had visited and never left when he was old enough and ready to face the world. Like Tobias, all the other children had grown up and made something of themselves. But Tobias was the only one who knew our secret.

Lately, as if she didn't have enough people coming and going, she'd gotten the idea of grandbabies into her head and been pushing me to marry and adopt.

I was forty-three and had no desire for children or to get married. My work was my priority, and finding someone to spend time with was never high on my list. But one mention of Draxton and Tobias, and suddenly, she's been bringing up the subject of grandbabies at every visit.

I let go of her and turned to touch the door handle with my thumb to unlock the door of my 2017 Mercedes 4x4. She smiled enthusiastically. Her soft, thin skin, crinkling like old paper at the corners of her eyes and around her mouth, reminded me of how fragile she was and that she, like my father, probably wouldn't wake up one morning, as she had little time left to live. "Ask them to dinner. I want to meet your new friend," she said as I opened the door and climbed into the driver's seat.

"I will ask him. But not for tonight. Maybe next week. We're still getting to know each other." I closed the door, found the button, and lowered the window. The cool morning air wafted inside along with the scent of her sweet rose perfume. She placed her arthritic hands on the side of the door, leaned in, wrapped her tiny hands around my neck, and kissed me again.

"Next week is perfect. Tell them both to come say hello, then the week after that, you can bring your man, and then we'll talk grandbabies, okay?" I rolled my eyes.

"No babies, Mama, please. He has no time for

children. I doubt he will stay, even if he finds what he's looking for. He is out of the ordinary and not the type of man confined by everyday expectations. His mind is locked onto things we can't see. He searches for those things, not for children and a home. I told you, Mama, I don't want more responsibilities. I have enough."

I started the car, and she crossed her arms. "You have no time to waste. You are almost fifty. Ask him about babies, if he wants that. Get to know him."

"I am getting to know him, but that doesn't change the fact that I don't want children. I'm not almost fifty, I'm forty-three. I love you, Mama, but I am happy. Whether I'm with someone or not, I don't want children. My life is full enough. I wouldn't mind spending it with someone who shares my interests, but it's time you nag someone else about babies."

She uncrossed her arms. "We'll talk again. Just be careful of those tsotsis at the crossing."

I shifted the car into drive. "I will, and no more baby talk, Mama." I pinned her with a stare. "I will call you. Love you." She grinned and waved. I pressed my foot on the pedal and leaned out the window, waving goodbye as I drove away. I was looking forward to seeing Draxton again today. I was definitely in trouble.

Ever since I saw his picture attached to the file submitted for an application to participate in our faculty's excavation, research, and mapping project focused on the caves in the Cradle of Mankind, I had fixated on him. The more I learned, the more I wanted to get to know him, shake his hand, and hear him speak to me. Those mysteriously deep, dark eyes gazed straight at the camera through unruly black locks of hair framing a face that appeared to be in a state of permanent scowl. But it wasn't just his dangerous look; the more I researched him, the more intriguing his background became, and I've been diligently figuring out how to get my hooks into him. He was like an ancient relic I wanted to own. He was extraordinary, and I wanted him to be mine, because he was a unique and complicated man.

His intensely dark exterior concealed a delicate mind. I never would have known he was different if I hadn't looked into his family history and found a diagnosis, almost as a footnote, indicating he was an exceptionally gifted individual with ASD.

I needed to find a way to tie him down and make him mine without sounding like I expected him to stay in one place, as he would likely get bored with me as soon as I agreed to fuck him. As much as I wanted him, I wasn't certain that Draxton could ever really belong to someone. *How do you catch a bubble without bursting it?*

That powerlessness drove me to understand him and win him over, which left me feeling vulnerable in his presence. He had a beautiful intellect and a personality like a rhinoceros. I loved it. I doubted he was even aware of this deep connection to another man. The way his grandfather raised him both shielded him and rendered him unaware of the intrinsic dynamics between people, between lovers. Draxton was clueless about society. He only focused on his work—maps and caves. I was besotted, infatuated, and just plain foolish around him—everything he said and did was innocently amusing and extraordinary. I was weak in my desire for him, and I battled both him and myself not to fall too hard and too fast for his brilliant mind, although he granted me free access to his body.

CHAPTER 5
DRAXTON

I WAS ALL KINDS OF FRUSTRATED. MY BALLS were full, and I felt like a bull, thinking being an ox must be better. As promised, Kellan had shown up a few times at camp, checking on us. So far, it was nothing more than a brief hello with a peck on the cheek and handshakes with Tobias.

Bloody fucking hell, I thought we'd had an understanding when I'd last been in his office. I wanted to feel like that again, but how could I if he just showed up to tease me?

Rolling my eyes, I set aside all my murderous, sexually frustrated thoughts. "Are you gearing up, or did you only come by to check on us?" I grunted.

Tobias snickered, and I nudged him aside with a hip bump to help him wash our breakfast utensils.

Once we start working, we won't return until much later. Without sunlight, cave explorers often lose track of time. It's also much cooler, a constant seventeen degrees Celsius, making the South African summer far more bearable inside the caves.

Kellan had arrived earlier than usual from Johannesburg and joined us for an early breakfast this morning. He got up from the camping chair he'd been lounging in, stretching his arms in various directions. That made his shirt pull up, revealing his narrow hips, belly button, and the fine black trail of hair that disappeared into his low-cut denim, secured by a black belt. I blinked and tried my best not to look at his bulge, but failed. Our eyes locked, and I looked away to conceal my desire. Bloody fucking hell!

"Yes, I'm gearing up today," Kellan announced proudly. The gears in my head clicked faster and faster until they created one loud humming noise. "If you two don't mind," he added as an afterthought.

Kellan was becoming increasingly difficult to understand. I wanted him close and pressed against me, yet also as far away as possible until he became just a speck of dust to me. This situation between us was way too complicated, and took up too much space in my mind, and I couldn't concentrate on my work. My work was more important because I'd promised my grandfather I would find that door. I shook my head to quiet it down. But, as usual, the voice inside my cock and head had different opinions about Kellan, and couldn't decide which had the final say.

If I told you I wanted to sleep with you, and you agreed, then what was the problem? I didn't have time to prolong the wait. We could have had incredible sex three times already. Three! Today could have been the fourth. But he had wasted it.

Hell, I didn't even know how to respond to Kellan. He seemed eager to explore, but unfortunately, it wasn't my body that captivated him, it was the cave.

Today, he dressed in work clothes like us. His fitted blue shirt, jeans, and boots gave him a look that made him appear like a seasoned spelunker. My fingers tingled, yearning to loosen that bloody buckle, unbutton, and unzip his pants to reveal the impressive bulge he was showcasing. I shook my head, telling my cock to calm the fuck down. I had to stop thinking about him like that. He's not interested in sex, he'd made that abundantly clear. Three times. I didn't want to hear it again.

"It's okay, Draxton. I'll finish up and pack our lunches. You and your professor can gather the urinals and backpacks." Tobias shoulder-bumped me with a strange, sly look as he dutifully packed our food into the small cooler. I snapped my tongue, throwing down the washrag.

"Thanks," I whispered through clenched teeth, leaning closer to Tobias's ear. "He is not my professor." Tobias didn't look at me, but judging by his shaking shoulders, he was amused.

I turned and pointed to the ablution block. "I'll be back," I said, ignoring Kellan, who stood with his hands locked behind his neck, teasing me. There was nothing worse than working with a full bladder and no urinal in sight. The general rule of thumb was to empty your bowels before entering the caves. We kept drinking and eating to a minimum until we exited again, then we rehydrated once outside. Unlike those assholes climbing Mount Everest, we speleologists never left anything behind. We carried glow-in-the-dark urinals with us, which we emptied, washed, and reused daily to ensure we didn't have to crawl outside prematurely or piss where we worked.

"I need to use the facilities as well," the professor said from somewhere behind me. I was doing my best to avoid him. He was becoming a real pain, and not the enjoyable kind. Since our meeting on campus, he had paid us three visits, and three times he had given me the *I'm-not-inter-*

ested treatment. I had work to accomplish, I had made my effort, and I wasn't going to belittle myself any further. I stormed into the bathroom, furiously relieved my bladder, gathered the urinals I had cleaned and sterilized last night, packed them inside their netted bag, washed my hands, and charged outside, colliding with Kellan's broad chest with an oomph.

"Careful," he said on a chuckle just before I could slam on my brakes.

"Excuse me," I burst out, my voice squeaking with nervousness.

In a flash, I cataloged his warm, tall, and sturdy frame against me. A constant cloud of exquisite smells hovered around him—a spicy leather scent with notes of citrus and lavender. His beautiful, dark eyes and wide smile revealed straight, shiny white teeth. Sweet hot sauce! I was jittery around this man.

His arms wrapped around me, pulling me in for an embrace. My eyes widened, and I inhaled sharply. It felt amazing yet horribly uncomfortable. This man made me edgy. He smiled, his expression almost playful, like a gorilla preparing to play with me until I was dead.

"Are you okay?" he asked, his voice laced with concern.

I nodded, attempting to steady my racing heart. "I-I think so," I stammered.

He chuckled again, not tightening and also not releasing me from his hold. "Sorry for scaring you," he said, his tone sincere.

I shook my head, still trying to regain my composure. "It's okay," I finally managed to say.

He flashed me another charming smile, still not stepping back. "Well, I should probably let you continue on your way," he said, gazing in the direction of the caves.

I nodded, grateful for the chance to escape his overpowering presence. "Yes, please excuse me. Please and thank you," I replied, eager to return to the caves, my heart still pounding.

"Draxton Dubois, you are excused, but I hope this is not the last time you end up flustered in my embrace."

Too close. Too tight. Too sexy. Too bloody much! I thought. His arms felt like industrial steel clamps around me. His breath carried a minty scent, like the gum he was chewing. His affectionate eyes and rigid body pressed flush against mine signaled that he wanted me. He focused on my mouth. The tip of his pink tongue swiped over his plump bottom lip. I stood mesmerized, forgetting that I was about to be broken in half by the jaws of life. He chewed and moved the spearmint bubblegum around. I wanted half of it. If we kissed, I would get half. I would steal a piece, bite it off, and then push his half back into his mouth. The thought had me panting. The heat between us was scorching. Too fucking hot. As much as I wanted to kiss him, I wasn't going to. This time, it's up to him to make the first move, and I don't intend to make it easy for him.

"Nope, not gonna happen." I wiggled my arms free and pushed him away.

"Do you want me or not, Draxton?" he asked gently. Damn it! He's creeping under my radar. That's precisely what he's doing!

Shaking myself like a wet dog, I tried to rid myself of the hooks he'd harpooned into me. If I didn't escape him, he'd reel me in—my mind and my body.

Before I could say anything else, Kellan turned and disappeared into the washrooms while Tobias was coming up the trail, laughing.

Screw this, I thought as I veered right toward the cave's entrance. "I'll get started," I muttered to Tobias, too embarrassed to look at him.

He clapped his hands once. "You two are so much fun to watch."

I turned my head up to the sky and shouted over my shoulder, "Tobias, I'm going to kick your ass one of these days!" Then I lifted both my arms over my head, pointing two middle fingers at him before entering the cave's mouth.

"You can try!" he taunted, then shouted back, "See you in two minutes!"

I pretended not to hear him. Asshole, I thought. Tobias found us so entertaining. Kellan flipped all my switches faster than Lady Gaga played piano. I didn't know how to act around someone so perfect for me, and yet not wanting to sleep with me. What was wrong with him? He was making me look like a fool running after him. I liked the challenge, but this was too much. I didn't pine for impossible men. I didn't have the time to...All I could do was ignore him and pretend he was ugly and stank like a decomposing pig.

CHAPTER 6
DRAXTON

"SINCE I GOT HERE THIS MORNING, YOU'VE barely spoken to me. You didn't even seem glad I came," Kellan said from behind. The rumble in his voice was even deeper at the mouth of the cave—a jolt of desire shot through me. My heart raced. I didn't turn around. I kept my head down, tightening knots.

"You can go first, I'll follow, and then Tobias can make sure I don't get lost or hurt behind you." He sounded amused.

I sighed and climbed into my harness, placed my helmet on my head, switched on the light, turned, and shone it straight into his eyes. "Whatever. I hope you're comfortable crawling Superman-style for two hours."

"I'm well aware of how narrow it gets in some places. Once we're through the chimney, you'll appreciate the extra pair of hands."

He climbed into his harness and copied me by putting on his helmet and blinding me back. Damn, his passive-aggressiveness was spot on—maybe even better than mine. I had to give it to him. He knew exactly how to mess with my head. I ignored him, pushed him aside, and started loading the loose goods into a net inside the small elevator.

"Please." I held out my hand. He handed me the cooler bag and scanner, and I packed those too. "Excuse me," I said as I reached past him to where Tobias was waiting to hand me his stuff.

"I wish we knew the dimensions of the door," Kellan said, flipping my last switch.

I took a deep breath but lost my composure anyway. "Listen, Professor. This isn't what we agreed on. Tobias and I were meant to work alone. I had hoped that if you visited, we could get to know each other better, but since you keep giving me the cold shoulder...I don't see much use for you here."

Tobias gasped. Kellan smirked. That's exactly what he wanted me to say.

"Draxton," he drawled. "Not all gay men jump into bed the moment they meet someone they're attracted to. I prefer to warm up to a person and get to know them first. Sex is the easy part, it's the getting to know each other that's the challenge. Can we please try to be friends first?"

I raised my hands. "Of course, we're already friends. Best friends ever!" Sarcasm dripped from my words. I sensed he was trying to let me down gently, but it only made me more irritated. Now I felt like I was belittling myself. "Just stop trying to get under my skin. Better yet, don't talk to me unless it's work-related." I slammed the button, and the elevator zipped down the thirty-meter shaft. Probably a little too fast. I slowed the speed by holding onto the cable with my gloved hands. The cable slackened, and a loud plop reverberated up the narrow shaft. Gods, I hoped the camera was okay.

"Tobias, perhaps you can explain to Draxton that everything isn't always about two bodies writhing and getting dirty. It's a game of the mind and heart. Anyone can have sex, but not everyone desires it all the time with just one glance. Also, let him know that the more he persists with this behavior, the more I enjoy getting to know him. I thought he was a man who understood the dynamics of power. But I see now, I hold the power while he is the one who is playing."

"For crying out loud, Kellan. Can you please be quiet? It's over. There is no game. I'm not interested in any game. Not anymore! You should have let me fuck you because now that I know you, I will never stick my dick into any of your fucking orifices." With that said, I handed Tobias the remote, clipped the seat belt of my harness together, and readied myself to be lowered. Tobias looked relieved.

Kellan waved. "I apologize for giving you the impression that this was only about sex. I didn't want to be rude by simply asking you to take it slow. Unfortunately, this is my cave, and I recall you being much nicer when you needed my assistance to approve your excavations. This is precisely why I love getting to know you better. I've heard about your skills...um, and we have amazing chemistry. You are making a big deal out of nothing."

"Bla-bla-bla," I snapped, signaling Tobias to press that fucking button. The sooner I plunged into the darkness, the better.

"You're upsetting him." I heard Tobias chuckle as I was lowered down. The rock face flew by, and I exhaled to make my chest smaller, helping me slide faster. Sparks flew as my headlamp scraped against the rock. With a dusty thud, my boots hit the ground. I unclipped the elevator cable and ushered Kellan down, followed by Tobias. No one said a word.

As we inched deeper, the cool dampness welcomed me, and a sense of calm filled my being. I loved it down here. While tight spaces made some people nervous, for me, they had the opposite effect. I felt safe, calm, and at peace in the quiet darkness. Constantly calling, *come further, a bit further. If you go further, you'll find protection from everyone and everything outside.*

The professor surprised me, he followed the instructions we gave him. An hour later, I had completely calmed down, and started to feel some- what bad for reacting to him like that earlier. To make matters worse, he was skilled at this. He re- mained quiet and slowly inched forward, much like a seasoned cave crawler scaling the ladder and over the dragon's back until we finally arrived at the chute.

I lifted my helmet to wipe the sweat from my forehead. "Let's rest here for a second or two," I said.

Once we caught our breath, I started corkscrewing my body to change direction. The space was getting so narrow that my helmet and chin scraped on the rock. "We're going to move downward and headfirst for this next section," I said as I crawled upside down at a thirty-degree angle. Kellan and Tobias followed me. "Here's the line. I'm moving over it with my left hip." With my boots touching Kellan's helmet on his head, I could feel him shakily turn his head in the space to, hopefully, see where I was indicating.

"It's a crack, not a groove," Tobias whispered from above.

Kellan was right at the spot where we hadn't scanned yet. "Kellan, I'll hand you the Doppler. See if you can scan all around you."

"Me?" he squeaked. I just now noticed this is the first time he hadn't said anything since we'd begun going down into the cave. "I can barely breathe," he whispered.

"Don't tell me you came all this way to freak out now. Tobias is behind you and has to reverse to let you breathe. There's more than enough air here, the Dinaledi Chamber is just around the corner. Do you want to come down to turn around?"

"I didn't say I wanted to leave. I said I can't move around enough to...what I mean is, I can barely breathe, so I can't move around. Ah, hell, you know what I'm saying..." Kellan sounded flustered.

I unclipped the new LiDAR head and attached it to the optic cable with one hand. "Here, on my left. Scan your left side, then hand it back to me. I'll flip it to the right and pass it to your right hand."

"Okay, give it to me. My left hand is...wait, yes, okay, ready." He tapped my ankle, then my left knee, and I handed it over. Tobias was quiet in the back, convinced I was wasting my time with this line, crack, or whatever it was. I'll agree it means nothing after I've studied the azimuth and inclination measurements. This new scanner integrates with our existing scans. It will capture a full 3D scan of the cave interior, all the way to the surface, and will hopefully identify any manmade structures surrounding us for one hundred meters. If I still don't see anything after today, then I will admit this was just a crack.

I craned my neck to see up my left side. Kellan was doing as I asked, and Tobias was measuring with the Caveatron. He lifted his head, and the light shone into my eyes. "From this angle, Draxton, would you say the roof of Dinaledi Chamber is directly in front of me?"

"Absolutely, because you're at about a thirty-degree angle."

"If I tilt it, the pan and zoom in the Line Plot Viewer flickers, and when I change direction, the screen returns to normal."

"That's strange."

"Yeah, it is. It's only for a couple of centimeters, just a flick of my wrist, and it's gone."

"Hm, let me think about that for a second. Kellan, are you ready to switch to the right side?"

"Almost done."

"Just tap my leg when you're ready."

"Will do." He sounded a little short of breath. We were boxing him in, I thought. I looked up at Tobias, who was now looking away from me.

"Yeah, Draxton. This is something noteworthy and new. This is the first time I scanned from this angle. I'm always feet first, never head first."

"This could be what we were looking for," I said as excitement rose inside me. A tap-tap at my left knee made me quickly take the LidAR and pass it to my right hand, then feed it back up to Kellan's right hand. "Kellan, I'm going to go deeper, into Dinaledi Chamber, so that you can breathe. When you are done…"

"Yes, yes, go ahead, please. I'm suffocating."

"Okay." I wiggled down until I could twist and then slid further into the belly of the famous Dinaledi Chamber, where the naledi brought their sick and dead.

"Tobias," I called.

"Yeah?" his voice echoed back to me.

"What if the door is on its side? What if you're seeing the door's edge, and if I look up, the roof is the door? We've been searching for a door that opens like ours does. What if it's some sliding or trap door?"

"It can be. Why not? Everything is possible, and looking at this screen, it seems plausible."

"I'm done, I'm coming down," Kellan whispered. I noticed his long, slender fingers first. He handed me the scanner and inched forward.

"Twist your torso and corkscrew out," I said, tapping him on the shoulder. "Turn this inside, yeah, that way. Yup, just like a baby being born headfirst." Gods, the sounds he made were beautiful as he grunted. I bristled at the thought of eventually coaxing sounds like that from him one day. I clucked my tongue at myself to refocus my wandering mind just as his white safety helmet came into view, followed by his relieved, sweaty face.

"Oh, glorious, fresh air," Kellan breathed.

"Yeah, thank the excavators who left the fan to vent the chamber for us."

"Really?" He sounded surprised.

"National Geographic left it here."

"Oh, now I understand the secrecy."

"Yup."

He leaned his head back against the wall, resting his elbows on his knees. He looked exhausted.

"Tobias, are you coming?" I called up the chute.

"You and Kellan can talk for a while. I'm going to work on this as I backtrack. Like I said, I've never worked this way before. I don't want to lose this sweet spot."

"Okay, do you need something to drink? I'll bring it to you," I asked.

"No, I'm fine. You know I don't like to drink too early in the day. I'll meet you guys outside." Tobias's voice was muffled. I assumed he had changed direction and was moving out of the chute.

"Okay!" I hollered, smiling at Kellan.

Tobias's chuckles echoed softly. "Have fun!" he added.

I sighed incredulously at Kellan. "Tobias had better have something to show us later, otherwise, I would think he's trying to leave the two of us alone down here."

"I think you're right. Come sit next to me, and let me explain, maybe you'll feel less offended if you understand where I'm coming from," Kellan said, removing his helmet and wiping his forehead with his sleeve before placing it back on his shiny, shaved head. I crossed my arms and widened my stance. He patted the cave floor beside him. I raised an eyebrow. He smiled back. My resolve crumbled, and I sat down, leaning my back against the wall like he was, crossing my legs at my ankles. We weren't touching, but I could smell his aftershave and feel the heat between our shoulders. I mirrored his action by dimming the light on my helmet. He was cleanly shaven as usual, and up close, under the light, the stroma in his irises revealed the most beautiful tiny golden patterns.

He cleared his throat. "I am crazy about you, Draxton," he said, laying a hand on my knee. Chilling feelings of guilt coursed through me. I should have realized that someone as perfect as him would require more than just a casual hookup. Of course he desired more. He sought an emotional connection—a relationship. Something I was not able to give him. Connection meant time, and I didn't have time to build bridges of trust before fucking him.

"You're making it difficult for me," I admitted. "I'm a self-centered, superficial man with a singular focus on my mission. I have my work, and we've been fortunate to cross paths. You know, like two islands in a stream and all that." I waved a hand between us. He shook his head as if what I was saying was a lie. "I'm attracted to you, I want to fuck you, and your whole package is like waving a bloody T-bone steak at a starving lion. The more you keep yourself aloof, the more attractive you are. Uncomfortable doesn't begin to describe me. I'm nervous, and I don't want to want you. Not in here. Not anymore. I don't know what to do with myself when I'm around you. I'm fucking bewildered. I'm never like this. You are in my space." I flapped my hands in the air. "I'm not sure if I have the time or capacity to indulge you. It's best if we put an end to this." I waved between us. "Whatever this chasing game is."

Silence.

"I confess I am sapiosexual. The way you carry yourself in a suit and your intelligence is as provocative as walking naked in front of me, teasing me. The sensation of my dick wanting to burst through my trousers is highly frustrating. Intelligent men exuding power are my Achilles' heel. I'm not an unattractive man. No one has ever given me the impression that they are interested in me only to deny me, the way you do, and it's giving me blue balls. It's as uncomfortable as it is confusing, to say the least. In my book, we cross paths, hook up, and then move on. But thank you for explaining. At least now I know"—I made air quotes—"it's a you issue, not a me issue," I said, patting my chest, relieved to have expressed my feelings honestly. He frowned, looking confused until his face scrunched up at me. Of all the things he could have said or done, he burst out laughing, and it echoed around us. I crossed my arms, which seemed to amuse him even more.

"You see, if we had slept together the day we met, I would never have learned that about you. Not all men are promiscuous or malicious."

"Now you're implying I'm promiscuous. I never leave camp. Just ask Tobias. And I never..."

"I know, Tobias has told me. I'm going to share a secret with you. Your friend and business partner has been trying to set us up for a long time. But somehow, you're always too busy." I sighed, looking at the opening of the chute as if Tobias were going to pop his head out. "That two-timing piece of..."

Kellan tapped my upper leg. "He's a good man. He kept saying you're not ready. I had your number on file and could have called you long ago, but I wanted to meet you in person when you had the time to think about something other than work. I know your job is your priority, and that people aren't your focus. I was intrigued when your file first crossed my desk, but listening to Tobias ramble on about your friendship and commitment to your work made you sound like a very busy man—someone with absurdly ambitious goals and visions. But you never had time, Tobias always came, confirming just how invested you are in your job. I was beginning to think you were ready to leave with National Geographic. Then you came to me, offering me your most valued possession—a family heirloom

—to find the door, not even wanting credit for it. You're a focused, handsome man, and I don't want to be just another fling. I like you. I also know this can't work long-term, but I'm not comfortable being treated like a toy either."

Now it was my turn to burst out laughing. It felt amazing, and here we sat in the Dinaledi Chamber, ancient crumbling bones surrounding us while our voices echoed like distant burial songs. I don't know if it was the noise or our backs resting against the wall behind us. Through the fabric of my shirt, the rock felt as if it were warming, maybe even vibrating. Kellan must have felt it too. We looked at one another questioningly, brows knitted as we swallowed our laughter. Kellan looked up and then behind him. "There it goes again!" he exclaimed. Astonishment and excitement surged through me as the wall vibrated once again.

"What the fuck?" We scrambled to our feet and stared at the wall, gasping for air and clenching our fists in anxious anticipation. We waited. Nothing. We pressed our palms against it. Nothing. It was cool rock, just like always. I kicked at it, knocked on it, and smelled it while Kellan did the same. Finally, I pressed my ear to it, and when that didn't yield any results, I stuck out my tongue and licked it. Kellan grinned at me. "And?"

I shook my head. "It tastes like dirt." He looked disappointed. With our hands on our hips, we waited for something to happen—anything.

"That was the weirdest thing," he whispered, shaking his head in disbelief.

"Yeah, it was," I replied, pulling my shoulders to my ears and inspecting it again by running my hands over its surface.

"Maybe we should try what we did before, see if it triggers anything again," Kellan suggested. It was a solid idea. I nodded, and we sat back down exactly where we had been before, then waited again.

Kellan checked his watch and sighed. "It's been two hours, maybe one of us should grab an EMP and sound blaster," he suggested, getting up and dusting off his pants. "I can go."

He extended his hand, and I grasped it as he pulled me up. "No, I'll move faster. I'll go. You wait here."

"I'll come with," he said eagerly.

"No, there's no reason for you to follow me in and out. I know these tunnels."

"If that's what you want me to do, I'll wait. But first, give me one of those glow-in-the-dark urinals. I'll need that."

"Sure, help yourself. It's in the net with our pro-visions," I pointed to the heap of tool bags. "I'll leave everything here with you. There's enough food and water for three people. I'll be quick. I promise."

Kellan opened his arms wide. "Come here."

I blinked, suddenly feeling dumb as stone. He stood there, waiting for me to process what he had just said. He wanted a hug. I pushed myself forward because I craved more. I stepped into his embrace, and our lips collided. A moan escaped my throat as I pushed him back against the rock, pinning him so he couldn't escape my onslaught. Like two magnets, we were irresistibly drawn to each other. He fisted my hair with one hand while the other slid to my lower back, anchoring my hardness against his. I propped myself up with my hands on the rock behind him as I leaned into him. We broke the kiss.

He's going to say this was a mistake. No, perhaps the opposite was running through his mind—maybe now he wants a wedding ring. Gods, I was conflicted.

"Holy shit, you're an amazing kisser," he whispered, looking dazed.

Breathing rapidly as if the oxygen in the chamber were depleting, we searched each other's eyes. My body tensed, and I wanted to bolt for the chute. His expression gentled, and he loosened his grip around me, then tenderly held my face between the palms of his hands. He closed his eyes. "No expectations, I promise," he said softly and waited. I allowed myself to lick and bite his plump lips. He moaned into my mouth. *First, he starved me, and now he lets me taste him.* I slipped my tongue inside and explored his mouth. The gum I had craved earlier was gone. In the deepest corners of my mind, something urged me to stop. To take notice. It warned me, but my thoughts floated around like candy floss. His hands slipped down to my waist, and he hooked his arms under my armpits, pulling me tighter against him to prevent me from breaking the kiss again. As passionate heat bloomed between us, a cool breeze brushed against my face. Our eyes opened wide in unison.

Beneath the palms of my hands, the black rock rippled and warmed once more. We locked eyes and broke our kiss in surprise, but before we could say anything, more wind filled the chamber, whistling like a kettle boiling water. I jumped backward, pulling Kellan with me, away from the undulating wall that was liquefying like the surface of dark well water. It moved faster and faster in a counterclockwise direction until the center dipped away like a spout forming. The high-pitched whistling transformed into a low, tooting noise. Frantically, I looked nervously from the wall to the chamber's exit. Kellan pointed toward it.

I understood what he meant. "Yes!" The wind, being drawn through the chute, created a whistling noise like a steam locomotive, warning us. Naturally, we didn't move. We just watched until we realized we were in the mouth of a vortex. First, the empty glow-in-the-dark urinals went flying, and then we dove for the chute. But it was too late. I shoved Kellan toward the tunnel opening to help him escape, but we ended up creating a vacuum by blocking the hole with our bodies. Kellan turned to reach for me. The vacuum broke, and we shot into the maelstrom of darkness and noise. Shouting was futile. I couldn't even hear myself in the pandemonium.

As we spiraled deeper into this chaos, the deafening noise drowned out any attempts at communication. Flashing lights cut through the darkness that engulfed us. We were falling through the sky! The disorienting, terrifying, and startling realization caused me to thrust my belly and hips toward the earth instinctively. I reached out desperately for Kellan, trying to find some sense of stability amidst the chaos. The sensation of skydiving was unmistakable. "Kellan, keep your head back and your feet up!" I shouted futilely. The surrounding forces pushed and pulled. I turned around, only to find that Kellan had vanished. The wind whipped like wet rags against my face, battering me. I steadied my body against the gravity that had its claws in me. I didn't know when this swirling abyss would release us, or where we would meet the ground.

Fear gripped me when I spotted him. "Kellan," I shouted. He was spiraling out of control into the un-known. He spun helplessly, with no sense of direc-tion. The deafening flutter of noise intensified as the chaos swirled around us—screeching, bellowing, and the booming crackles of lightning. *No, no, no!*

The air grew thinner and warmer. Smoke! Or-ange-brown flames loomed far below. Damn! I pressed my arms against my sides, palms open, shoulders shrugged, head tucked down, and dove, propelling myself toward Kellan. I reached out, wrapping my arms and legs around him. "Got you!" I shouted. His body felt limp. "Kellan!" His head flopped back, wearing an expressionless look. He was unconscious. I clung to him, refusing to let go as we continued to somersault, ass-over-head. When we hit the ground, we would do so together, I thought, bracing for impact.

But still, we fell. We should have hit the ground by now. How far were we falling?

"Shit! Ouch! Ouch! Damn!" The hot, smoky air

turned to ice pellets. "Bloody hell!" I shielded Kellan's face as golf balls of ice bombarded us. With a long, drawn-out *whoop-whoop-whoop* sound, the tornado we were riding disappeared, and we plopped down into ice-cold powdered snow, knocking the wind out of me.

CHAPTER 7
CALLISTO

I STOPPED MY POINTLESS WAILING AND CLOSED my mouth to keep my tongue from slapping me across my snout. The singing wind sliced through my thick fur like a thousand swords, while my small ears flapped, creating a rumbling wrrrrr-wrrrr droning.

Horrified, petrified, and completely rattled, I tumbled. It seemed to go on forever, and at one point, I thought I was flying.

"Don't be afraid," countless voices of my brother whispered, funneling, pushing, and pulling me toward another point in time.

I was on a mission. I couldn't fail, I thought as I was falling—falling—falling, being pulled into a swirl of colors and lights. Concentrate and think of home, I told myself. A wave of relief washed over me as I veered to a time of peace, to the calming blues and greens, away from the raging fires of war. But at the thought of war, the wind changed direction. The blues and greens disappeared, replaced by blacks, reds, and oranges.

No, no, no, no! My paws trotted nothing but air. Refocus! I should have only thought of home, not war. "Go back home, go back home!" I howled until I couldn't howl anymore. The fall seemed endless. The further I fell, the more urgent it became to change my destination. The smells of burning below grew sharper. I tasted sulfur, melted rock, and the charred, dead Anzulla—approaching too quickly. Fear kept me from thinking of the right kind of home. The speed squeezed my lungs, and the air wasn't filling them. Urgency, fury, disappointment, and a fleeting flash of courage flooded my mind as I tumbled.

I kept trotting. I was going the wrong way.

Choking, coughing, suffocating, burning blue-black clouds shrouded the dead surface below.

Fatal speed and forces pulled and pushed me. I wasn't soaring like a bird; no, I fell as gracelessly as dried shit. The loose skin of my cheeks forced my eyes shut as a vicious gust of hot air rushed through my fur. My lips flapped, spit flew, and my gums dried as I continued slipping through the layers of darkened sky. In the distance, volcanoes spewed lava, with flames licking the sky impossibly high. "Don't land in the lava," I told myself, then started howling again. The faces and echoing voices of my friends flashed like lightning around me—whispers of hope and survival, the crucial reason for my fall.

The temperature changed from scorching hot to ice cold. The wind changed direction. The fires died down, and the red and orange hues darkened. Embers suddenly turned into snow, slicing through the darkness. Still, I fell.

"Warn them...find home...remember!" the voice of my brother boomed in the swirling vortex of time.

"Please help me. I'm going to die!" I bellowed futilely.

In the final moments before impact, I realized that I was the only one who could save myself. I closed my eyes and repeated the words, *I am a ball, and I am going to bounce like a ball. A big white ball! I'm going to bounce. I'm not going to die.* I curled my body as if lying down, covering my eyes with my paws, and waited to hit the frozen ground.

I am a ball. I'm going to hop like a rubber ball.

CHAPTER 8
KELLAN
THE DARK CONTINENT

A THUNK AND A WHACK TO MY HEAD JARRED me awake. I flailed, trying to get Draxton to release me. He swore, letting go.

Blinding, ice-cold gusts of wind battered my face, and I realized we were sitting neck-deep in snow. "Where are we?" I asked.

Draxton pushed me up. "Fuck knows!"

We wobbled, struggling to stand like a pair of drunk friends who wouldn't make it to the after-party. I was dazed, trying to find my equilibrium, and losing my battle with the icy wind, knocking the breath out of me.

I reached around Draxton, holding onto him as we kept each other upright. "We're gonna freeze to death!" I told him.

"No shit!" he yelled, and his words disappeared into the storm.

We sank back on our haunches, clinging to each other for warmth. Minutes ago, we were warm inside the musty cave. Now we sat in the center of a tumultuous snowstorm, with nothing but white as far as we could see.

"Where on earth are we?" I shouted, futilely wiping the snow from my face. Draxton's head was covered with the stuff.

"More like, where *did* we land?" Draxton yelled. Our teeth chattered loudly, like an AK-47 block party.

Icicles clung to his nose, and his exposed skin was covered in angry-looking red and purple blotches. Even his usually dark, furrowed eyebrows were now as white as the surrounding snow.

Panic overtook me. We were in serious danger. I shot to my feet, bringing Draxton with me. "I don't kno-o-o-ow," I yelled into the wind. "We must find shelter! Get warm...um...light a fire!"

We turned, scanning our surroundings. Through breaks in the whiteout, I could see we were on a level patch nestled between a sharp incline and a decline. "We're on a hillside!" I gestured, then yelled, "Up or down?"

Draxton turned, bringing me with him. "There!" he shouted into my ear.

"Yeah! Light!" My hands were numb, and I stuck one under my armpit and hooked the other under Draxton's stiff arm.

Little by little, we carved a path at a slight upward incline. My legs were numb, shaking, and unbalanced. Thank the stars Draxton wasn't wearing his denim shorts today, I thought fleetingly.

"Fire!" he croaked, waving his arm as the snow abruptly ceased, the wind died down, and the edges of a huge opening under the overhanging rocks came into view. I estimated about twenty more paces to go.

"Yes, that's a fire...and people. We have to go!" I clung to him, and he held onto me just as tightly. We pushed and pulled each other forward, straining to keep ourselves upright as we forged ahead.

"Fuck!" Draxton yelled as he toppled to the side, pulling me down with him.

"Come on, we're almost there!" I grunted, teeth clenched with effort as I hauled him up by the arm. Halfway closer, we stumbled again, and this time, he looked like he just wanted to sit there and hide his head between his elbows. He was exhausted... maybe terrified. "Keep going. We're close. Do you smell smoke?" I asked, trying to focus him on getting inside. He let me help him back up, and we started moving again.

The first thing that hit me was a wall of heat. "Thank the stars, several fires!" Draxton exclaimed as we shuffled inside. My frostbitten cheeks stung as I wiped the ice from them. I coughed and choked with the sudden change in temperature.

We stopped once we were safe from the storm raging outside. Surprised faces locked on us as we stood on the doorstep of their cave. It was instantly clear that we were far from home.

The sharp scent of woodsmoke mingled with cooking food, carried on the waves of heat rolling over us. "Could we...perhaps...share your fire?" I asked, half-dragging Draxton, as I shuffled a little further into the cave toward the warmth.

The cave ceiling soared, easily two stories high—I could've parked ten cars inside. Several fires cast a warm glow, their flickering light dancing on the walls and the faces of the men, women, and children staring at us. Smoke curled upward in deafly silence, disappearing into natural air vents formed by the rock crevices, creating a warm, hazy atmosphere.

For a second, we all stared as if frozen in time, but then I almost swallowed my frozen tongue. Draxton and I both gasped and jumped at the suddenness of it all—everything happened so fast. In an instant, swords, spears, and bows were drawn and aimed at us, as people hunched around their fires scrambled and leaped into fighting stances, with wide-eyed, fearful expressions.

The biggest man I've ever seen, dressed in white fur pants and boots, with a magnificently sculpted naked chest, leaped up, ready to pounce and kill us with his spear.

"Bloody fucking hell?" Draxton barked, stepping backward.

The women hid their screaming children behind them, moving to the back of the cave.

I threw my arms up in surrender.

Then it registered. *Arrows? No guns? What the...* I blinked, trying to process what I was seeing. Draxton tripped to the side, untangling himself from me, but froze in place, also realizing what we were seeing.

My breath hitched. "We've walked into...um... the Ice Age," I said low and very slowly, mimicking Draxton by retreating, keeping my hands raised. "Whoa, whoa, whoa!" I yelled. They froze, poised to attack, then puzzled expressions spread across their faces. "Good God, it's homo troglodytes!" I whispered, blinking in disbelief.

Draxton side-eyed me, hands up. "Cave

dwellers?" he told me in a hushed tone over his shrugging shoulder.

My heart thumped inside my constricted chest. "They are human," I whispered, noticing the different races on the Fitzpatrick pigmentation scale, but most had dark to yellow-olive complexions with straight brown to black hair. One guy stood out like a white painted exclamation mark among them.

My eyes flicked faster than paparazzi flashes as I scanned the rest of the cave. No electronics or anything that suggested that this was from our era. No backpacks, no sleeping bags, no camp lights, no tents, or foldable chairs.

A low rumble broke the silence. It was behind us. I dared not look. That was the sound of an animal.

"Kellan?" Draxton warned as we stood shivering side by side.

Turning and running, I figured, meant either being mauled by whatever was behind us or freezing to death outside if we got away. They could kill us now, or later, either way, Draxton and I were dead.

Even more confusing was seeing the big man's smile. He tossed his spear aside and opened his arms wide as he fell to one knee. "Cal-listo!" he shouted, astonishment etched on his face. "It's me! Ouroboros!" He looked upwards, which felt strange, as he seemed to be gazing over our heads. How big was the animal behind us?

Stiffly, but very slowly, Draxton and I turned and noticed four shaggy legs. Cautiously, we tilted our heads upward.

"Holy crap," Draxton whisper-shouted, gazing up at the underside of something covered in white fur. "What the...?" Draxton's teeth sounded like sand hitting a windshield. "K-K-Kellan, don't m-m-move, it's a f-f-fucking beast."

I couldn't move my legs anyway. The beast was enormous, its white furry chest towering above us. The rumble coming from it echoed off the walls as it huffed at the large man, calling out to him. We'd been walking through the storm beneath a massive polar bear with glowing blue eyes.

We're about to be eaten, either by this bear or by these people! The man kept calling in a deep, thick voice, "Callisto, Callisto. Is it you, my friend? It's me. It's Ouroboros. Remember me? Ouro?" The rugged-looking man pounded his chest like Tarzan, and I saw the others approaching with smiles on their faces. They ignored us, becoming rowdy and excited about the bear. They chattered in a strange dialect of English mixed with their local tongue, but it was still understandable. Their leader was a tall figure with large hands and a booming voice, giving off the impression that he could survive ten Ice Ages. He definitely wasn't someone I could take on in a fight. Everyone was dressed in similar animal skin and fur clothes. My eyes darted toward their fires—my frozen body thirsted for that warmth. Draxton's eyes were wide, shock having jolted him from his half-conscious, hypothermic state just moments earlier.

Terror gripped my frozen chest. Callisto only had to bend down and eat us. The tip of his big black nose was as large as my face. Long black toenails, as long as my lower leg, retracted as he curled into himself. As if hearing my thoughts, its four legs moved away, and Callisto shrank to human size.

"Unbelievable!" Draxton croaked, lowering his hands. "No way! Did you see that?"

"How is that even possible?" I couldn't believe what I was witnessing.

"Yes, it's you!" The man laughed, diving past us and into an embrace with the magical creature. "Oh, Callisto, where did you come from?" he said, burying his face in the snow-covered fur around the animal's neck.

Oh my god, was this my father's fantasy story?

The bear suddenly erupted in a series of wet, snotty sneezes, then nodded its head as if it were excited and communicating. They mobbed the bear, seemingly forgetting about us, as they rushed toward it, petting it and babbling excitedly.

Instead of rushing to the fire to warm up, we stood shivering, hugging ourselves, waiting for them. I cleared my throat and shuffled my feet. Finally, Ouroboros appeared to remember us and rose from one knee, giving us a suspicious look. He ran a hand through his hair, brushing off the snow he'd collected from the bear's fur. The fine white pellets glistened like diamonds as they flew in all directions before melting into tiny droplets on the warm cave floor.

I bit my bottom lip, unsure of what to say to convince him we were nice people, then moved closer to Draxton, ready to defend him if needed. The soft whining and panting of the bear confirmed my suspicion that they were communicating. This warrior and his people sounded friendly—they laughed affectionately as they petted the animal, clearly as old friends reuniting.

"Where did you find them?" the leader asked the bear before stepping over to our side.

A confused expression crossed his face as he left the chaos behind and pointed at our chests. I inhaled deeply and carefully, mimicking Draxton's actions—tucking our chins to our chests and straining to see what he was pointing out on our wet shirts. "Why are you dressed like that? Are you from the Light Continent?" he asked us in a deep, thunderous voice, contrasting sharply with the friendly tone he had just used when speaking to the bear.

The chatter of voices in the back faded as everyone turned to listen to our answer.

"L-l-l light c-c-c continent?" Draxton stuttered, his jaw trembling and lips blue.

I shook my head. "B-b-better explain to us whe-where t-that is. W-we are n-not from he-here."

"I can see that you are not from here. The question is whether you are traitors?"

The bear huffed, drawing everyone's attention. It almost seemed as if he was telling them something. Judging by their faces and gestures, they were listening intently and responding with serious looks and nods.

Ouroboros turned his attention to us where we were waiting, shivering and freezing, eyeing longingly the multiple fires deeper inside the cave. "Callisto seems to think we can trust you."

"Y-yes, we are harm-less." Draxton's words were nearly incomprehensible. He crossed his arms to keep warm. Most of the men, women, and children returned to their places around the fires, giving others who had waited in line a chance to hug and talk to the bear. Others curiously edged closer to their leader.

"May we share your fire while we get acquainted? We've been wandering in the cold, hoping to find shelter with you," I asked.

"Da! Come on!" He gestured toward a large fire in the center, and we didn't need to be asked twice before darting toward it. Thankfully, everyone had lowered their weapons, though they kept them close.

"Wait, let me." I bent down, loosening and removing first Draxton's boots and then mine.

"Th-thank you," Draxton whispered through vibrating lips. We tiptoed carefully to avoid getting dirt on their furs and pillows spread around the fire pit. We stood as close to the flames as we could without getting burned.

"Take off the wet clothes. You'll get sick if you stay wet," the white-haired man said.

"Undress...better...follow their advice," I told Draxton in a low tone, and he nodded, already tugging at his tucked-in shirt.

My fingers felt foreign and dumb. I moved sluggishly. "It's true, we wouldn't warm up if we were wet," Draxton noted, avoiding eye contact, glancing up now and then. Most people gave us privacy by turning away. Draxton joined me by taking off his shirt, jeans, and socks. The white-haired man gathered the clothes and handed them to a woman, who hung them over a line stretched across another fire deeper in the cave. We huddled, breathing in the smoke and heat deep into our lungs, coughing weakly. I soaked in the warmth, closing my eyes for a moment in relief as the prickling sensation of life returned to my limbs.

Draxton tapped my bare knee, inviting me to sit. I joined him, crossing my legs and leaning toward the fire, palms open. Ouroboros then spoke to the man with pure white hair. The man grabbed a fur coat next to him and removed the one over his shoulders, draping it over us.

We smiled gratefully at them. "Thank you."

The reunion in the background had run its course. All attention shifted back to us. The bear was approaching. "Kellan?" Draxton asked softly, sounding uncertain beside me. Strangely, Callisto circled the fire as if looking for a seat, then came to sit right next to Draxton. He dug his fingers into my upper leg. I shifted, and Draxton cautiously narrowed the space, away from the danger. I kept an eye on the bear while Draxton sat right next to him, leaning into my shoulder.

Gods, this was weird.

"Where did you come from? Where did you find Callisto?" the leader asked.

I ran my hand up Draxton's arm, over his shoulder, and down his side, just as he did to me. The movement helped blood flow. Life returned to my numb, prickling, burning skin.

We sat in our underwear, and I noticed them stealing glances at mine, which had white skulls and crossbones splattered over the black fabric. Draxton's plain white underwear didn't attract as much attention as mine.

Ouroboros cleared his throat, waiting for an answer.

Startled and glancing between Ouroboros and Callisto, I placed a hand on Draxton's knee, checking in with him. He didn't look like he minded if I spoke, so I answered. "Uh...no, we didn't find him. I honestly didn't know he was following us. We'd landed...uh...right outside your cave. We saw the fire, but we didn't see the giant bear until you mentioned it."

"Callisto protected you. You wouldn't be alive if not for him. Thirty minutes in that freezing blizzard and with those clothes, you should be dead."

Draxton and I looked astonished at the bear. His piercing, intelligent blue eyes shifted from me to

Draxton and then back to the man who had just offered us the thick white fur coat off his back.

They acknowledged each other again, as if engaged in a silent conversation. The animal lowered its head, bowing to the friendly warriors, before resting its chin on its paws while watching us with a pleased expression, or at least what might resemble a smile in an animal. Wordlessly, I glanced at Draxton and then back at the beast. Everyone appeared both creepy and friendly. There was nothing else to do but smile back at them, especially at the warriors.

"Something to warm your bellies," a woman with friendly hazel eyes offered us each a cup.

"Thank you," we said together. I cupped the warm clay mug in both hands. It smelled delicious, so I carefully took a sip of the hot milk. "Hm, it's heavenly. Thank you."

"And sweet," Draxton added. She was correct. As soon as the milk filled my stomach, I felt warmer and stopped shivering.

"Yes. We put a little wild berry juice in it for the children," the woman said. She was short with long, straight brown hair braided into a single, long plait. Her teeth were clean, and she appeared well-groomed. Her big, round, friendly eyes scanned us up and down before she retreated to another fire.

A loud sneeze from the bear startled me. Its fur was now pure white and fluffy as it had dried. Shaking his head, he rolled his snout between his paws. His short tail made small, happy movements before relaxing against his backside, looking as content as an iguana on a hot rock.

"Where are we?" Draxton and I blurted simultaneously at each other.

Ouroboros answered, "Callisto says he was sent back in time and that you two are meant to be here with him. He vouches for you, saying you are here to help him." Draxton stiffened at the mention of moving back and forth through time. "What?" I looked at the man's face. He seemed serious. "Can you really understand each other?" I asked.

"Da! Callisto walks with Atlas. They are brothers, and we speak in spirit. They are our protectors." The polar bear grunted, with his eyes closed, as if in agreement.

"Protectors?" Draxton asked.

"Yes!" the others around their fires replied in unison, as if disagreeing would betray their beliefs.

Draxton tapped my knee. "Tread carefully, Kellan."

Acknowledging Draxton with a nod, I scanned their faces. Callisto chuffed again, this time meeting my gaze directly as if to confirm. We held eye contact for a moment before he broke it and rested his large head once more. He was clearly affirming their words, ensuring we understood that we'd earned their trustworthiness solely because he was the reason we didn't die out there. Having the bear on our side was a good sign—one of trust.

Soon, the younger children started coming closer, and we instinctively huddled together, unsure of what to expect. They giggled, and a brave little girl ran up and touched my bald head. A man and woman scolded her, chasing her and the other little ones, whom I estimated to be no more than five years old, back to their firepits. I assumed they were the parents reprimanding them. I smiled sheepishly, rubbing my smooth-shaven head. "It's okay," I said. "They're just curious and playing. I'm the only one here without hair, so it probably seems strange to them."

Ouroboros looked disgruntled. "Not strange, but scary and abnormal," he scoffed. I frowned. That was a strange observation. Were shaven heads taboo around here?

As the laughter and upset parents calmed down, Ouroboros reached for three spears, and I froze. Draxton threw his arm around my waist. The woman who had brought us cups of milk helped another tall, muscled woman to slide the wire handle of a large cauldron over the spears. Together, the three balanced it over the red-orange coals of the fire. Okay, so he wasn't going to kebab us, I thought, feeling Draxton relaxing beside me.

They were cooking something that smelled like a meaty stew. It smelled delicious, and my stomach clenched, reminding me that breakfast had been our last meal before we went caving.

Ouroboros stared at the pot hanging from the tripod of spears. "We thought Callisto and Atlas were dead, or perhaps trapped inside the mountain. We believed they had died like everyone else, or maybe they had been taken as prisoners. Most of our people are dead, or taken, or have deserted us," he muttered, trailing off.

Silence hung oppressively heavy over us. Seconds later, joy replaced the somber expressions as Callisto let out a disgruntled chuff. I realized he was saying something to them.

"Callisto has good news!" Ouroboros said cheerfully. "You brought him here, to us. I thought the gods had lied or forgotten us. Look at us. Only a few of our people are still alive." The sagging faces and nodding silent agreements from the onlookers confirmed that.

Ouroboros raised his voice. "So! Where did you come from? Did you escape? How did you run into

Callisto?" Hope flickered in his eyes. "Are others coming? What happened? Why now, after a hundred winters?" His eyes widened with glee. "Or did you come through the time box?"

I glanced at Draxton. He sat up, looking less pale and more alive than he had ten minutes earlier. "Time box? Yeah, like a portal." He beamed, giving me a sexy look. His whole posture shifted to what I saw the first day I met him—full of confidence and swagger. "So it was a star door and not a crack! I thought it was a groove, but it turned out to be just a crack. The door wasn't where I thought it was. Tobias was right," Draxton croaked with a sparkle in his eyes. I wasn't sure if they caught his meaning, but I stayed quiet and smiled back at him.

"Da! Did you fly through the stars?" Ouroboros asked.

Draxton coughed, then, while plucking at the fur, muttered, "Falling through time boxes and flying through stars is normal around here?" He lifted his chin, shaking his head. "We didn't fly. We fell."

Ouroboros waved a nonchalant hand. "Fly, fall, walk, jump. It's all the same to us. The point is, you came from another time and place?" He grunted.

I squeezed Draxton's upper thigh. He was doing great. "You answer," he murmured to me. "Because I don't have a fucking clue which version of Twelve Monkeys this is," he said cheekily, rubbing his hands and holding them over the fire.

"How should I know?" I scoffed as the dawning confirmation of my location crept closer and clicked into place.

"You know everything. You're the professor," he said teasingly.

I narrowed my eyes at him. "Are you jealous? Or do you admire my academic standing?"

"I told you I like intelligent men," he said over his shoulder, showing me that pretty dimple when he smiled. It felt like it was only the two of us sitting at a fireside as my world narrowed to only him.

Dammit, he was stunning. "You also said I was like a T-bone steak," I teased hotly.

He gave me a pointed look. "Yes, and you said you are in charge."

I chuckled. "You searched for the door," I retorted. "We found it. It's your grandfather's map. It's your dig. You should explain."

Draxton bristled. "No, it's your map. I had no clue the door was a vortex to the bloody Ice Age. I thought we'd step into a shiny, steel-floored, hyper-futuristic place. Not this," Draxton exclaimed.

"Hey, Ouro asked you a question!" the man with

the white hair shouted, pointing a finger at each of us.

Chin to chest, Draxton hid behind a curtain of black curls. "We're in deep trouble," he whispered jokingly under his breath while returning to plucking at the fur and running his fingers through it.

I sighed. Gods, I couldn't tell if he was serious or not. I'd promised Tobias a long time ago that I would never treat Draxton differently. It seemed it was time to gather my pretty bubble and pray it didn't burst. He was much more cunning than I thought. If there was one thing Draxton hated, it was being babied, but he seemed okay with me doing the talking. I also didn't want to upset our audience. "Um, let's start at the beginning. I'm Kellan," I said, thumbing my chest, "and this is Draxton. Thank you for your kind hospitality. The fire, the milk, the warm welcome— it's wonderful."

They waited.

We waited.

The big man sighed. "Looks like I have to take the long, polite route to get my answers." He patted his chest. "Hello, Kellan and Draxton. I'm Ouroboros. Most call me Ouro. That kind woman is Sopora, the mother of my only son, Libre." He pointed to a friendly, dark-haired boy who waved at us. "All my other children are girls," he muttered. Tension stirred around the fires as Ouro received foul looks from the other women. He quickly recovered. "Which is a good thing, women are most precious. We wouldn't have survived without their keen abilities to hunt and gather," he announced uneasily. I thought maybe this was a sensitive subject. Ouro continued introducing them. "That is Rocket, and this"—he tapped the man with the white complexion on the back—"is my best friend Snow...um." Snow was the perfect name for him, I thought. Ouroboros continued naming each and every man, woman, and child. "Over there is Silky, Bendre..."

I stopped keeping track of the names of all the men, women, and children as he pointed and named each of the fifty-three people inside the cave. At least now, I knew the white-haired warrior's name was Snow. He was tall and skinny, with brown leather pants hanging low on his hips. Just like Ouro, he wasn't wearing anything to cover his attractive abdominals. We parroted, hello, hello, hello, and so on, and so on.

They waited.

Beneath the coat, I felt warmer and more at ease. The fire crackled in the silence, illuminating their leader's familiar-looking face. A feeling of unease and recognition flickered a spark. I thought I might know who this was.

"Alright, it's my turn to speak," Draxton finally said. He placed the palm of his hand on his chest and sat up straight. "I am Draxton Dubois, the third. I was the only son born to my mother, Jestina, from Salt Lake City in the northern hemisphere on the continent of the Americas. In the time two thousand years after the birth of Jesus of Nazareth and twenty thousand years after the last Ice Age. I am the seeker of hidden doors to forgotten worlds and record the never-written-down history about human mysteries." My jaw dropped at Draxton's announcement. He was doing an excellent job of making himself sound important. He was giving them a reason to keep us alive longer. "We were working, excavating the Dinaledi cave chamber in the Rising Star Caves, located in the southern hemisphere on the continent of Alkebulan, later renamed to Africa, at the southern tip, to be exact."

Ouroboros frowned and glanced at the others, who shook their heads at him. I didn't interrupt him. I was eager to confirm where the hell we were. Draxton blundered on. "My grandfather gave me a map of a cave system that leads to what I believed would be a large door to an advanced world." He raised his arms, looking up as he explained. "I imagined huge gold doors opening to another world, maybe another reality. One with advanced technology and mythical creatures"—he gestured to Callisto and grinned—"so far, I have gotten half of it right. Now, if all I need to find are perhaps golden goblets or sundials, something shiny, to prove my theory of advanced ancient civilizations." Draxton paused, probably waiting for an answer or reaction, but Ouroboros waited longer, expressionless—not a twitch.

Draxton sighed and kept going. "To make a long story short, we were kissing when the wall vanished. Suddenly, we were sucked into a portal. We spun through the air like dust motes for what felt like forever. Finally, we landed in a heap of powdered snow."

"Hm." Ouroboros looked at Callisto, a thoughtful expression on his face. The animal shook its head once, and a few seconds later, Ouroboros said, "You came with Callisto. You brought him here. He was supposed to go to the time before the invasion to warn our people about the war. But you brought him here."

Draxton and I turned, facing Callisto. "*Us?*" we asked simultaneously. He just blinked back. "Is that one blink for yes and two blinks for no, or the other way around?" I asked.

"If Callisto says you brought him here, then you are here to help us get rid of the invaders," Ouroboros announced with finality.

"The fuck?" Draxton asked.

"Yes, fuck!" Ouroboros scowled, pointing at us.

"What invasion, Ouro?" Draxton and I blurted out simultaneously. *Was that the war my father had escaped?* I had to know.

"Not now. It's time for dinner and bed. We all need to eat and rest. We don't share bad stories before bed. Tomorrow is a new day. Are you warm now?" he asked.

I looked at Draxton silently, seeking his thoughts. Our limbs had gradually intertwined, resembling a koeksister, with our legs draped over and under each other. A line of permanent surprise and curiosity formed across his forehead. I suspected I had one as well. Draxton glanced at Ouroboros to respond, "Yes, we're warm, and thank you." Our gazes shifted from person to person as we expressed our gratitude.

"Good. We'll talk tomorrow when the children are out of earshot," Ouroboros announced softly.

Everyone else took that as a cue to bring their wooden plates, passing one to Draxton and me. I was surprised to see potatoes, pumpkin, and pork being served. Glancing around, I saw no garden or farm animals. "Where do you grow your vegeta-bles?" I asked.

"We have another cave for that," Ouroboros said. "We'll show you around tomorrow."

Draxton widened his eyes and shook his head at me. "Stainless steel forks?" Draxton asked aloud. "Where did *they* come from?"

"From before the war. We have wooden ones, but tonight is special," Sopora, who had brought us the hot milk earlier, answered.

"Impressive, this is a big surprise," I whispered to Draxton. "They have a massive steel pot on the fire, and their tripod of spears is also steel."

"True, and curious," Draxton said.

It was quiet in the cave as everyone dug into their food. It seemed like we had waltzed in right at dinnertime. Even Callisto got a plate.

"This is so good, thank you," I mumbled, my mouth full of hot potato. The pork stew practically melted on my tongue.

"Kellan, do you think these people could be sur-vivors of some advanced race?" Draxton asked qui-etly. He'd been stuck on that theory since the day I met him. I had a lot I still needed to tell him, and I dreaded how he'd react knowing Tobias and I had been keeping secrets.

"I told you we don't talk about bad things when

it's bedtime," Ouroboros reminded us with a whip of his eyebrow.

"My bad, sorry," Draxton said softly as he finished clearing his plate.

After dinner, our clothes were dry, though they smelled like campfire smoke. We got dressed, and then Ouroboros and three other men led us to a small alcove near the front of the cave, where a tiny waterfall trickled between the rocks. "You can empty your bladders here, but for your bowels, you'll need to wait for the storm to die down. A little further down the mountain, there's a natural hot spring and waterfall where we'll wash and handle our business tomorrow," Ouroboros explained.

Draxton chuckled. "This is the perfect start to an amazing adventure."

We joined them, urinating into the stream that disappeared into an opening where the sound of rushing water grew louder. I playfully nudged him with my side. "It's quite civilized. Maybe you've found what you've been looking for," I whispered. We zipped up, and he gave me a little push forward, then playfully smacked my rear. I jumped in surprise and amusement. "You sneaky, sexy man!" I yelled. He gave me a sly smile, promising more, and slapped my backside again.

We laughed as we headed back to our earlier

spot, watching everyone settle in, cozying up around their fires. I was exhausted from the busy day and thought I would fall asleep instantly as I pulled the animal hide higher. We locked eyes and flopped to the side, sinking into the soft fur cushions, while the fur covering our heads created a small, private space.

"Kellan. I think I'm the luckiest speleologist ever," Draxton breathed. He leaned in, pressing his warm lips against mine. It was brief, intimate, and filled me with relief.

CHAPTER 9
DRAXTON

MY HEART POUNDED. INSIDE OUR WARM private cocoon, Kellan and I exchanged breaths. The air was heavy with the smell of the stew we just had, woodsmoke, and our sweat. It was as grounding as it was intimate. I didn't do intimate, but I had nowhere to go and nothing better to do. So I lay painfully still in the silence, enjoying the calmness I always found in darkness.

Kellan grasped my hands, holding them tightly between our chests. I couldn't see his eyes, but I knew he was staring at me, just as I was at him.

Our breathing stabilized, and my heart rate slowed. He threw a leg over my hip, scooting even closer, our cocks touching, his forehead on my chest. A wave of heat consumed me. Gods, this man was such a contradiction. I thought he hated the idea of having sex too soon. He told me that less than a day ago.

"Hold me if you need to," he whispered into my chest.

I rolled my eyes. I despised romance, *but* after falling through a time door, Kellan's whole "wait until we know each other better" must have seemed pointless. On second thought, we were about to get intimate before we got sucked into this time and place.

If my grandfather were here, he would have told me to reassess and look at my options.

Groaning, I threw an arm over Kellan's shoulder. I pulled him closer and kissed the top of his bald head. "Come here," I said, snuggling closer as my cock stirred.

"You can hold me for as long as you like," he whispered.

I jerked my head up. "You say that as if I were hesitant and resisting you. I'd wanted you from the beginning, and I'd made it obvious. How many more invitations do you need?"

"Is your hair dry now?" he asked.

I held my breath, wondering why he'd asked that. What was really going on? Was our survival his justification for wanting sex, right here, right now?

Should I even let him get this close to me? And what does the humidity of my hair have to do with it?

I haven't had sex often, but when I did, I preferred topping. It felt less intimate, and I could avoid eye contact. But as he shifted closer, fitting perfectly against me, I sighed. "Yeah, I'm warm and dry."

He snuggled into me, resting his head under my chin with a soft, contented, "Hmmm, that's good," his hot breath searing like a coal on the center of my chest. Was that a signal? Was he trying to arouse me?

The heat intensified between us, and I began to sweat.

His body relaxed in my arms. I lay perfectly still, waiting and listening for further cues.

Callisto's inhuman snores rattled rhythmically behind me. Since our first meeting in Kellan's office, my mind had finally been silenced. Kellan wanted to have sex with me.

I was rock hard.

Why was Kellan's breathing slowing down? Shouldn't he be breathing faster?

I gently rocked back and forth, giving him a little shake. His head lulled back. Oh, he was drifting off.

Dammit, he was falling asleep, while my heart rate picked up its tempo. Perhaps I should turn around? The longer I lay there, wanting to fuck him, the worse it got.

He sniffed and snickered, making light snores when I extracted myself from him like an octopus escaping through a porthole—extremely skilled, and careful, like I did stuff like that every day.

Like he was my boyfriend, and I actually cared about waking him up.

I threw the animal pelts off us.

Fuck this!

In one smooth move. I pushed him away, flipped over, and, for good measure, *accidentally* elbowed him.

"Hmmm," I scoffed, frustrated. I had other things on my mind. Besides, we weren't alone; Callisto's crystal blue eyes reminded me. He'd stopped snoring and was watching me.

The unknown waited for me to be discovered. The best next step was to get to know my surroundings. I was on a mission, after all. Not a mission to fuck Kellan, but to find the advanced race my grandfather believed held the answer to our broken society. I'd found the door, which I didn't expect to open, somewhere in the sky.

All because I had kissed Kellan. "Hmmm," I scoffed again. I should kiss Kellan more often.

Irritated, I crossed my arms. "What?" I asked the

bear, still staring at me. He shook his head and closed his eyes.

"When these people wake up, I'm going to befriend a woman. They tend to babble." Callisto nodded a yes.

So, that was my plan, I was going to turn up my charm and start a proper investigation.

Kellan moved his knee between my legs, all the way up, right against my balls. Bloody hell, even in his sleep, he was a tease.

My murderous feelings about my rejection three times over resurfaced, and I lay awake stewing.

CHAPTER 10

KELLAN

EVEN DURING THE DAYTIME, IT SEEMED LIKE the sun never showed itself. The land was shrouded in constant semi-darkness as thick black clouds gathered in preparation for the next storm. Snow and ice covered everything, so I followed the flattened icy path, my steps filled with bewilderment and shaky apprehension. The smell of smoke and manure hung thick in the air when I arrived at the farming cave. Men, women, and children worked, played, and socialized while braiding each other's hair. This is what their daily activities looked like, I thought, as I searched for Draxton's tall figure.

I didn't expect him to be interested in mingling with strangers, but when I woke up and saw that he wasn't with me or nearby, panic set in. I called out like a madman until Snow told me that Draxton, Callisto, and Sopora were on a walk because Draxton wanted to see the other cave. I huffed and puffed, slipping on the ice, frantic to find him. I worried that he might panic and run off, getting lost and freezing to death. But as I came out of the stairway carved into the rock, Draxton caught my eye immediately. He didn't seem distressed, standing with his hands in his new fur coat pockets, listening to whatever Sopora was saying. The relief I felt upon seeing his relaxed and happy face was overwhelming, and I wondered if I had underestimated him. It seemed he hadn't thought of me or worried about me—no, he had purposely left me behind.

He couldn't just leave without a word. We needed to stay together. If we split up, how would I ever get us home?

I needed to talk to him, but I had no idea how to approach him. Our survival, *his survival*, depended on staying together. My father was a king, which meant Ouroboros was now the king. He had survived a series of attacks, the same attacks Ouroboros had mentioned last night. I saw and heard the truth of the fantastical things my father always spoke about, that he had battled alongside a magical polar bear and a dragon. All my life, I struggled to believe that, including his miraculous healing abilities. It was utterly unfathomable until last night, and I *had* to let Draxton know before he grasped what was going on here. *That I've hidden the truth from him.*

I went directly toward them. Sopora noticed me coming and smiled, but she must have seen how upset I was because she spoke to Draxton. When I reached them near the far entrance, she turned to go. "Morning, Kellan. I'll be over there," she said, gesturing to where two goats were being milked.

"Morning, and thank you," I said to her before turning to Draxton.

"There you are. Did you finally wake up?" Draxton said, his tone was sarcastic.

I scowled. "You could've woken me up or at least left a message. I was worried you'd wandered off to piss and got lost, or worse, attacked by something," I blurted.

Draxton removed his hands from his parka and crossed his arms. The children were running around us, playing so loudly that I thought Draxton would appreciate a bit more quiet. I pulled him by the arm to the side for a serious conversation. He looked at his arm in disbelief before glancing back at me. Then he lifted one eyebrow, giving me that brooding, sexy look I wanted to lick off his face. But now that I had found him, I was lost and had forgotten what I wanted to say. It made sense while I was trekking over here. Now I wonder, maybe I was overreacting, because here he stood.

"How old are you?" I asked the most random question ever.

Draxton tapped his foot. "Thirty-eight. What is this all about, Kellan?"

I rubbed the back of my neck. "Yeah, maybe I was treating you like a child just now. I'm sorry. I was caught off guard when I woke up this morning and you weren't there. My mind instantly went to the most unlikely but worst-case scenario. Please let me know where you're going, and I promise I'll do the same."

"I didn't want to wake you," he barked at me. "You fell asleep instantly last night. I figured you were dead tired, and if I wanted you awake a little longer tonight, I would have to let you rest up. You know, so you don't have an excuse to be rude to me."

"Rude?"

"You turned me on and left me hanging."

"Gods, you are..." I turned away, breathing deep, thinking what to say, before facing him again. "I'm sorry, yes, I was exhausted."

"That's why I let you sleep in," he grunted.

I blinked. He was so sharp-minded. I had to step up my game. I took a deep breath and tried again. "Okay, thank you, I understand that now. But I would never have done that to you. I would have waited or woken you because I would have thought about how scared you would have been..." I stopped speaking when I realized my explanation wouldn't get through. "Just try never to leave me alone, because I need you, um...I feel better if I know you are safe, please," I chose to say, making it clear to him that we should stick together, to get home together.

"Okay, I will. Just remember, you were the one who said you didn't want to have sex with me, and then last night, you were all over me. At first, I thought you weren't that into me, since you turned me down. Three times. Then, we kissed. Last night, you were grinding on me, only to fall asleep in my arms. I told you, relationships aren't my thing." He broke eye contact and turned to watch the goats being milked.

My eyes darted from him to the goats. "Draxton?" I said to get his attention.

He turned back to me, but his eyes were focused on something else behind me. "My work comes first, and right now, that means finding proof of an advanced race. I wanted to check out this cave. Now that I have, I can tell you it's basically a mini farm, and it's smart to keep the animals and humans separate. Did you know diseases can actually jump from animals to humans, even worms, and some can be deadly?"

I shook my head and smiled at him. It truly bothered him that I was resisting. Perhaps if I pursued him and engaged in intimacy, he would see that as a sign of my interest and desire for him. My heart raced as I realized that it was him, his gaze upon me, making me feel nervous. I looked up at him like a shy maiden. Draxton challenged all my preconceived notions of myself. I had always been the one in charge, the bossy, self-assured type. But now we were entering another realm, and I suddenly contemplated how it would feel to submit to him. He appeared regal, so confident and unfazed.

Draxton widened his stance, arms still crossed. "You sound like a boyfriend ensuring I know my limits and boundaries. I don't like men who think they can control, manipulate, or change me. You had your chance. I see now who you are. You kissed me in the Dinaledi Chamber because you felt it was time. Last night, when you were cold, you used my body for warmth, and now you want me to keep panting after you like a puppy, hoping to be petted and trained."

My mouth fell open. I couldn't believe what I was hearing. Is this how he sees me? I didn't know how to respond to that, so we stared at each other, our eyes doing the talking. The fear of losing him and the relief of finding him safe while he was mingling with others felt good. His assertive words were commendable, and I didn't want to change him at all. My tear ducts began to prickle, and my nose stung. He'd hurt my feelings on such a visceral level that I was about to cry. I was never one for drama, but here I was, causing it, doing exactly what I'd told myself I wouldn't do.

He surprised me. The vicious look on his face softened as he uncrossed his arms and reached out to my icy face. I stood in awkward silence. Draxton's warm hands cupped my cheeks, and he wiped away the frozen tears with his thumbs. I didn't push him away. I waited to see what he would do next because whatever I said and did was interpreted both wrong and completely accurate.

"It seems we were both wrong. I'm sorry," he whispered. He was unpredictable. Then again, I didn't really know him. I had seen him for just a few minutes on a couple of occasions, and he was so obsessed with either having sex or finding the door that we didn't have much else to discuss. I thought I understood him based on what Tobias had told me and what I had read about him.

"I'm sorry too. I don't know anything about you, *or even myself.* I never wanted to train or manipulate you. That was never my intention. That's not what I want you to believe. Can we go back to our kiss in the cave? Can we start over from there?" I asked, sounding foolish.

Draxton's dark eyes were nearly black, resembling the caves he enjoys exploring, searching for things no one believed existed. And yet, there we were. He was searching my eyes, my soul, for something I didn't think was there. I shrugged, attempting to seem innocent and casual. Then again, maybe he saw through my act.

He gave me a lopsided grin. "So, I'm spoiling *your* plans, Professor."

"Yes, all of them," I said breathlessly. "I don't want to cramp you, but I also don't want to be just fuck buddies. I think you should show me what you want because I do want you." I want all of you for *myself*, I thought.

Draxton gave me the softest kiss. Nothing wild or furious. Just a gentle lips-to-lips while maintaining our intense gaze. "We are in a predicament because I don't know how to be intimate without running away. In that sense, you need to understand. I have this fear. I don't want to owe you anything. I want you to be independent since I can only focus on myself. I'm not good at putting myself in other people's shoes. I don't care much about what boyfriends want. I take it day by day, moment by moment, and if you're here by my side, great, if not, that's fine too, because our paths will cross again. There are ways to show you I care, and I would if the opportunity arises. But I don't have the mental capacity to worry about *your* feelings and things I can't control. I can only manage what I feel and what I do. So, Professor, let's take it day by day and moment by moment. I promise I will try to do better by letting you know where I am at all times—only because you need me to."

I swallowed loudly and gave a slight nod. "Yes, thank you. Our messed-up situation has changed, and what we needed back home, we don't need here." Draxton glanced over his shoulder to ensure we were alone, then stepped closer, pushing against me while still holding my face in his hands. Fire ignited in my belly as he brought our lips together and kissed me until my knees buckled. I was on the verge of collapsing and about to pull him down so I could grind against him.

"Careful, Professor Kilroy. Children are watching us," he grumbled with a grin that sliced my insides into fluttering ribbons. If he only knew I had a weakness for him. *What was it about this man? Maybe it was this place that made me lose all my rational thoughts.*

CHAPTER 11
DRAXTON

OURO'S STORIES WERE NOT ONLY inconceivable but also never-ending. It felt like he finally had someone new to talk to and fully seized the opportunity to go on and on about unbelievable things, especially the one in which he claimed to be an Igigi.

I made a face of disbelief. He waved his muscular arms in the air and proclaimed, "I was born with the blood of gods. Before the invasion, my family lived in these mountains," he said fondly, his eyes crinkling at the corners as the bright orange flames danced in his warm yellow-green eyes.

Kellan was captivated. He fit in perfectly, which led me to wonder if I had misjudged him. I had thought he struggled to adapt because he walked around with a puzzled expression when he thought I wasn't looking. But I'm always watching him from the corner of my eye, even when my head is turned away. He leaned closer to Ouro, soaking up every word. The four of us had just skinned a couple of rabbits and were gathered around the fire, waiting for our dinner.

I shook my head. "Prove it, I want to see it. Don't tell me I have to believe, and if I don't, I will go to eternal hell. Prove it right now to us." I pointed to Kellan and me. I know I acted a little hostile, which was out of the ordinary here. Religion was pushed down my throat as a child, to the point where my grandfather had removed me from school and home-schooled me, saying he could do a better job.

Ouro narrowed his eyes at us. Snow snorted a challenging chuckle. Wordlessly, Ouro reached for his knife and pulled it from its sheath, where he had just inserted it after gutting the rabbits. He pushed the white fur sleeve of his jacket back, then pushed the tip into the soft flesh in the middle of his forearm. I cringed when blood bloomed, as he slowly slashed a deep four-inch-long line up his forearm. I wanted to squeeze my eyes shut, but I waited.

Nearly slobbering over Ouro and not hiding his

hard-on, Kellan patted my leg. "Watch this!" he said, like a boy showing his best friend porn for the first time.

I shot him a sharp glance, wondering what was going on with him. Even if Mister Perfect Professor was puzzled or unsure, he had the heart of a child within his chest. He thrust his chin toward me, keeping his eyes fixed on Ouro's forearm. "Look, you're going to miss it!"

I was fucking looking. I peeled my eyelids back, showing him my eyeballs. Placing the warm palms of his hands on my cold cheeks, he turned my head like a psychopath, forcing his victim to watch the carnage. Bright red blood ran in a thin rivulet down Ouro's arm.

"Fuck, Kellan! What's wrong with you?"

"Look!" he exclaimed.

Then, as soon as the cut revealed tendons and yellow fat popping up like mushrooms from his flayed open wound, the blood stopped running, and the gash knitted itself closed, healing in seconds.

I gaped. My eyes felt like gumballs about to roll out of their sockets, "Ho-ly shit," I exclaimed in awe of what was happening before my eyes.

Kellan released me and extended his hand, asking Ouro to see his forearm up close. We inspected his flesh. With his forefinger, Kellan swiped at the drop of blood that was disintegrating into dust on his arm. His forehead scrunched, and he suddenly looked sad as a deep, contemplative frown cut between his eyebrows. His lips puckered, and he chewed the inside of his cheek. "Ouro, Draxton and I believe you," he said softly.

For a second, I wondered why Kellan's mood had changed, but then he smiled at me, and I thought maybe I was reading too much into his reaction. *Was he hiding something?* I shook my head. Ignoring Kellan, I turned to Ouro. "Yes, thank you for showing me. I apologize. It's just that—"

Ouro settled back. "No worries, I understand. Hearing is not seeing," Ouro said as he sheathed his knife.

I wasn't about to ask about infection or tetanus if he healed like that. "When you say blood of gods. What do you mean? Did you or your parents drink it from a cup?" I was thinking about the holy chalice and the blood of Christ. Perhaps there was a connection to the time even before Christ was born.

Ouro topped off our mugs with fermented berries. The tartness was intense, but it gave a pleasant buzz. "I doubt anyone drank it from a cup; it was easier to just bite or suck on them. Maybe it was their cum…probably. We loved the taste, and we drank tons of it!" He laughed.

"Oh my goodness, are you joking?"

"No, it's true. Ask Callisto," Ouro insisted confidently.

I toasted them. "If Callisto says it's so, who am I to question it?"

"You arrived at a perfect time in Anzulla. It's nearly time for the ice to melt and for us to leave the winter caves," Ouro announced as he passed around pieces of rabbit meat. It lacked salt, but they rubbed mint leaves and garlic into it. The meat was charred on the outside and juicy on the inside.

This is not a cave. I know caves. This is a man-made alcove. A hollowed-out overhang not big enough to house fifty-five people, and judging by the number of pregnant women popping out babies, it's soon going to become overcrowded in here.

Kellan pointed outside. "You said the people go down to the shore to catch fish."

Snow nodded, and after chewing said, "Yes, many things happen in the summer. We get ready for winter and war."

"Da!" Ouro agreed and fell to the side, crossing his legs at the ankles. Kellan shook his head. Talking of war made us nervous.

"I was going to suggest we build weather-resistant housing for the people."

"You were?" Ouro asked skeptically.

"Yes, you said we are here to help. We believe that teaching your people how to build safer houses could be a way for us to help." I tried to keep my voice friendly and steer clear of the subject of war. We knew nothing about warfare except that it kills innocent people, leaving everyone worse off than they started.

"We'll talk about houses later," Ouro said, dismissing the topic.

Kellan snuggled closer to me and whispered in my ear, "I can share more stories about the Igigi if you'd like. I have firsthand memories of the phenomenon." His warm breath sent tingling through my body. Maybe this is why he was sad earlier. He probably wrote a book about the Igigi and discovered his research was wrong and all nonsense.

I shrugged. "I want to learn more about the invaders. I'm curious about their advanced technology. That was what I was originally searching for when we got pulled through the door."

"There are many tales about invaders, wars, and our survival." Ouro sat up to flip another rabbit over. The meat smelled delicious, and the one taste I had a few minutes ago was just enough to keep my stomach crying out for more.

"It looks ready, Ouro," Snow said as he helped him remove the meat and offered it to us.

I savored every bite, then licked my fingers clean, following their lead.

"Yes, for us, your stories are incredible," Kellan said as he placed his hand on my knee.

I had slowly become comfortable with him, especially with being touched in this way—gently, meaningfully, and with care. I didn't enjoy being smothered with affection; it made me nervous. But this was okay. It wasn't loud and overwhelming like the buzzing of flies, constant, relentless, and irritating. Unwanted affection made me want to cover my ears or pop in my earbuds, making me crave solitude in the darkness. However, our circumstances were quite different from those at home. This was for support, for sturdiness in the unfamiliar. Back home, I would have seen this as an attempt at a relationship, which meant being torn away from my work. I never had time for dinners and movies, and that's what boyfriends wanted. As soon as a man started asking when I'd be done working, I knew it was time to let them go. My work meant everything to me. But my situation had changed. I wasn't working, and I only had Kellan. I was glad about it. Lacing my fingers with his, I knew I had done the right thing when I looked up and found him smiling at me with fondness.

Ouro's voice broke through my reverie. "Our world was peaceful, lush, and thriving. The invaders were its antithesis—cold, calculating, consumed by hatred. To them, we were mere scavengers, dwelling in the mud. Those humans who allied with them viewed them as saviors, desiring their half-machine existence. The invasion destroyed Anzulla, and thousands died. Our homes were shattered, leaving only us—the last of the San."

"So, are they machines with mechanical arms and legs?" Kellan asked what was on the tip of my tongue.

Ouro shook his head. "No, they are hybrids. They look like us, but they aren't like us on the inside. No blood. No bones. No organs. Nothing but hate and machine. They pretend to be good, but they're not." Ouro scowled and clucked his tongue. "Some think they saved us. They did not save us. They killed us! Their technology spread across the land, flowing into the rivers and the ocean, consuming and polluting everything. We were caught by surprise. It was chaos. Those who understood guns and war and technology fought and fell like embers from the skies. They invaded in numbers I cannot count. They swarmed us, over and over, until nothing was left. We never stood a chance. Like wretched phantoms, they brought death, darkness, loss, and despair.

"I am the fallen son, forgotten and alone. With the people I've gathered, we now prepare to fight before we die, on a dead mountain, on a dead land, and surrounded by dead waters." He clenched his fist against his chest. "But we will endure. The war is not over. They think it is. However, your and Callisto's arrival has unleashed a dangerous ambition within me to destroy them on a massive scale. We will be ready, there will be war, and you have delivered the message that we have not been forgotten, that we must persevere. I will open the mountain and bring my people from the brink of extinction, and we will be renewed. With calculated and fierce strength, we will annihilate the nest of our enemy. They will burn like we burned, they will be flattened to diamond dust. Their hybrid bodies will explode out of their meaty confinements, scattering wires and machine parts over their Light Continent. Their electronic brains will smoke, and with the hammer of my wrath, I will splatter their mechanical bones into an oily sludge that Atlas will set afire so they may never rise or invade anything ever again." Ouro's shoulders sagged. "Most have forgotten the war." Ouro pointed upward. "The traitors believe the invaders protect us from the sun. The sky is covered with an invader blanket."

I turned to Kellan, banging my fist on my thigh. "I knew it! What did I say last night?" I waved my arms around animatedly. "We're in a freaking snow globe! We're being watched. I can feel it. We're in a huge ball-shaped studio." I laughed alone. Somber faces stared back at me. Kellan looked deathly pale, as if he might be sick. *Was I the only one who thought it was funny? Probably.* I swallowed my laughter. My grandfather would have said I was being insensitive...

Ouro seemed all talked out, and Snow didn't look much better. Kellan appeared sorry for me. "Thank you. We can share more later, and we'll tell you about our homes in a time and place far from here..." My voice trailed off.

Kellan scooted closer, whispering, "We're lucky to be here. We could've landed anywhere, anytime, but we're here." Leaning in, I breathed deeply to steady myself.

"I agree, we are lucky. Imagine if we had arrived just a little over a century earlier, we would have witnessed the fallout," I added, relishing being his sole focus with fire dancing in his eyes. He seemed to like me, no matter how awkward I could be sometimes.

He rubbed the cold tip of his nose against the scruff of my beard. It's been three days since I last shaved, I thought. "I have something to tell you." He stroked and purred, murmuring like a cat against the shell of my ear.

My head snapped up with interest as I instantly forgot about what I had felt shitty about just seconds earlier. "Yeah?"

"Yeah." He breathed against my face. My toes curled, and my cock uncurled like a spring. His warm breath in my ear kept me in place.

"Ah-hum, I do," he rumbled against my cheek. "I knew about the door," he said, and I froze in place. It's stuff like this that makes me want to run and explode somewhere in private. I turned my head down. So many emotions started to boil inside me. But my traitorous cock liked Kellan up close, and near me.

"I have recorded direct accounts, apart from my research, on African myths about people and animals emerging from another time, especially around the Star Caves area," he whispered with a purring rumble.

"*What?*" Curiosity surged, and it started to sound like a beehive inside my skull. My eyes widened, gleaming with interest as I looked at him. He smiled, knowing he had me hooked.

"It's not supposed to be news. If you've read the research papers and books on the subject, you probably discussed it with Tobias, and he knows that. He should have told you." Kellan's words pierced my heart and mind. *Why do I allow this?*

I almost told him that I didn't want to know. I nearly jumped up and ran away. But for some inexplicable reason, he fucking waited for me to process it all. The noise in my mind dissipated, and my heart rate returned to normal. We sat in silence for a while as the four of us stared at the last rabbit waiting to be picked clean, and then it hit me. I straightened my back and narrowed my eyes at Kellan. "That's why you weren't surprised when I showed you the map. I thought you were either hiding your surprise or that it was no surprise at all. Why lie by omission?"

"I couldn't spill all my secrets on our first date. I had to keep it cool. Make you work for more, Mr. Dubois. For instance, my family...no, not family, my father, has been living in that Cradle for many generations, and I've heard some strange stuff about the Igigi."

I dramatically raised my hands. "Like what? Please share." Sarcasm dripped from my words, but I was secretly annoyed with myself for not doing my homework and trusting Tobias too much.

Kellan waved his hand in a circle, gesturing everywhere. "Earth's name is Anzulla, not Earth."

Ouro clapped his hands at us. "That's exactly where you are! Callisto was supposed to go to the time before the invasion to save Anzulla. Now you've ended up here, in this time. I'm convinced Callisto will protect you while you help us get rid of the invaders. We must prepare for war!"

At the mouth of the cave, Callisto lifted his head from his front paws. He was eavesdropping, not sleeping as I had thought. He perked up and let out a joyful bear bark.

I let my head drop. "Damn, Anzulla. Fucking Igigi. I've never heard of that before. I thought I was an expert, but now I hear I've only been scratching the surface. I bet you know even more, which is why you resemble Ouro's family!" I blurted.

Kellan didn't freak out. He didn't even try to deny it. "You noticed Ouro and I resemble each other?" he asked.

"Yes," I said, pointing a finger at Kellan. He reached for the charred rabbit, plucked the hind legs off, and handed one to me. We sucked the bones clean in uncomfortable silence. Ouro and Snow lay on their sides, staring at the cave's roof.

I grunted in irritation and wiped the meat fat from my mouth, then pointed a finger at Ouro to respond to his earlier remark about war. "We're going in circles, anyway, Ouro. That's not what I wanted to hear when I asked about advanced technology. We aren't fighters, warriors, or bloody soldiers. I don't want to start a war with your invaders." I waved my hand between Kellan and me. "We know nothing about fighting."

Kellan clutched my shoulders and whispered, "Shhht, calm down, Draxton. Remember who you're talking to."

I shook off his grip and jumped up. "How can you just pretend and go along with this crap? What the blazing hell, Kellan! Perhaps your blood does the same as Ouro's. Have you ever bled and seen what it does?"

Kellan looked in surprise at me and shook his head. "How did you reach this conclusion? Gods, you have an amazing mind, Draxton. No, not my blood," he replied. "My father's, yes. But not mine."

I was right. He did look sad. He thought about his father's blood earlier. I turned and started marching to leave the cave. Callisto growled at me as he sat up, forcing me to skid to a halt. I blinked as he *poofed* like the Ghostbuster Marshmallow Man. I turned back to

Kellan. "Look at this. It's bullshit. This is not okay. Kellan, you knew about the door and this place, and again, why do you look so much like Ouro-fucking-boros?"

"Hey!" Ouro jumped up. "You don't come in here screaming in my home. First, it hurts my ears, and second, it looks like you need to blow off some steam."

"Blow off steam?" I stomped my feet. "How? Where?" I pointed at Callisto, blocking my way. "And why the fuck would I do that, if you say so?" I shouted, pinning Ouroboros with a grave stare.

"Draxton, you're overreacting!" Kellan said calmly. I panted like a dying mammoth, glaring at him. He slapped his hands over his mouth. That felt like dousing me in oil and setting me on fire. My fists clenched, and my eyes widened as my blood boiled and flames of anger reddened my neck. "Oh my god, I'm sorry, Draxton. You have every right to be upset, but..." Kellan backtracked.

I ignored the monster bear, Snow, and Ouro, then turned my fury on Kellan, shouting, "T-t-t that's it! You never ever say that to me, ever again. And for fuck's sake, explain yourself now!"

Kellan lifted his palms, trying to calm me while speaking over me to Ouro. "My father...he...Yeah, I think we could be family, yes."

I ran my fingers through my hair. "What the hell, Kellan?"

"What?" Ouro exclaimed. Callisto made a grizzly mewling noise.

Snow sprang to his feet. "Yes, I agree with Draxton! Please explain because this is news to all of us."

Kellan nervously shifted from side to side. I moved closer, and with the help of freaky Callisto, we cornered Kellan at the back of the cave. He seemed to grasp what was happening and dropped all pretense, his shoulders sagging like a deflating hot-air balloon.

"Talk now!" Ouro commanded in a low, menacing voice from behind me.

Kellan sighed. Meeting my gaze, he said, "I needed to make sure you were trustworthy. I wanted to tell you, but the moment never came. We hardly know each other, Draxton. Please understand that. I'm telling you now. I wasn't hiding anything. Please forgive me. I will share everything I know. Being here makes my father's story much more believable." He spoke, looking heartbroken and innocent.

The pleading look on Kellan's face stirred a tinge of sympathy for his trapped misery. To relieve the pressure, I stepped aside to make room for Ouroboros, who was grunting behind me. He tilted his head, eyeing Kellan as if seeing him for the first time. We waited. Callisto's toenails scraped against the cave floor as he plopped his hefty body down. His warm breath brushed over the back of my neck, oddly comforting, and I glanced at him. He blinked his crystal blue eyes at me, holding my gaze. *Was he asking me...what?*

"Well, start talking," Ouro barked.

Snow stood, chin in hand, sizing up Kellan. "Yeah, talk."

Kellan grumbled an *okay-here-it-goes*.

CHAPTER 12
KELLAN

MY AUDIENCE WAITED FOR ME TO SPEAK. I chewed the inside of my cheeks as if it were gum. I never thought I'd reveal my father's secret here in a cave where he could have stood, had his friend not pulled him away from the fires and shoved him to safety. I drew in a long, heady breath and let out a sigh like a dying geezer. Facing three attractive men, a white bear included, I rolled my gaze from one to the other as they waited with bated breath, piercing me with question marks in their eyes. Best audience ever to reveal the one thing I promised my father never to share with another soul unless I trusted them. I had no choice, and the circumstances were such that it didn't matter whether I trusted them yet or not. Ironically, it was in the time and place my father had left behind, so this leader, Ouroboros, had to pick up the pieces. Alone. He better not call my father a deserter or, worse, a fleeing coward. "Hmmm." I let out a long, rumbling grunt, staring at them. I would not allow those words to come near my father's name.

I narrowed my eyes and assessed my audience. Each one was unique and exotic in their own way. Snow appeared as an elf-like albino. He was tall, pale, and slender, with soft white hair, white eyebrows, and blue eyes so light they shone silver in the firelight. I agreed that Ouroboros resembled me a bit, but if he was my brother, it would certainly be from another mother. He was taller, had a much broader chest, and a sculpted physique. My eyes were a shade darker than his, but the shape of our eyes, noses, and even our lips were identical. The first time I saw Ouro smile, he reminded me of my father.

Draxton, with his curly black hair, long eyelashes, and dark, calculating eyes, was strong and his body was honed like a typical spelunker, fit and athletic, designed to endure hours of climbing, crawling, and chasing dreams while sometimes neglecting to eat. We shared the same build and height. I was lean and tall, thanks to the excellent genes I inherited from my father. Earlier, Draxton and I navigated the icy terrain together. I stayed on pace while we watched and learned about hunting rabbits. I wasn't a gym rat, but I carved out time for the occasional solitary rock climbing session to escape the office and alleviate the stress built up from constantly dealing with needy students and frustrating faculty staff.

I lifted my hands. "Just back up a little. I feel like I'm being attacked and put on the spot for something I never did and only heard about. So back up, please," I requested regally.

"Yeah! Let's sit back down," Ouro said, and we returned to where all of this began around the fire. Callisto shrank back to his normal size and sat beside me. I smiled at him, feeling like he was on my side. Ouro took the leftover rabbit bones and tossed them into the cold fire pit. Snow added another piece of chopped wood.

Staring at the dying coals spitting embers and the wood igniting into flames, I came to as Callisto nudged me with the tip of his snout, urging me onward. Okay, I thought, catching a glimpse of Draxton's clenched jaws. "A few hundred years ago, my father emerged from the Rising Star caves through the same door we've fallen into. He mentioned arriving just a few years before the English and Dutch settlers, which I estimated to be around the late 1600s. He passed away peacefully in his sleep at an estimated age of nine hundred years old."

Draxton gasped. "You sneaky shit! Why did you hide that from me? You are a liar!"

Ouro's silence sliced through Draxton's resonant, accusatory words. He signaled for Draxton to be quiet and then put me on the spot. "Who was your father?" he growled.

"His name was Gu," I said, sitting up straighter. "As you might know, Ouro, his name was Gu, and Gugusan means—"

Ouro's eyes widened. "King of the San people," he trailed off, and I pushed on.

"Yes, and he talked a lot about birdmen and baby gods—said he was friends with them, drank their blood, just like you. He stated that he had been severely burned and that his friends had abandoned him." I cleared my throat. "Ahem...at the time of Anzulla's destruction."

Ouro looked confused at Snow. "It can't be. My father...Gu died in the war. He died. Didn't he? I saw him being covered by rivers of flaming lava. Didn't I say he died?" he asked Snow.

Snow shrugged, confusion evident on his face. "I wasn't there," he said. "I wouldn't know, Ouro." He touched Ouro's lap gently. Ouro looked puzzled, his gaze drifting beyond the cave, as if his thoughts were wandering. Then, he took a deep breath.

"So, he wanted to return, but he couldn't?" he asked, his voice cracking.

I stared into his devastated eyes, so much like my father's. I was glad he asked that and didn't attack my deceased father's character. "He waited over four hundred years for his friends to come and get him. But they never came."

The distinct sound of teeth grinding caught my attention. Draxton shot me a sinister scowl. "No wonder you knew every inch of that place by heart. No wonder you joked about the gates to heaven. Did you know where the door was? Did you activate it?"

I met his gaze. He looked hurt and betrayed. Lowering my voice, I looked him in the eye and shook my head. "No, Draxton. I promise, my father didn't even know. He woke up alone and burned severely. He thought his friends had left him behind to go hunt for food, and he waited inside the cave, disoriented and badly injured. He moved deeper, searching the cave system, convinced he was stuck inside the mountain, but ultimately remained in the Dinaledi Chamber after realizing it wasn't his home. He thought maybe his friends had brought him and placed him there for safety, away from wild beasts." A wave of trepidation spread through me. Now, I had to tell Draxton the most unbelievable part. I scratched the back of my head. Please don't laugh, I thought as I gathered my courage. "He said his friends traveled in a time-jumping machine."

"Da, that is Ishtar! I thought he was dead or had deserted us! He's still alive? So he *did* abandon us!" Ouro exclaimed, thumping his chest and then mimicking a bird taking flight with a flourish of his hand.

"I don't know, maybe he did die, since he never came back for my father," I replied. "But I doubt my father was saved by a time machine. Remember, we fell through a door?" Callisto sneezed, and Ouro's head snapped in his direction. He stared at the bear and then said, "Callisto says Atlas pushed Gu through the door. Right before him."

Looking stunned, Draxton raised a crooked eyebrow.

I pressed on. "Crazy, I know. My father lived and waited inside the cave for many, many years—his words," I said, using air quotes. "He only went outside to look for food and water."

Draxton exclaimed, "The fire pits and layers of charcoal in the chamber!" The awe in his tone suggested that I could lower my guard. I was anxious about scaring him away, but this felt promising. The atmosphere around the fire grew more relaxed, and I settled into sharing my father's story.

"Yes. Eventually, he ventured further from the cave, returning each night and leaving early in the morning to survey the land in all directions. As the years passed, he always came back, looking for clues related to his messages or any signs that someone might be searching for him. With each disappointing return, he stayed away longer and explored further. He had come to know the people and tribes moving up and down, over the mountains, and back along the coastline."

Snow poured each of us a cup of fermented berries, and Draxton passed mine to me. "Thanks." I sipped a mouthful and continued, knowing that Ouro was waiting for me to get on with it.

"To the leader of the San!" Ouro smiled, revealing a set of berry-stained teeth for the first time since I began telling the story. He looked pleased.

Relieved, I leaned forward, eager to continue. "Yes, this is where it gets really interesting—"

Draxton interrupted, "No way! Your father had something to do with the Khoikhoi and San Tribes. The Bushmen?"

"I think, maybe, he did. He always said they were there before he arrived, that they were originally the people of the land."

Draxton folded his lower legs underneath him and sat on his knees. He bounced excitedly, clapping his hands on his upper legs. "So, so, so, your father saw everything, the history from before the Zulu wars?"

I gathered Draxton believed me and nodded proudly. "He did. He had many friends and just as many enemies. He called himself the ghost of the Dark Continent for his ability to be fast, in and out of sight."

"He was an Igigi?" Draxton asked.

I grinned. "Yup." I pointed at Ouro. "Just like Ouro."

Face flushed vermilion red, from the alcohol, Snow slurred, "Are you Igigi?"

I chuckled. "No, unfortunately not. My mother is a regular human. They met when she was a student in one of his classes. My father was an exceptionally intelligent man. He was extraordinary. He wrote textbooks on various subjects, including history, science, and biology. They fell in love, and he invited her to visit his home. My father, who had lived near the cave, waited all his life and finally accepted us as his home. When I turned eighteen, he took me inside the cave and told me about Anzulla, which sparked my interest in paleontology. My mother still lives in the house he built, just a few kilometers from the caves. I believed him because we would visit the caves, and his expression would be sad, as if mourning yet unable to verbalize his pain. I was always aware that he was different—wise beyond his years. He looked about forty years old, his entire life. That's why I believed him. It's impossible to remain unchanged throughout the years, yet he appeared forty in all the photos of my upbringing."

"Did he tell you about me and my brothers?" Ouro asked.

I smiled warmly at Ouro. "Yes, but he never shared your names with me. He mentioned he had beautiful and strong sons and daughters. He believed he was in love with his best friend, but he never truly fell in love until he met my mother."

Ouro perked up. "Da, that's true. I am like my father. I had one love for my best friend, but now I have multiple lovers to build a strong tribe. I have only one son, but thirteen daughters," he said, trailing off with a disappointed tone and a down-turned mouth.

I wasn't sure how to respond to that, but I was glad when Draxton cleared his throat and spoke. "You know, Ouro, where we come from, they have tested the seed of strong men. It is known that virile men like you usually have daughters because you need one son to take your place, but many daughters to provide you with countless grandchildren, and by that number of grandchildren, you are seen as rich and powerful."

Ouro sat up straight. "Really?" His eyes darted from Draxton to me. I nodded in agreement, even though I knew Draxton was twisting the facts to cheer him up. "You hear that, Snow? I'm rich and powerful!"

"Yeah, big man. You are!" Snow laughed.

"So, you are Igigi, but not because of our father's blood?" I asked.

Ouro nodded, his expression serious. "Da, I'm my father's son, but I have the strength of the mountain, like Atlas and Callisto. Many of us did." The sight of Ouro's downward gaze and furrowed brows spoke volumes about his loss. "All the others died. It was us, the youngest, who were told to stay inside, who survived. Atlas made the fire so hot that he caused the volcano to erupt and buried himself underneath the lava. He was incredibly upset after witnessing everyone being killed by the electricity and light spat at us by the Zelk machines." Ouro raised his arms. "He became so furious that he spewed balls of fire until the Zelk retreated to the Light Continent. He returned, roaring with madness. We were terrified of him. He was in a frenzy. I chased the last surviving people away with the animals beyond the mountains while I watched him fly into the mountain, heat it up, and shut the opening with melting rock."

Callisto grunted something at Ouro.

"I'm so sorry that happened to you. I know if my father had the opportunity, he wouldn't have been able to stay away. My mother would have made him come back. I'm not sure why the door opened for me and Draxton, though," I said.

Callisto snorted loudly through his nose. Ouro's gaze shifted toward him. "Callisto is saying that you are here for a reason and that you are meant to help in your father's place. You and Draxton were in the right place at the right time."

Draxton jumped up and dashed away from our circle, settling into a dark corner as far from us as possible. We watched him lift a leg, fling it over a massive log, and turn his back on us.

Snow leaped to ask a question, but I stopped him with a raised hand. "No, give him time. He doesn't mean to be rude. He just wants silence. To think," I whispered, worried that Draxton might need his earbuds and music. He hadn't said anything, so I didn't pry, trying to avoid reminding him about something he couldn't have anyway. If he freaks out and puts his hands over his ears, I'll make a plan to help him cover them. I didn't want him to know that I understood he was different, nor did I want to embarrass him by drawing unwanted attention.

My statement appeased Snow. He took his place next to Ouro. "More wine?" he asked and began re-filling our cups with bitter berry alcohol. "I understand. We all do because living in a cave with a bunch of people makes everyone feel that way at some point."

"Yes, leave him for now. Let's focus on happier things. I want to share more about Gu." Ouro raised his cup in the air. "To our father!"

Snow and I lifted our cups. "To Gu, king of the San!" we cheered.

CHAPTER 13
DRAXTON

I DIDN'T TALK TO KELLAN OR ANYONE ELSE for the rest of the day, and by the time the clan returned, ate, and went to bed, I couldn't bring myself to be merry. My mind was a whirlwind of thoughts, replaying Kellan's words from the first day we spoke until last night.

Ouro smiled, Snow looked concerned, and everyone kept their distance, as if solitary sulking were perfectly normal. Their indifference baffled me. Why didn't they think my behavior odd? Why didn't they urge me to join them, to snap out of it? They never pushed.

I didn't eat or sleep near Kellan or anyone's fire—the shock of it, the audacity. But worst of all, I felt something else beneath the anger—a pang of envy.

Kellan had it all—a legendary family secret. I shouldn't begrudge them. I should be happy for them. Ouro was surprised and now so content. He and Kellan talked nonstop about their father, Gu.

I was a mess of emotions, and seeing them rekindle their father's memories filled me with guilt. The longer I ignored Kellan, the worse I felt about my reaction to him opening up. Gods, I freaked out even before I heard the whole story. My grandfather drilled it into my skull, and still, I'd reacted like a ten-year-old throwing a tantrum. Kellan could've stayed silent, kept it to himself, or only shared it with Ouroboros. However, he wasn't hiding anything. What troubled me the most was Kellan's confession about his need to get to know me before sleeping with me. I was still grappling with whether his desire was genuine or if he was just worried that I would discover the door or expose the secret to National Geographic.

Kellan gave me a skewed grin as he sauntered over. He brushed the powdered snow from his head and shoulders before joining me. The cold air that followed him chilled me, and I wiggled deeper under a blanket of furs. I held one side up, silently inviting him to sit beside me by the fire. The three of them were up to something. They claimed they were taking a leak, but I knew they were plotting something. Ouro had once again sent the clan to work in the agricultural cave, and afterward, I heard them whispering just outside of earshot. Maybe they wanted to go rabbit hunting again. That's another thing. I should stop trying to figure everyone out. I'll go crazy if I don't stay in my lane. I should let them talk and bond with each other. I don't need to know everything about everyone.

Callisto also vanished without a sound while I was deep in thought. He was probably trying to catch something to eat. He came and went independently, not relying on us for food like a pet would.

"Brrrr!" Kellan shivered and snuggled closer to steal more of my furs and heat. "Are you feeling alright?" he asked, crossing his long legs while tugging and tucking the open ends closed.

"Always," I lied, forcing a smile as I fiddled with the seam of my jeans. "Thank you for sharing all that yesterday. You and your brother had a lot to catch up on. Did you enjoy it? You must have, being the only child, and now finding out you are not alone."

"Yes, I always wondered, especially after my father died. I wish I'd asked him more about his other family. Thank you for asking," Kellan said, looking hesitant and speaking carefully. I hated that. I hated pushing him away. I don't want him sulking or walking on eggshells around me.

I leaned forward. "Tell me more," I said, trying to bridge that gap I'd created between us.

Kellan smiled. "Ouro still didn't get his father back, but he's happy to hear that our father died peacefully without war or violence, and in the end, having found a mate, my mother, and having another son." Our dark eyes met. The brown and golden flecks disappeared behind his enlarging pupils as he stared longingly at me.

Pushing my hair from my eyes, I lifted my chin, keeping my voice calm and distant. "I have one question. It's the only thing bothering me. It makes sense you were at the site, checking on us. But tell me honestly—because I know you're not interested in sleeping with me—was that the truth, or just an excuse to avoid sex? Are you even interested in me at all?" That wasn't very good; I should have kept it light—a sharp pain twisted in my chest.

Kellan laughed awkwardly, and I just sat there, waiting for an answer, trying not to let my vulnerability show. "My wanting to get to know you is real, Draxton Dubois. I was sure about your trustworthiness long before we even met." His solemn gaze bore into my soul, and heat flushed through me. It must be the constant buzz from the alcohol. Otherwise, I was in deep trouble.

"So, I guess this is us getting to know each other?" A tiny flicker of hope trickled through the steel wall, encasing my heart.

"Yes. Never doubt me. Always ask. I promise you, I'm not a man who hides behind lies," he said, and I believed him.

"So, are you attracted to me or them?" I asked, trying to figure out the undercurrent I felt in the air between the three of them and me. I braced mentally. A head-on collision was imminent, I thought.

Kellan leaned closer, gripping my ankle. "It's a bit more complicated than that. I want you, as a person, I'm attracted to you and your mind. I know you need space, and I don't want you to think you owe me anything. I also don't want you to think I'm the jealous, possessive type of man. I'm very open to hearing a partner out, and I'm versatile about sex, once I make an emotional connection. Still, if I develop more than attraction towards you, which I believe is a strong possibility, I want you to know that's where I think we should have another serious conversation. I will never put my feelings and needs above yours. I'm just not that kind of man. Just promise to come and talk to me. I see you as a solitary man, unaccustomed to constant social interaction. You take longer to process your feelings, but you are also impulsive, which makes it difficult to determine if your actions are merely reactions to stimuli you haven't had time to process. Are you doing okay in that sense?" Kellan was strange in his impressive way. He knew me, I thought. He was the first person, other than my grandfather, who saw me.

I forced my eyes to stay connected with his. "I'm acclimating like a lizard, slowly becoming one with my environment while I'm learning to be an iceman dwelling in a cave," I admitted.

"Now, for the second part of your original question. Luckily for us, Ouro said that he respected us for being gay and that a couple of men and women preferred the same sex as well. But as the tribe leader, he would have appreciated us sharing a bed or two with a few willing women. He has a tribe to rebuild, after all." Kellan snorted a laugh, shaking his head, which lightened my mood. "Don't freak out. I'm only the messenger. As things are, some women do not want men either, but they are willing to carry a child. They don't know who the father would be because all the willing men's seed is collected and injected into her vagina by her partner."

"Uhm." I realized where this conversation was headed. I admit, it's not an absurd request from a leader trying to save his people from the precipice of extinction. "I won't mind depositing a few contributions into his gene pool, but not in the traditional way. I'm physically incapable of staying hard around a vulva. It scares me. But where there's a will, there's a way. Maybe he can tie me up and blindfold me," I said as Kellan's eyes grew larger and larger, staring slack-jawed at me. I gave a slight shrug. "I'm also not a man who puts my needs above others."

Kellan laughed, the sound filling the cave and lifting my mood. "Ouro would be glad to hear that, I guess." Kellan's smile lines were pronounced. He looked stunning when he was pleased with me. "Ouro said if we didn't want to talk war—"

"Yeah-yeah, then orgies were always a mood fixer," I interrupted, chortling and making a face by sticking my tongue out and pulling my eyes askew.

He snickered, his shoulders shaking. "Yep, that's why Ouro sent all the disinterested parents off to work the livestock and plants in the cave this morning."

"Oh my goodness, Kellan, I was never a porn enthusiast—either watching it or making it. Judging by the current mood in the cave, I can tell this is where we are headed. Give me an old map, and I'm intrigued and entertained for hours. I would memorize every inch and plan to find and explore those places. I thought you weren't interested in public displays of affection, either. I guess priorities re-arrange themselves when you get sucked into a vortex and get spat out in another time and place."

"Take it easy. And you are right, Ouro has plans for us. Trust me, he promised he would never force us to do anything we're not up for," Kellan said softly.

"Their frankness about sex is growing on me," I joked, "and I'm not made of stone."

"I know, believe me, I know," Kellan teased, sounding like a playful ogre, and we laughed.

Ouro and Snow had invited us repeatedly, openly entertaining numerous lovers, but Kellan and I found solace only in each other. Lately, though, Kellan seemed drawn to them. It was strange knowing they were half-brothers, but it didn't faze them, because I suspected *inbreeding* was occurring to maintain the human population numbers.

Since our first night, we'd stolen moments of in-timacy before sleep, but it became clear they were accustomed to complete openness. I was still ad-justing to undressing, washing, and feeling comfort-able in their presence. Kellan adapted far quicker and seemed to thrive.

My stomach flip-flopped a few times when he leaned closer to kiss me softly on the mouth.

"Would you mind if I joined them in washing and oiling?" he asked with openness and interest, patiently waiting for my response. I didn't feel trapped or backed into a corner.

"Sure, I washed earlier—no need for me. I'll watch you," I whispered. Kellan leaned in and kissed me again. I felt as light as a feather, as if I could float away when I opened my lips for a lingering kiss. Still, I felt frustrated and didn't understand why, even though I was getting hard.

"Join us if you'd like," he said, rising. He undressed with his eyes locked onto mine. My breath caught in my throat as heat flooded my neck. His knowing smile confirmed his teasing before he joined the others. Ouro swayed to a silent tune, washing and oiling Snow. Kellan grabbed a cloth from the boiling water over the fire and began working on Ouro's back. Naked, they washed and oiled each other, their genitals swaying freely. I wondered if the cleansing and oiling, said to promote healthy skin and warmth, had a completely different purpose.

The cave filled with the crackle of fire and the soft sounds of water sloshing and dripping, caused by the men swaying like tall grass on a calm, windy day, as they dunked and rinsed their rags.

They were humming something peaceful as their

bodies rubbed together, enticing me as I sat there gazing at Kellan, who was taking care of them. I pushed my awkward feelings down, reminding myself that what mattered most was that Kellan and I were safe, and this was an experience of a lifetime. I have never been good at hiding my feelings. I'd much rather hide myself, spelunking.

As my cock started to beg for more space in my jeans, the cave was getting hotter inside. *I guess being naked must feel good.*

Snow kept turning Ouro's hips to bring Kellan into their trio. Their long, uncut cocks were now nudging against Kellan's erect one. Ouro turned, giving me a full view of his front as Snow and Kellan continued to rub their hands over his shoulders, down his back, into his lower body as if Ouro was a pole and they were giving me a show.

Ouro smiled seductively at me. Inviting me. His cock hung low and thick, the weight of it too much to stand erect. Snow turned Ouro slightly sideways, so I had a view of his front and back. I watched transfixed as Snow slid his washcloth between Ouro's tight butt cheeks, his muscled glutes glistening, moving up and down.

These men have perfected the art of starting an orgy, and the longer I watched them, the more I thought my skin needed oil, too.

Kellan was mesmerizing. With not an ounce of fat on his muscled, tall, hairless, dark body, he swayed alongside Ouroboros with a yellow-brown complexion, slightly lighter in pigmentation, holding his cock at the base while rubbing his cock head filthily against Snow's hip.

Living in such close proximity, we're getting to know each other intimately and very well at an accelerated speed. Maybe that's why Kellan enjoyed it so much. This place and way of life of the San people were in his blood. His body became instantly accessible when we escaped death and needed heat to stay warm.

It was the reality, the trust, and the comfort.

Watching Snow insistently massaging Ouro's back while Kellan stared into my eyes, calling me over seductively and wordlessly, had me hard—hurting and wanting. My heart galloped, urging me to get up and join them.

Fuck, I wanted that! I wanted Kellan to do that with me. I wanted to do that with Kellan. His lips slid down Snow's neck, down to his torso, then as he sucked on the ivory hoop through his nipple. Kellan bit down, pulling on it with his teeth, stretching it paper-thin, while not breaking his gaze with me.

My breath sped up, and sweat beaded on my forehead. They turned to give me a better view of

Ouro moving in behind Snow. I glanced at their chiseled abs as Kellan went down on his knees to grip the swollen head of Snow's leaky cock.

My gaze jumped from face to face. The rawness of want in their eyes, an unspoken dare to join them, made me want that too. The heat in the cave climbed even higher as Kellan's lips trailed downward.

Shivers of delight sizzled down my spine, and I began toeing and removing my boots while loosening my belt.

For a second, I broke the intimacy between the four of us, momentarily hopping on one foot, and then the other to remove my jeans and undress.

I quickly regained my balance, making my way over to them. Gods, the sight of Kellan, on his knees, firmly grasping that engorged cock in front of him.

"Do it," Ouro commanded, his voice thick with lust, "make him rock-hard so his balls are bursting. Draxton, help Kellan suck Snow's thick cock."

The urge to join Kellan was overwhelming. The cave air chilled my skin, cold sweat ran down my naked chest, while a fire raged within. My cock and balls throbbed. Doing that together while they watched ignited an intense yet erotic buzz inside me. I trembled, mesmerized by the heat radiating from them. Like a junkie, I knew it was addictive—I knew once I'd done this, I would remember and crave that forever.

Snow, an exquisite albino, contrasted sharply with Ouro and Kellan's glistening, darker physiques, resembling a high-fashion gay magazine spread. Snow, as fit as Ouro, possessed a leaner, smoother build, closer to Kellan's. My lips tingled, and I licked them when Snow hissed as Ouro's erection slid between his firm buttocks. Snow steadied himself on Kellan's shoulders. A satisfied groan escaped Snow as Ouro's impressive length entered him. The sheer thought of a warm cock penetrating a hole shifted my gaze to Kellan, kneeling perfectly, as he pleasured Snow with his soft, full lips.

The world swam. I was dizzy with lust, and why was I still watching? *I should join him.*

Kneeling in front of Kellan, Snow's long, pink cock between us, we started to pleasure him, our tongues dancing over the vein-bulging cock.

Our four bodies swayed, pressing together in a slow, rhythmic motion.

My gaze locked on Kellan. He was constantly touching me—a hand, a mouth, a leg, even an ankle entwined with mine. And when physical contact ceased, his eyes burned into me, ravishing me with their intensity.

Snow smelled like lavender oil, a fresh scent so sharp and intoxicating, and unlike anything I had ever encountered. I copied Kellan, wrapping one hand around Snow's lower leg, and anchoring myself as we swayed. We bit and nibbled his groin, all the way to the head of his cock, gently, testing Snow's reactions, gauging his pain and pleasure.

My masochistic nature pushed me to discover Snow's limits. I bared my teeth at Kellan, signaling my intentions. Together, we synchronized our bites, teasing him to the brink of pain, nibbling his cock from the tip of his engorged purple head, up the shaft, into the wild nest of pubic hair.

We took turns savoring and sampling Snow's delicious precum, alternating between his heavy testicles, laving his magnificent cock with our mingled spit. Passing each other's mouths and kissing as we traveled along Snow's lengthy member.

Snow whined and moaned. "Fuck, this is intense...almost unbearable. I'm fighting not to come."

Snow gripped our shoulders tightly. He was holding back the inevitable, I thought, imagining Ouro pounding his prostate from behind and us torturing him from the front. *The mixed onslaught must be intense.*

"Take it, Snow, take it all," Ouro breathed heavy as he spoke, his voice tight with exertion. "Yeah, relax that hole. Uhm…Yeah…look at me…I'm so deep inside you." From the corner of my eye, I saw his hips moving slowly, sliding in and out with paced strokes.

Snow groaned, his eyes rolling back. "Yeah, drag it along my insides, just like you know I like it," he cried out shakily, rising onto his toes.

Sweat slicked between our skins as the four of us moaned.

Snow's weight nearly crushed my shoulder. I gripped Kellan's shaft with my free hand, and his eyes snapped open, locking with mine. The look we shared, drunk with lust.

I bit down harder. We moved rhythmically like willow branches in the wind, knowing Snow couldn't hold out much longer under this intense pleasure and pain.

"Just…one more…stroke, Snow," Ouro whispered, "then we stop."

"Da, da, da!" Snow snapped, retracting from our mouths. Dazed, we wondered what to do next. I craved Kellan right then and there—to push his face into the fur, mount, and ride him hard.

I realized I was an orgy virgin as Ouro pulled us to our feet and brought us to a large tree stump deeper in the cave. I looked at Kellan, unsure how to proceed.

"What the hell?" I looked at Kellan, who shrugged, gasping for air. His lips were as swollen as mine felt.

"Just surrender to the experience. Enjoy reveling with me in the giving and receiving, touching, sucking, licking, and kissing whatever ended up in front of you tonight. Ouro has plans, let them...I trust them," Kellan told me with a mischievous grin and a wink.

"Snow, show our visitors what we do here," Ouro said, turning to leave the cave, naked.

Snow pointed to the massive log I'd sat on last night. I'd never examined it. At least ten men would have been needed to move it. "Drape yourselves over the wood. Grip the handles," Snow ordered.

"What is this thing? I thought it was a dinner table. Is this a BDSM ice dungeon?" I asked.

Snow chuckled. "You'll love it. Everyone loves Ouro's log."

"Oh my goodness, the double entendre!" Kellen laughed, sprawling naked across the smooth, polished wood. His feet dangled on one side, his head and arms on the other.

"It's probably this smooth from years of use," I observed, feeling a mischievous thrill. It was like we were school kids getting away with something. I thought this was going to be fun.

"Yes, come on!" Kellan chortled, bouncing on his toes. "Let's live a little. I think I know what they're planning. Earlier, outside, Ouro and Snow were chipping icicles and smoothing their ends. They said it was a surprise. I bet he went to get them."

Hesitantly, I kneeled on the furs Snow had thrown down in front of the log for us before I sprawled myself across the smooth wood. My backside was up, mimicking Kellan's position, feet dangling toward Snow, hands gripping the wooden pegs hammered into the ground like handlebars.

"Are you comfortable?" Snow asked, crouching down in front of us. "Make sure there's room between your thighs. We're going to collect your seed, so spread your legs wide." His long cock swung stiffly between his knees as he bound my wrists with leather strips. The air felt heavy. I wasn't sure this was safe. I glanced at Kellan, to my left, waiting for his turn.

"Are you sure we are not about to be slaughtered and eaten alive?"

"Very sure," he answered. "Snow, if Draxton wants you to stop, will you?"

"We will, Draxton. Just say stop, and we'll stop," Snow said, tying Kellan's wrists. This was unsettling, and the tension as Ouro approached made me glance back at Kellan. "I'm only doing this because we're doing it together," I whispered. Kellan's eyes darted to something behind us.

The silence, the mystery, the suspense—it made me whimper with anticipation. Blood pounded in my head as I hung upside down from the log. Seeing Kellan helpless beside me hardened my erection.

"Oh yes," Kellan groaned just as warm oil was drizzled and slicked over my backside, dripping down my wide-spread thighs and balls.

"My thanks for the seed, brother," Ouro rumbled, a deep growl accompanying his words from behind me.

"Your turn." Snow chuckled, and Kellan moaned, roaring sounds that hinted at both pain and pleasure as his eyes squeezed shut and his knuckles whitened on the grips.

I realized the icicles were going to be carving canyons, judging by the size Ouro was pressing against my crack. The icy feeling disappeared, and I closed my eyes when more warm oil was worked into my tight hole. He spread me open first with one, then more fingers, then pressed the ice against my ass again.

I was about to be thoroughly fucked, and I should've shouted stop—common sense screamed it, but as Ouro held the ice, teasing my sphincter, I wanted more.

The moment his fingers wrapped around my balls and tied something there, I knew I wouldn't cum until he had allowed it. It was tight and heavy, like a sack of rocks dangling from a rope as it encircled my cock, like a weighty condom. I tested it, swaying my hips. Something definitely swung from my genitals. Suddenly, I understood Kellan's earlier shout. The ice vanished, replaced by a hot poker resting against me.

"Would you like me to warm you?" Ouro whispered in a deep, husky voice.

"Perhaps just a bit."

"How about just the tip?" he suggested, as he breached my sphincter.

"Holy, shit, shit, shit, shit!" I huffed and puffed. The next moment, the poker was gone, and it felt like my cock was dipped inside a snow cone. My legs were shaking. The strain on my muscles, being pulled in opposite directions, took me to uncharted levels of subspace. I yelled, my throat raw, and not once did I call out, *stop*.

The sensations of heat and cold, the fear of losing my cock to frostbite...or whatever was being done, it was absurd. He tortured me with heat and ice. Stretching me to the maximum. "Fuck yeeeees!"

I yelled when he rewarded me with heat against my prostate.

Shuffling and pumping my hips, my balls and cock stretched. I planted my toes, searching for purchase so I could open my thighs in an attempt to ride the resemblance of an orgasm building. I started begging, needing that ice to stretch and burn more. "My hole, stretch me wider, fuck, me, yes. Put your cock and that ice inside me at the same time!" I lifted my hips. This was something I wanted to experience again and again, just for the sake of sharing it with Kellan.

I heard him panting and giving Snow orders, just like I was begging Ouro. It was like I felt what was being done to him. Kellan told volumes and volumes of Outlander stories, traveling all over the place, never arriving at the end. Between the two of us, it sounded like we were being slaughtered, skinned alive, and liking it. Our voices must have been echoing down the mountain—no wonder the rest of the clan had left in such a hurry.

I lifted my head, the movement of shadows on the cave wall danced as Ouro and Snow's silhouettes stirred our asses with baseball bats, looking like witches stirring their cauldrons. "Ah fuck, ah fuck! I'm being coned with a motherfucking icicle!" I hollered, holding onto my handles while my hole was being worked like never before. I bit my shoulder in frustration. Sweat dripped down my face and down my arms. In and out, fingers, cock, warm oil, and ice. Over and over and over again.

"Please, Ouro, I want to come, I need to come! My prostate, my hole, my balls, and my cock. All of me needs to come!" I was deliriously high, dumb, and disoriented by the brain-damaging, extraordinary sensations of blood pooling in my head, mimicking being choked. "I feel like passing out," I muttered. I'd stopped trying to swallow. Spittle dripped out of my mouth. I was being used while I begged for more. It dragged on and on until the ice was gone. My whole mind and body were a mess of water, oil, and the need to come.

"It's time, Snow. Their balls are full. Now we're going to fuck your ice-cold holes and collect every drop of seed," Ouro announced. There was shuffling, and I hoped they would hurry up and fuck me already.

My hands were loosened. "Lift your hips," Ouro said, moving between my thighs, doing something to my nether regions. Life returned to my cock, and I sighed. It tingled and prickled. Enhancing the feeling of him entering me.

"Yes, yes, yes! Push that monster cock inside me." I begged.

"Are you ready? Are you going to come for me? Are you willingly giving us your seed?"

"Yeah, I'm...I'm so ready. But I don't know if I can do this without you or I touching me."

Ouro slowed to a halt. "You will. How's your cock feeling? Do you feel the suction?" *Suction?*

"Yes, that does feel good." I had no idea what was happening between my legs, but whatever it was, it wasn't enough to make me come. I lay still, concentrating on that trigger to help me blow my load. "My cock is tied. Please loosen the weights or whatever you have hanging from them."

"There's nothing. It all melted a long time ago."

"Am I imagining it now?"

"Yes, it's all trickery. Feel the heat of my pulsating cock inside you." He grunted into my ear. "Think of the heat, the good feeling. Let go," Ouro said, and unhurriedly sank into me. "Do you feel it now?" Ouro asked and started to move. I swear I felt his cock in my throat.

Deep and slow strokes. Sensual. It didn't take long for me to enjoy that good feeling he was describing, and after the fifth thrust of being pumped full of warmth, I *gloriously and finally* ejaculated as volley after volley of waves pulsated through me.

"Fuck yes!" My eyes rolled back, and I sagged, deflated, and sated. When I came to my senses,

Ouro removed the suction from my cock and dragged me by my ankles off the log. I landed on warm, thick fur. He cleaned me, and I thanked him and checked in with Kellan.

I saw what was done to me. Between Kellan's legs was a small pumping and sucking contraption. I assumed that as the ice melted, a vacuum was created that sucked semen into the tin test tube, covering his cock from base to tip. They were milking our seed to impregnate their woman. Yeah, I did give permission, and I have to admit, not knowing what was happening made it highly erotic.

"Be still, I'm going to mount you," Snow told Kellan. He turned his head, his bloodshot eyes meeting my sated gaze. Kellan was a shaking, trembling, blubbering, cold fucking mess, just like I was seconds ago.

"Ah fuck, you are so hot. You are burning my insides. What are you doing?" Kellan exclaimed.

Snow chuckled in the shell of his ear. "Maybe I'm pissing inside you?"

"Oh no, that's not okay, that's not my thing! Oh, my God, I'm coming." Kellan looked like he was convulsing as he orgasmed.

"Yes, come for us, brother. Make my tribe strong! Snow, keep going. I want another load from him." Ouro cheered from the sideline. "It feels good, doesn't it, little brother?" Kellan spasmed, and Snow panted, slowing down like a steam train rolling into the station and moving his hips extra slow.

"You're not pissing inside me?" Kellan blubbered.

"How can I fuck you and piss at the same time?" An evil chuckle bubbled out of Snow's mouth. Kellan lay splayed open, arms and legs draped lifelessly. His head was turned my way. I sat up carefully. My ass was raw. I don't know if he saw me. His eyes were half closed as he was murmuring incoherently while Snow started pumping into him ferociously. I stared at Snow's magnificent body, undulating faster and harder until he grunted. His body stiffened, and he reversed rigidly, pinching the tip of his penis shut. Kellan coughed and sucked air into his lungs, "No! Do not stop. I can go again!" Kellan begged like an insatiable pirate.

But, to my surprise, Ouro jumped into action. He removed the test tube thing from Kellan's cock. Snow swung around like they had mastered this move and let go of his blocked slit. Cum sputtered into the tube Ouro held for him, mixing his seed with Kellan's. Spiderwebs of cum dragged between the tube and the tip of his cock. Ouro put a cork into the tube and then kissed Snow with a smile. He was happy about his *catch* for the day.

"That's so fucking hot," I croaked through my raw throat. "One hell of a fuck." I scooted over, helping Kellan from the log and onto the furs. Suddenly, Snow was there, assisting Kellan to clean up.

I heard a wolf whistle, then the pitter-patter of feet. "Take this to Sopora!" Ouro said from somewhere far away.

"Yes, Father." I think that was one of Libre's older sisters. I heard rushing feet disappear, and then seconds later, I felt Ouro climb in under the furs, lying down, all four of us on our right sides. I wrapped an arm and leg over Kellan, spooning and holding him. We closed our eyes, and no one said a word as we fell asleep with smiles on our faces.

CHAPTER 14

DRAXTON

I FELT LIKE A COW, MILKED DRY TO THE PUBIC bone. Still, that didn't prevent me from engaging in it over and over again. "That semen-juicing, enlarging the gene pool, cum-banking, icicle fucking session was the last bloody time," I had said just yesterday to Ouro, and here we are, one day later.

We were drifting in and out of slumber, baking like a ball of wet earthworms next to the dying fire, when a clatter of wings and squawking entered the cave. The bird kept going at it until we started to move and undulate, retracting aching limbs and flaccid dicks until we were just four separate humans. Dismantled and awake.

Ouro rolled my legs off him. "Hm, we have

news," he said, wide awake, and got up at a speed that told me this was important.

I got up and cleaned myself. "Kellan! You have to see this!" I mouthed silently.

The bird squawked and hopped closer. Ouro yawned while stretching lazily. "What do you have there? Please show me," Ouro asked. The large black crow was hopping sideways and back and forth, as it continued squawking and dancing. "Oh, I see. Thank you," Ouro praised it with a sweet, happy tone.

This was interesting. I quickly washed all the stickiness away, then hurried over to where Ouro stood naked, still talking to the crow as if they knew each other. Scared it would fly off, I approached carefully. I was starting to love it here, *living the Dubois dream*. I affectionately squeezed Ouro's ass-cheeks with one hand and joined him, listening to their conversation, which only Ouro and the crow understood. He smiled at me. The crow's beady black eyes looked at us, still happily sitting in Ouro's big, cupped hands.

"Here." He showed me a small rolled-up paper between his pointer and middle finger.

Carefully, I picked it from between Ouro's fingers. The crow wasn't scared. "What's this? Was it tied to its claw?" I asked and reached out to stroke the bird's head.

Ouro turned to Snow and shouted ecstatically, "Snow, it's time. We have the design for the tattoo."

Unrolling the paper reminded me of the lollipop paper I used to unroll as a little boy. Something was scribbled on it. I couldn't read it, but below that was a small square barcode with the same fucking geometric shapes we found in the Rising Star Caves.

"Good," Snow hollered. I stood speechless and frozen, staring at the square with familiar-looking ciphers.

"Draxton, if you agree, when it is time, and we are certain that the tattoo will get you inside that tall building, will you go?" Ouro asked, tapping me on the shoulder.

Absentmindedly, I gave him a nod, still staring at the design. "Um, why me?"

"You wanted to see the invaders and their machines, didn't you?" Ouro asked.

I didn't say anything to Ouro but turned to talk to Kellan.

My face must have been ashen. Kellan looked at me and asked, "Are you okay?"

My heart galloped. "Look at this!" My hand trembled as I handed Kellan the small piece of paper. The temperature in the cave dropped as I waited for his reaction. He unrolled it, looked at it, and then gawked at me. His lips moved, but no sound escaped his throat. Tiny hairs rose on my neck like someone had walked over my grave.

Kellan shook his head. "Un-fucking-believable."

"Yeah, un-fucking-believable, in-fucking-deed," I said.

"So, what does this mean?" Kellan asked.

"Ummm." I was grappling for explanations when I remembered Ouro's question. Wide-eyed, I said, "Ouro asked if I would let them tattoo me and go inside the invaders' tall building, and I think I agreed. Are you willing to go with me?" A smile cracked my astonished face while I was pumping up the charm to get a positive reaction from Kellan. He shook his head in disbelief. I bit my bottom lip. I took the piece of paper to inspect it more closely. I pulled the same deciphering code of the alphabet my grandfather had written in milk from memory on the side of the map. "*Entry. Pass. Trusted. Human.*"

"Hm?" Kellan leaned closer until our foreheads touched.

I whispered, "You were correct when you said I'd hidden something by waterproofing the map. My grandfather had written an alphabet code along the side of it, and I had memorized it." My gaze met his. "This says, *Entry. Pass. Trusted. Human!*"

"No, fucking way!" Kellan playfully hit my left upper arm with a fist. "This is exactly what you've been searching for."

I nodded eagerly. "Maybe slipping inside and checking the place out will help them, and also be my chance to see it. We can't ignore this. This was in the tomb of King Solomon and Dinaledi." Excitement popcorned inside my chest and wanted to explode out of my mouth, but I held my breath, practically jumping up and down.

Kellan stared at me, perplexed. He furrowed his brow, and again, he examined the paper up close, then straightened his arms, studying it from afar. His weathered fingers pinched the sides as if holding a spider. "This is it, then? The key to unlocking their language?"

"Say yes!" I urged him. "I believe I've finally cracked it." I wanted him to come with me, but if he said no, I was going to go anyway. I didn't search all my life only to come this far and give up. I owed it to my grandfather. I have to see this through. My mother and father died while searching for these clues. All my life, I've worked so hard to give their deaths meaning—the Dubois family secret. The deciphering code is ultimately for this. To read the missing advanced race's alphabet. Okay, they are the invaders, but that's because we landed on this continent. What if we landed on that side? Would we still be thinking the same about the invaders or Ouroboros and his people? Perhaps we are not here to start a war; maybe we are here to bring peace.

A radiant smile gradually formed on Kellan's stunning face, and we were grinning like two mischievous clowns. Snow noticed our barely containable excitement and approached. We quickly straightened up, trying to appear casual, as if we weren't just discussing something secretive—the biggest find of my life.

"Hey, guys," Snow greeted us with an inquisitive smile.

"Hi, Snow," I replied, handing him the small piece of paper with the coded message on it.

Kellan and I exchanged excited glances. "We'll go when the time arrives," Kellan said, bumping shoulders with me. I was beyond excited—my hopes were fulfilled.

"Yup, just like I told Ouro would happen when the crows came home!" he exclaimed over his shoulder so Ouroboros could hear our response.

"How will this work? How will we get there?" Kellan asked.

Ouro waved the question away. "Don't worry, we

have Simon! He'll get you inside!" Ouro sat cross-legged, writing something on another small piece of paper. "I'm busy replying to him right now. I'll feed the crow, let him rest for a bit, then send him on his way."

CHAPTER 15
KELLAN

OH GOD, OH GOD, OH GOD! I WAS, WITHOUT reason, clueless, lost, and soon-to-be brokenhearted. I'm falling in love with Draxton! My walls were crumbling like old polystyrene—the pieces, floating away, taking my brain cells with them.

"It's been over twenty-five days since we arrived. I want to be alone with you," I murmured to Draxton while rolling up my furs to prepare to leave the cave.

"I agree. There are too many people talking, wanting, and suffering. It's driving me crazy," Draxton whispered.

"You've forgotten fucking, hunting, and surviving," I cough-whispered into my sleeve.

"I'm nervous. I need time to wrap my mind

around everything. There's so much to process and think about," he said, and helped me tie my bedroll and started rolling his so we could carry it on our backs. "I'd much rather prefer you wrap your lips around my cock," he said as if he was joking. I loved that about him too. He tries his best to make it look like he is the sexual butterfly. I *pfft*, rolling my eyes and not saying that I knew the sex was too much for him.

"See it as an outreach movement and a quest to do good, Kellan. We will have more alone time once we show them how to build better homes when we have our own place. Then, when we are settled, we can explore the unknown. There is no way for us to search the clouds for the door we fell through. It's somewhere in the sky, and I have no clue where to start looking. Let's find out what's beyond the borders of the magnetic field. They saved us and have been nothing but good to us. I'm a firm believer in paying it forward. See it as a learning opportunity, Professor. You can find out how those ciphers ended up in the tomb of King Solomon and Dinaledi," Draxton said. I rolled my eyes at him. He tittered. "Think of all the books you could write someday."

I let my head fall and stood chin to chest. He gave me a peck on the cheek and held up the bedroll for me. I turned to stick my arms through the loops.

"I guess. I can try to see it that way. We do owe it to them for keeping us alive."

"Exactly. But don't feel too obligated. Remember, we let them milk us dry to repopulate Anzulla. My attachment to these people continues to grow. I'm starting to feel like one of them."

"That's what happens if you get to know people and talk to them. Now we both made promises, making it sound like we are staying forever." I held his bedroll for him, and he hoisted it onto his shoulders like mine. "We already stayed the quarter of the winter, and now we're part of their summer routine too. It's a lot of responsibility. I don't want you to feel overwhelmed." I spoke in a low tone.

"But think about it. If this is where we're destined to meet our end, we might as well fully embrace it," Draxton joked, but I was nervous about the uncertainty. I think subconsciously, Draxton wanted to go because exploring was his default mode.

"I had a good life back home. I want to go home. My mother must be worrying herself into a heart attack. Heck, what about my job?"

"Yes, I hear you, Professor, but we have to find the door first, and to do that, we have to start somewhere because I have no fucking clue where we are. Being a loner and an only child, I have only Tobias waiting for me. I have no clue what the Dinaledi

Chamber looked like after we fell through the door. Did it close, or is it still open? For all we know, the cave collapsed, and they think we are lost inside, and if not, I wonder what Tobias is saying about our disappearance. We've never planned for this."

"Why would you think the cave could have collapsed?" I asked, picking up on the unnerving tone in his voice. This was the third time he had mentioned the cave could have collapsed.

"My parents died in a mudslide while exploring the Tears of the Turtle Cave in western Montana. They never found their bodies. That's why my grandfather raised me." Draxton wasn't looking at me and kept his hands busy packing cups and other loose items in his leather knapsack.

I put my hand on his shoulder. Touching him without smothering him, although I wanted to wrap my arms around him. "How old were you?"

"Four. I don't remember much. Missing my parents never dampened my curiosity about exploring caves. My grandfather taught me everything about exploring and reading maps. Finding the door to an advanced world was always my biggest motivator," he said, standing up and smiling at me.

It was fake. He was thinking about something. I could tell when he genuinely smiled. The expression on his face showed he didn't want to discuss it any further. I recognized his tells. He would turn his head a certain way the moment he finished talking to someone or when he disagreed, but chose to say nothing.

I pretended to laugh and turned away to give him a second.

"Ready?" he asked, grabbing my shoulder and turning me to face him minutes later.

"For you, always," I said, patting Draxton on the chest with my palms. "Your curiosity is the reason for our predicament. The question is, are you ready?"

"I've been ready all my life. I guess we might as well see for ourselves the extent of our"—he kissed my left cheek—"predicament"—he kissed my right cheek—"satisfy my curiosity, and assess our chances of getting home." He kissed me until my insides fluttered with adoration and delight. When he broke the kiss, I smiled like a fool. "There's my professor. I only want you, not Snow and Ouro," Draxton said as he began to load more stuff onto my back. I was dumbstruck by his words and my premature love—out of my mind, with no intellect involved in my feelings for Draxton Dubois.

"Just us, from now on?" I asked not seeing his reaction behind me, and I waited.

He gave a small, "uh-hum," and that was it.

Most men, women, and children were also ready to go and waiting for us. I was glad to get out of here. Our lives have regressed to killing our food, skinning, drying, salting, and softening the leather for new furs to wear. To survive the cold, sex has become something as familiar as brushing my teeth. Daily. Yes, I do brush my teeth. We floss too. Other than having sex, making homemade toothbrushes was a legitimate way to pass the time.

I enjoyed getting to know Draxton better. Seducing him has become something of a modern-day luxury. I was living in such proximity to him that I feared the physical and mental closeness had blurred the lines of intimacy that came very easily to me. I was falling in love too soon, and I didn't want to suffocate him, so I made a conscious decision to spend time with others to show him I was not a weight around his neck. If he felt the same way about me, he would need a lot of time to figure that out. Maybe he would never figure it out.

As the days passed, Draxton and I promised many things. We are on our way to help them build houses during the summer to withstand their vicious, deadly winter storms—nothing fancy, but something practical. Although I grew up with many people coming and going into our house, I realized now that surviving with strangers was on another level. One surpassing familiarity. Fifty-three survivors are all that was left on this small patch of land surrounded by dark, frozen ocean waters. Draxton and I had no choice but to stay and learn to survive in this unforgiving, weird world. We have a summer to look forward to. They say the summer lasts only a few weeks, and during that time, people built, hunted, and traded.

Among all those plans, Ouro was waiting for Simon's reply to confirm he had made contact with their informant, who had promised them information and a tool they needed. We had a hectic schedule ahead of us before the next frozen season arrived. Ouroboros said the living conditions weren't as horrid as they had been a century ago. They've adapted and survived, making things as bearable and livable as possible. However, it was still far from what Draxton and I considered comfortable living conditions.

Draxton and I quickly learned how to use weapons, like spears and long knives, when we'd survived an attack from wild boars. We'd gained new leather for our shoes and meat to eat. I grew up in South Africa and thought I knew what suffering and survival meant, but I didn't. I've realized I was wrong about many things. My ancestral history went much further back than the Cradle of

Mankind, and I admit, if I ever get to go back, I will never be the same. Not me or Draxton.

I was in a state of limbo. I felt part of this group of survivors. In a way, I could say I was visiting forgotten family members. For now, I was guarding my secret—I was thriving on Draxton's nearness. I craved him. When he wasn't with me, I felt like a foreigner who was not meant to be in this time and place. There were periods, even days, when I experienced love, camaraderie, freedom, and even deepening friendships so profoundly that I forgot I was taking part in other people's lives. I didn't feel forced to adapt, survive, and be one of them because I knew this was temporary, but if Draxton weren't here with me, the situation would have been so different. He didn't know it, but he held my sanity in his hands. I tried my best not to be a pathetic, needy man. I tried to show him that I could endure, that I was strong and brave like him, and that I could make this work until we found that door.

Draxton discovered his advanced civilization, but it was much more complex than he initially thought. On cloudless days and nights, I could see the sun and moon far beyond the artificial ozone layer. My father described Anzulla as a melting pot of species and technological advancement. But the Dark Continent, Ouroboros's world, was a post-apocalyptic ice world. The only technology that remained was that of the invaders on their Light Continent, and they were apparently the most advanced.

Soon we would have to cross the ocean. I realized Draxton wasn't just searching for a door. He wanted to know what lay beyond it, and now he had to decide whether this was enough; to me, it clearly was not. I worried because he was always looking ahead, searching beyond what is right in front of him—me.

I was telling myself that any archaeologist would give their left eye or a limb to experience history like we were. That shit like that couldn't be imagined.

Although I wanted to go home, I knew that if the door opened right in front of him, he would turn around and ask me if he could stay just a little longer. So, I didn't want to be the man nagging him. I wanted to give him everything he had ever dreamed. I cherished everything about him, but I would never be a man who restricted his optimistic, adventurous spirit.

I was willingly stuck and one hundred percent here with him. We've agreed to see what is waiting beyond this cave. If I had an airplane, even a drone, I could get a bird's eye view to see what this world looks like, maybe even find that hole we fell through.

Callisto had adopted Draxton and me. The massive polar bear, with his icy stare, never leaves our sides. I guess I was wrong about that too; the spirit animals of ancient kings weren't just statues, imagined or born of superstition.

Pointing his spear to the melting frozen landscape below, Draxton said, "Let's go explore!" The excitement in his voice pushed over the last pawns guarding my heart, toppling the chessboard game I was playing with myself.

He was brave for both of us. "Yes, let's go! I was thinking about how thankful I am to be here with you."

"Oh, my Kellan. I would not have any other man falling through a sky portal with me. But please don't thank me. It sounds like I planned all this." He jested with not a single mark of dread on his face.

"No, probably not planned, but thank you for normalizing the weird and twisted stuff." I knew I had said the right thing when he smiled that genuine smile, the one he reserved only for me. I was in deep trouble; I was swooning on the inside.

"It's better to make light of this. I'm just trying to make the best of our situation. It's useless to go to Disneyland and never ride on anything," he said.

I barked a laugh, shaking my head. "Ha! I doubt this is the happiest place on Earth!"

"Probably not," Draxton said. "No, I think the best is yet to come."

"It's a toss-up," I said. "Anything is possible. Our known history hasn't happened." He handed me a spear and gestured for me to walk.

"Yes, let's do this. Let's go build some clay igloos."

"Draxton, Kellan, are you coming, or will you stay in that cave forever?" Sopora called, her words sparking laughter from those nearby. I'd initially thought she was queen, but Ouro had no queen; he ruled like a lion amongst his pride.

"We're coming!" Draxton and I replied as one. I took a deep breath and stepped onto the wet foot-path leading us to the ruins of the harbor village destroyed during the war a century ago. The children were the most excited, hopping like crickets, joking, playing, and enjoying the freedom of summer.

We walked, slipped, and slid down the mountain for more than half a day at a brisk pace. By the time we reached the crumbling city walls, Draxton and I were completely exhausted. I was sweating under my fur coat, but I didn't want to take it off because then I would have to carry it in my hands.

It wasn't snowing, but it was dark as we followed the group up some ancient steps to a flat area where they set down their belongings and started building bonfires. Everyone was quiet but seemed to know what they were supposed to do. From about half a kilometer south, the sounds and smells of the ocean drifted toward us on the cold wind. As far as we could see, there was only rubble, rusted roof panels, and all kinds of debris, covered in mud and snow. It was truly the remains of a deadly war zone.

I was catching my breath, taking off the hot and heavy fur coat, and surveying the area when Draxton tapped my arm. "Look! Kellan, look!" he urged impatiently, and when I didn't move quickly enough, he cupped my cold face in his gloved hands and directed my gaze into the distance. Sometimes I think he treated me like people treated him. Like now, as he forced me to look.

When I saw it, I stifled my laughter and amusement. Among the rubble stood an ancient structure several meters high. It was hard to see the detail because it was already dark, but it pointed skyward like a beacon.

"Let's go check it out! I think it's an obelisk, Kellan," he said excitedly.

"Don't go there! You don't know the area. It's unstable. It's better to explore in the daylight, or take Libre with you," Sopora warned us.

I stopped Draxton by linking my arm through his. "Let's just take a look from here, and then check it out up close as the sun rises. We don't know if there's anything dangerous out there," I cautioned, hoping he wouldn't run off.

"I won't get lost in the dark. I'm a speleologist," he replied to my dismay.

"I know, but I'm talking about unexploded bombs, loose rubble, or even wild animals," I said as we stared at the needle-like object. "But I agree with you. It does look like an obelisk—a severely damaged one, missing pieces as if it had been chewed on."

"Probably shot at or crashed into," Draxton said in awe. "It looks a bit like a jagged tooth."

"From this angle, it has holes like Swiss cheese. Tomorrow we'll go take a look, and then we have to start cleaning up, making space, and laying out the city plan for the streets and clay huts," I said.

"I need to go take a piss," Draxton said.

I rolled my eyes as he hurriedly unhooked his arm from mine. I knew he had just gone an hour ago, and we hadn't drunk much since then. This was where I reminded myself that I wasn't his parent. I never wanted to be his keeper. I was his lover and wouldn't treat him like a child.

He was already moving when I called out to him. "Sopora warned us. We don't know the area, so I'm staying here until daylight." I sighed and started to unroll our furs so I could sit down and start a fire for us.

He wasn't even twenty meters away when a string of children grabbed their fire torches and ran after Draxton.

"Leave him. He'll be fine. The kids play here every summer. Libre will show Draxton where to go!" Sopora laughed.

I buried my head in my hands. "I'm hungry and thirsty. Please don't tell me I have to hunt for food." I chuckled awkwardly. I was exhausted and hoped Sopora would share her food with us.

Sopora kneeled, breathing into the fire, which flared to life. "Make yourself comfortable," she said, pointing to the leather knapsacks. "Help yourself. I want to build two more fires over there." She gestured toward the spot where I assumed the children would sleep. "I'll bring fire to you. Start by placing stones, then small pieces of dried grass, wood shavings, and goat pellets. We can share your fire. I made sure we packed enough supplies for everyone for two days," she added as she began to build the next fire, moving with the energy of a teenager. She had kids. She couldn't be that young. How on earth were these people hiking all day down a mountain and still looking ready to walk right back up again?

I gulped cold water from my canteen, unpacked

our gear around the fire pit I had built, just as I had been taught, and then made my way to the supplies. I saw the others getting their food and could already smell the meat roasting. As I watched groups of people gather around the fires, I realized I didn't look much different; I was bare-chested, wearing jeans, sitting on my haunches, and searching for provisions in the dark. My hair was growing out, and my beard was unkempt. "Where is that bitter berry wine?" I muttered. "I want to get snot drunk!"

CHAPTER 16
DRAXTON

KELLAN AND I HAD ARRIVED AT THE END OF winter. We'd fallen through the door almost two months before.

I couldn't say which month of the year it was because I didn't know if we were in the northern or southern hemisphere. Most days, we hardly saw the sun and moon, making it difficult to tell which equinox it was. Usually, an equinox marked the beginning of spring in the northern hemisphere, and the sun crossed the celestial equator going north. While in the southern hemisphere, the equinox occurred when the sun moved south across the celestial equator.

The skies in summer differed from those in winter. They shimmered as beams of light danced and reflected off the honeycomb-like structure above the clouds, shielding Anzulla. Summers there on the Dark Continent hovered just above freezing, about thirty degrees warmer than winter. The weather was so extreme that there were no spring or fall seasons. It was either cold, freezing, or fucking cold with ice blizzards. From what I had heard about the Light Continent, it was the opposite of winter. Summer temperatures were sweltering. The invaders desired heat and dryness so their machines wouldn't rust.

We had helped our hosts as best we could by teaching them about building dome-shaped homes strong enough to withstand blizzards and hurricanes. With our extensive archaeological backgrounds, Kellan and I both had extra experience in identifying the types of dwellings that endured for centuries. The ones we constructed resembled igloos built with geopolymer bricks, which we cut from layers of volcanic ash and clay. We also laid passageways that connected the huts, allowing people to move around from pod to pod while avoiding the extreme weather elements. After a week of teamwork, we completed the first structure, which was large enough for five to seven people to live and sleep comfortably inside. After that, the others jumped in, enlarging their new village, clay dome by clay dome—home by home. We kept going, working as fast as we could to finish as much as possible before the short summer was over. Rocket showed us something amazing by unearthing old water and drainage canals. We opened those up and started to repair and connect them, thus planning the layout of their new village. It felt good to help and to see their thankful faces.

Here, with these people, I never needed to search for a dark spot to hide. Ouro's people were kind, accepting me without question or judgment. We laughed at the jokes, and they genuinely thought I was funny, catching my meaning instantly. We swapped stories late into the night and planned the next day's activities to occupy our time. Kellan made it easy for me to be myself. His easygoing nature and laughter were contagious, just like his sincere smiles. This dark and cold place felt warm and bright when he was with me, and it didn't scare me. Even in a crowded room, I felt safe from judgment and expectations.

After a long day, we all came together for dinner and campfire stories, much like in the winter cave. It was our turn to host, so we gathered in our hut and used our new fireplace for the first time. I missed Ouroboros. He had gone on a walkabout, apparently like he did every summer. So, he wasn't attending our get-togethers at the end of the day. Kellan and I had more alone time, and he allowed me space, just as my grandfather used to do, so living with him was easy. I never felt trapped or obligated to act in a certain socially acceptable way.

"Why is Ouro not helping?" Kellan asked Sopora after a few too many cups.

Sopora tilted to the left, and Rocket nudged her upright. "He isn't against us trying to build houses," Sopora, our new neighbor, told us, also a few too many potato ales later. "Ouro's set on moving our people back into the mountain. But if building houses keeps us happy and busy during the summer, he's not opposed to it. He feels responsible for everyone on this Dark Continent."

I didn't want to badmouth their leader, but I thought maybe he had spent too much time in the wild and was avoiding civility. After all, it sounded like he was eager to get away and be alone. Something felt missing without Ouro's enormous presence. We ended up talking about him several times a night. We were being rambunctious and gluttonous. The summer brought different varieties of food, such as fish instead of red meat or fresh potato ale instead of wine, thus making mealtimes a festive get-together despite Ouro's absence. I was stuffed with flame-grilled fish and enjoying the homemade beer. Most of us looked tired after a day's physical labor and were not in the mood for our loud questions and discussions. Duty-bound fathers hoisted up pregnant mothers, gathering the children to go home, settle down, and sleep in the newly built houses.

"Goodnight, everyone," the younger boys called from outside.

"Libre, are you ready for bed, or would you like me to walk with you?" Sopora asked.

"Mom, I'm too old to be tucked in. You know that." He pouted, clinging to the doorframe. His mother made a disappointed face, prompting him to come over and hug her anyway. He was almost ten years old. Like Ouro, he was tall for his age and had his hair braided on top and shaved on the sides.

"You are never too old to have your mama care about you." She held him tightly as he stooped and leaned into her. Her love for him was evident in her happy smile. Kellan looked fondly at the sight of mother and son hugging. I bet he missed his mother dearly.

Picking up the conversation before everyone started to leave, Sopora continued, "Ouroboros prefers to go see and talk to the herds of animals when the mountain passes open during the summer."

I handed her a fresh, full cup of potato beer. "He

had said something about animals. We want to see what he's doing, but he said that it's for another summer. That implies he is sure we are not going home this year."

"Ouro has one thing on his mind, and that is to get inside the mountain and free Atlas to help us wipe out the invaders," she said with unfocused eyes. She wiped her mouth and continued. "He means no disrespect by not helping. He is just working on something else that is more important to him. We all work hard and try our best to stay cheerful and motivated. It's our way of life to spend our short summers like this. It's our tradition on the Dark Continent. When the ice shows signs of melting and the darkness turns to perpetual twilight, we take a break from digging into the mountain. It's our tradition on the Dark Continent. It's our vacation time while we prepare for the next winter and more darkness. Ouro has to check on the animals, ensuring they stay away from the invaders. But this year is different. You are here. Callisto brought you to us. To help us," she explained jovially with flushed red cheeks.

Kellan was licking and sucking on my neck, and I was waiting for an opening to say goodnight to Sopora and Rocket.

"Speak of Ouro. There he is now with Snow."

Sopora pointed to where they were entering from the long hallway of our house, with Callisto leading them.

"Ouro! Snow! Welcome, come join us!" Rocket shouted.

Ouro pointed to me and Kellan with his spear. "No, we came to get those two," he said authoritatively, meaning don't ask again, I have business with the Outlanders. Callisto chuffed, flinging his head up and down and sideways. I swear he meant to say, *get up and move your drunken asses.*

"But you just arrived. Sit with us. Tell us about the animals. Are they good?" Rocket said anyway, ignoring the urgency while he made way for them to come sit down. Sopora was just as ecstatic to see them. She patted the open space next to herself, waving them over.

"No, sorry, Rocket, Sopora, that will have to wait for another fire. Kellan, you and Draxton, please meet us outside," Ouro said, sounding serious. Snow gave us a small wave, then left, following Callisto and Ouro out.

I untangled myself from Kellan's long limbs. "Looks like we have to shelve those beers for another time," I moaned and groaned as I got up. Kellan rolled to his hands and knees, crawling and complaining about the untimely summons. Holding an unfocused hand to Kellan, I pulled him upright, nearly toppling backward. We found our footing, holding on to each other, then continued stumbling over each other as we put our boots back on.

We left Sopora and Rocket alone on the floor in front of the massive hearth. "See you later." Kellan waved goodbye as if swatting mosquitoes. I grabbed our parkas and spears, handed Kellan's to him, and then followed the two men and the bear up the mountain to a small clearing where they were waiting for us. By the time we met up with them, we were sober enough to stand up straight.

High above the mountains behind us, a plump moon hung. Ouro's spear swept from the land's edge, down to the village, and out to where the black water met the blue-gray horizon.

"A hundred long winters ago, when I was a young man, all that was green." He pointed to the far right with his spear. "There was a river, fed by waterfalls, flowing past the San village, where I lived with our father, my mother, and all my father's other children, your half brothers and sisters," he told Kellan. "That river forged a path through the jungle, splitting into two smaller rivers that cut off a piece of fertile land from the mainland before disappearing into the ocean. It was a special place, with a old, large tree, and among its roots, the warm water from inside the mountain mixed with the river water, possessing healing qualities. Now it's covered with ice and frozen waters." We listened and swayed to Ouro's rhythmic description of the land from before the invasion.

Far in the distance, the small summer village showed signs of life as smoke from the newly built hearths and campfires evaporated into the cooling air. Ouro followed our line of sight. "You've done well, thank you. The winter was harsh, and summer was short, but if need be, my people would always have a cave to flee to. This cave has saved my people many winters." He gestured with his spear "Come, let's go, walk where I walk so you don't fall into a hole and disappear." Ouro laughed, teasing us about our reputation for falling through holes in the sky.

I tittered while scratching my itchy beard. Kellan and I have both turned into troglodytes. We didn't shave because it kept our faces warm.

Ouro stopped and waved his spear in an arc over our heads. "When the skies opened and Anzulla burned, everyone who could fly took to the air to fight the invaders. But as they attacked, they either fell, exploded, or crashed. I saw it every night in my dreams for many years," he said somberly. "You know I don't like wasting my time in the village. My time is best spent working on the mountain. I decided today that you have built enough houses for my people, and we don't have enough time for summer. You helped build those safe houses for the people, but they don't need them if we can get inside the mountain."

I shook my head, a frown creasing my face. "Ouro, this doesn't make sense. Why live in caves when you could be safe and happy in the village? Everyone's open to new things."

"Draxton, we are vastly outnumbered. The invaders' numbers fill them with self-righteousness. If they were to attack while we live in those houses, we would be unprotected. We are like ants scurrying when we aren't inside the mountain. They can zap everything in half with a single swipe of their laser cannons from left to right," Ouro said.

Kellan raised his voice. "But even ants can kill, brother," he said.

"Now you sound like our father. Believe me, the invaders know that. For now, we have time because the machines are useless here. Thanks to Atlas and this mountain. We must find a way to fight them. You must help us. I am building an army, while we still have time, while they can't reach us. Together with the beasts, we will destroy their machines and take back what was ours."

I loved hearing Ouro's melodic, deep voice, but I

didn't like it when he spoke about war. He says he is over a hundred years old, but he looks like a solid, healthy, virile forty-something to me. I could tell his people came from a developed, hygienic, and intelligent time, despite how they looked and lived now, and opening the drainage canals and water systems this week only confirmed that fact.

Kellan stepped closer. He kept his voice low and respectful. "But you need guns. Proper weapons. If these invaders were able to kill all your people, even when your gods and kings were fighting, surely it would be reckless to start a war."

Snow shook his head at us. "We know, and that is why we need you."

Ouro tapped Snow's shoulder. "I've got this." He gestured to me and Kellan. "Snow and Rocket will help get you to the Light Continent. You are experts on buildings and those things of technology. Besides gathering intel on the invaders, you'll retrieve the rock cutter to break the hard rock covering the mountain's entrance. The winter cave had taken us a century to carve with hand tools. We need that machine to tunnel in...we'll fight. We've lived in darkness and despair, losing hope, consumed by fear. But the Gods haven't forgotten us. Your arrival with Callisto is a sign. Atlas and Callisto will fight alongside us. Atlas will bring beasts from far beyond this mountain to smash their flying machines. They will lose if they come to battle," he declared resolutely. "We believe in you!"

I rubbed my forehead. "What beasts, Ouro? Like Callisto? I ask because Callisto's a phenomenon I can't explain. Are there more like him? After seeing Callisto shrinking and talking to you, I don't have a choice but to believe in the supernatural."

"What is the supernatural?" Ouro and Snow asked simultaneously.

"Things we humans can't do, things coming from the Gods. Like Callisto. I've never believed in such things. In the time and place we come from, we never saw animals growing and shrinking at will, like Callisto. I was searching for proof of mythical beings, but most people from our time think it's fantasy. Most think mythical creatures are, well, a myth. Made-up stories. I've always said it is uneducated tunnel vision, through a straw."

They laughed. "You say the strangest things, Draxton. No, unfortunately, there aren't more bears like Callisto. But there are herds of animals, even predators like wolves, beyond the mountains. I have to go around and through many valleys to get to the wild animals. But, deep within the mountain, however, the beasts are so far away that only Atlas knows their location. He must guide them out, just as he would lead you home," Ouro said. "And what do you mean by...straw tunnels?"

I made a tunnel with my fist. "Where I come from," I said, "we look at things through something like this—a tunnel. Even though so much is happening around us, we only see what's behind and in front of us." I looked excitedly at Kellan. "This is confirmation that history is not what was written—"

"We need tunnels, yes, not, as you say, straws," Ouro said, latching onto tunnels and missing my meaning.

I gasped and turned to Kellan with wide eyes. "Oh! Holy shit, Kellan, my scorched earth theory. The evidence of a massive global fire dates back approximately twenty thousand years. I theorized it was a fire likely triggered by an electromagnetic storm, leading to a worldwide lightning storm that destroyed the grasslands and turned the lithosphere into rivers of melted rocks that shaped the surface to what we saw in our time."

"Smart man." Ouro slapped my shoulder with a flat hand, interrupting me. "I don't have a clue what you just said."

"What the fuck, Draxton, twenty thousand years? It can't be?" Kellan said, ignoring Ouro.

"See?" Ouro said. "That is why you and your Kellan are going to the Spire place. I can't go there.

They know all our faces. You have unfamiliar faces. Simon will set up a meeting. Snow and Rocket will help you."

"You still want us to go there?" Kellan asked.

"Da! You learn fast, see?"

"But, staying here is safe. If you stay here, your life goes on. Why not share the Earth? You are already sharing. Aren't you?" Kellan asked.

"You mean Anzulla? No, they are not sharing. They can't come onto the land; if they could, there would be no sharing. Only the mountain keeps us safe."

"Yeah, and now you want to drill a hole in it. Why?" Kellan asked.

"Because it's our home, and because Callisto said so." Ouro embraced us, pinning us with those determined yellow-green orbs, and spoke. "You can do this for me. Snow will help you. You can take Callisto with you. You are smart, and you will need Simon's help to bring me a tunnel maker," he said with conviction.

"I've never even killed anything but bugs in my life," Kellan said as Ouro hugged him.

"Yes, me too," I said, waving a finger between us. "I can't slit throats or defend myself. I'm not built for war! One loud boom and I'm paralyzed with fear," I admitted.

Ouro squeezed my shoulder. "That's exactly why I need you to go. You don't look like us. You look like them. You shave your hair and beard. Snow and Simon will help you. Then you go inside those tall buildings. Ask them for a tunnel maker and bring it back to me."

We stood in silence. I didn't know what to say. I was sure Kellan was also thinking about the twenty-thousand-year theory. Kellan scratched his head. The muscles of his jaw clenched, unclenched, and clenched again and again. I read it in his eyes. We wouldn't be told that it was okay, that they could send somebody else. No, we were their only hope. Atlas was our only way back home, and then it hit me. "So, Atlas has powers like Callisto, but is he a bigger, stronger protector, blowing fires, melting rock, a fire-breathing...dragon?"

"Yup, he is our protector, like Callisto. They are brothers!"

"A dragon!" I whispered, hardly daring to hope. "I'll only believe it when I see it," I added.

Towering over my shoulder as I sank deeper into the melting snow, Kellan let out an agreeable rumble. "Hm, yup!" he said, popping the "p" loudly in my ear, tugging me closer while pushing his hands deep into my jacket pockets, and lacing his fingers with mine.

He let go of my right hand and pointed over my shoulder to something far beyond the city wall. "There. What is that?"

"I thought you were never going to see it," Snow said.

"Ahhh!" Ouro exclaimed, pointing with his spear. "The ice has melted to reveal your surprise!"

Kellan bellowed, "Is that an airplane?" His voice echoed down the hill.

My gaze finally settled on the wings of an airplane lying askew on the shore of the icy waters. "Oh my goodness, why didn't you say you had an airplane?"

"It was not needed to tell you," Ouro said with a chuckle, sticking his spear into the ice, standing tall and proud.

Snow gave a teeny grunt. Shrugging in shame, he said, "It has a reputation for struggling to stay in the air. At the end of last summer, I crashed it. So, we've started to adapt it to land on ice and water. But..."

"A water landing airplane?" Kellan asked excitedly. He had mentioned a few times that he would like to see Anzulla from the sky, and no one ever said they had an airplane.

Ouro smirked proudly. "Yeah, if it weren't for Rocket, it would have never flown. He makes the fuel in his pots, pipes, and other things."

I shook my head. "Kellan. You can fly, can't you?" I asked, and Ouro and Snow waited for the answer.

Kellan answered carefully. "I can...It's something I did in my free time...but that thing looks like it crashed and is stuck upside down."

Waving his hand, Snow said, "Nah, that's no problem," as if crashing an airplane weren't a real setback. "When the ice has fully melted, we'll go get it. We'll fix it up."

"Ah! Very good," Ouro said. "See, Callisto and Atlas knew what they were doing by sending you to us. Now fix the airplane, Rocket will make the sauce on his fire, and you go to Spire City."

"Where did you get the airplane in the first place?" Kellan asked.

"It came through the crack with the invaders," Ouro said.

"I swear, Ouro, as soon as I think I know what's going on, you say or show us something new and extraordinary."

"I have stories meant for many fires," Ouro chortled, meaning there were going to be many more long-ass amazing stories. He waved his spear in the air, pointing to the sky. "The invaders came through the crack, *pow-pow*! They attacked and killed anyone who resisted—and everyone resisted, of course, refusing to hide, but to fight their flying machines."

"Are we talking about spaceships or airplanes?" I asked.

"Both. Everyone was fighting until Atlas had had enough. He flew up and up, then sprayed his fire to destroy them. I was hiding with the young ones, and we watched how he covered Anzulla in flames. Now, things have changed; the war is not over. We need that tunnel-making thing. Please!"

"Ouro, it must have been traumatic seeing it firsthand. So you were watching the smaller children?" Kellan asked.

"Sopora was one of them. I'm an Igigi. We were the oldest of the children, and now they are my people. Together we hid near the mountain, while we watched and listened to those fucking things killing our parents," Ouro spat, pulling a face as if the words tasted sour.

Ouro's tension and hatred radiated from him. Kellan remained levelheaded. I checked in with him by tilting my head back and looking up at him, upside down. I silently asked with my eyes, "What's your answer? Are we in or out? I will do whatever *you* decide."

The cold wind sang. Frozen twigs rustled. Owls

hooted. Callisto grunted. Ouro and Snow waited. Kellan gave me a slight, agreeable tip of his chin.

"Alright. Kellan and I will check out your airplane and let you know tomorrow," I said as I turned fully and climbed back onto the elevated ground he was standing on.

He whispered in my ear, his breath warm against my skin, "I have a hangover. I need some time to talk and process this."

I whispered back, "Me too."

He smiled cunningly at me. "You said this is an adventure." I turned my head toward Ouro and Snow. "We'll help as much as we can, but first we need some quiet time to think before fully committing to your summer plans to get a tunnel maker for you."

"Before we fly to our deaths," Kellan added skeptically.

"Hm, good point," Snow said, giving Ouro a strange look.

"Before I forget," Ouro said, a gleam in his eye, "I want to show you something else. Something...supernatural, as you might say. We call them bloodstones, or gifts from the Gods." He reached into his thick fur coat and revealed a bright, glowing pinkish-red gemstone in his palm.

My eyes widened. Kellan gasped. "Holy crap, Ouro, what is that? A giant ruby?" he exclaimed.

Ouro held it up, between thumb and forefinger. "A secret we've kept from you," he said. "We weren't sure you could be trusted." It wasn't polished. Up close, it looked like sea glass, sanded and weathered. The moonlight intensified the glow. We stared in astonishment. Their smiles were pure delight, as the reddish hue pulsed like an Olympic torch, stirring palpable promise and hope within me. "It's part of the mountain's magic," Ouro revealed excitedly.

"Where did you get that? Does it burn?" Kellan asked.

I offered my hand. "May I hold it, please?" I asked, captivated. Ouro placed it in my outstretched palm. It was warm, but not scorching—not like fire, more like an LED. I passed it to Kellan, who was equally mesmerized, cradling it gently as if it were a handful of fireflies.

"It's crystal. It grows like moss inside the mountain. I am the leader, and I say who is allowed to have the light. You've proven that you care about my people. These crystals enable my people to live a *long, long, long* time, just like Igigi. This is why we guard the mountain and hide it from the invaders. The light gives life. They use diamonds for their technology, but they want crystals for powering their batteries. If we have a war, we need this light to give us the strength to fight the invaders. Lots of it. I give this one to you. You will live a *long, long, long* time, like me. Like all the others. We trust you because you came with Callisto. You built houses. But summer is short, and we have smart plans for you. Da? You bring me the tunnel maker?"

I was so confused. My mind spun in all directions. Calculating. Recalling. Rewriting. Everything I've ever known was not nearly a drop of what was truly going on. "Are you saying if we carry these, we will live forever? Is this light some elixir for everlasting life? Should we grind, mash, strain, inject, or swallow it?"

"No, you just never get sick or old. You put it inside your pocket. That's all."

I gaped. "Ha-ha! That's all?"

Kellan's brows furrowed as he shook his head, looking dejected. "We are never going to go back home, are we?" he asked, and I laughed nervously.

"Maybe, maybe not. It depends on Atlas showing you where to go once you finish helping us blast open the mountain. The door Gu fell through is inside that mountain," Ouro said.

Curiosity piqued, I wondered if it resembled a colossal tank or perhaps something as compact as the diminutive Men in Black Noisy Cricket gun.

Eager to satiate my curiosity, I asked, "What is the size of the tunnel maker?"

Snow chimed in before Ouro could respond. "It's a small, easily portable machine. Simon told us about it—he'd heard rumors of its use in underground prisons. He contacted an informant to confirm, who then sent us schematics for the skin branding needed to meet him and get the machine.

The thought of prisoners trapped underground chilled me, reminding me of the loss of my parents, lost forever.

"Simon confirmed the informant worked in Invader Technology's design and manufacturing department," Ouro said. "All you have to do is get inside and bring it back."

CHAPTER 17
DRAXTON

KELLAN BROKE THE INTENSE SUCTION AROUND my throbbing organ. "Do you know who the Igigi are?"

I flung aside the pillow that was covering my face to muffle the sounds of my impending orgasm. "For the love of...could we discuss whatever is on that stunning mind of yours in thirty seconds?" I lifted my hips, poking his chin, nose, and lips a few times.

He didn't grasp the urgency of my message. He blabbered on, and I let my head plop back in hopelessness. I was two strokes away from losing it. With blurry vision, I sighed, relaxed my clenched jaw, and surrendered. This, right here, is what happens when you jump into bed with genius professors.

"I've been thinking."

"You have?"

"Yeah."

"Kellan, please tell me what's so important that I needed to hear it right this second."

With his right hand still firmly gripping the base, he looked like he was using my prick as a microphone. I won't tell him that, it would only give him more to talk about.

"I was contemplating the Sumerian myth that describes the seven Anunnaki descending from the heavens and creating the Igigi to serve them, similar to the creation of Adam in Genesis. In the myth, the Igigi revolted against the Anunnaki and their servitude. Ouroboros may be a mysterious watcher or guardian, like my father."

"Yes, and?"

"That's it. I just wanted to mention that."

"For no reason?"

"Well, aren't you intrigued?"

"Not-at-fucking-all!" I poked him again and again with my cock to give him a clue what was actually on my mind.

"I see I'm not going to get anything sensible from you, unless I suck it out." He opened his mouth and slid my foreskin back. I waited with a supplicated, pleading, lustful gaze. He rubbed his short beard up and down my sensitive member, giving me a danger-ously teasing look.

"Gods, you're driving me crazy," I groaned. I felt intense pain shooting from my groin to my eyes. He licked his lips, causing my breath to hitch and my heart to race. His warm tongue circled the head of my penis, making it wet. I watched closely as his lips approached the tip. We locked eyes before he finally began moving his lips up and down. Overwhelmed, I leaned my head back and covered my face with my arms when he deep-throated me, taking his time.

Intense pleasurable sensations overtook me. "You're starting to make sense now," I groaned, my eyes closing as I felt like I was levitating. I was so very close. "Damn, you are good with that mouth... I'm going to come," I hissed. He stopped sucking, squeezing the base of my cock again, wrapping his left hand around my balls, and pulling them. My body convulsed once and squirted only wind—nothing.

"You're edging me out of my damn mind!" I heaved. I welded my eyelids shut as I recuperated from the onslaught of the delectable pleasure build-ing. My legs vibrated. I splayed and curled my toes. Gripping the fists full of the fur below me.

"You are at my mercy, Mr. Dubois." He chuckled evilly.

I took a long, deep breath, calming myself and anticipating more of what he was doing to me. "I am," I admitted. *He doesn't know the extent of it.* "I'm going to return the favor, and you'll be crying rainbows, begging me to end the torture."

"You are not in the position to make idle threats," he said, releasing my balls and running his finger along my taint. Playing and teasing, not quite fingering me.

"Ah, fuck, yes, make me come, please."

"I have you all alone for the first time in our house. You said you wanted to play just with me—only me, not Ouro or Snow. You also mentioned—"

"Kellan, I know what I said...just push that finger inside me, please!" I threw my arms over my face again and waited, ignoring him. I wasn't a patient man. When I wanted to come, I fucking wanted to come! "This is torture for me. I'm not playing." I sounded like I was about to cry.

He chuckled as his finger blissfully slid inside me. I groaned with relief. "We don't have time for this. Snow and Callisto are waiting for us."

"Let them wait. If we fly to our deaths today, at least we had this."

"Ah, thank fuck." I breathed as his finger pressed deeper, rubbing against my prostate at the same time his lips covered my cock.

Kellan thinks we are going sightseeing while testing the rebuilt airplane, but I was planning something different. I had decided to explore the mining prison alone.

Simon, our informant on the Light Continent, had given Snow and Ouro the coordinates for the working prisons via crow mail over the years. After I orgasm, hopefully, within the next few strokes, Kellan was under the impression we were only doing reconnaissance while he showed us his flying skills.

Ouro and Snow had initially objected. They tried to talk me out of my crazy idea and warned me that escaping from the prison was nearly impossible. I wanted to show them how much they meant to me and how much I appreciated them, but most importantly, I wanted to do this for Kellan. It didn't take much convincing after I told them I was a champion at breaking in and out of places. I knew I was because my grandfather mentioned it frequently, especially when I overcame my fear of being trapped, and crawled deeper, or heights, and went skydiving. So, it made sense to me to do this for them. Instead of putting everyone in danger, particularly Kellan, I should be able to achieve the same result on my own. They agreed, albeit skeptically, after Ouro asked Simon by crow mail if it was possible. Simon replied within two days, stating it was extremely risky and that no one had ever entertained the idea because breaking out was nearly impossible.

Ouro then insisted that Callisto join to help me. Initially, I protested because a big white polar bear is not exactly inconspicuous, but I was quickly reassured that his size wouldn't be an issue once he shrank to something resembling a cute, fluffy sewer rat or an ugly Chihuahua. Now, the plan was for Snow to direct Kellan on where to fly, as Simon had provided the best time for sneaking inside the working prison. I was going to jump out of the airplane and then sneak onto a prisoner truck to be taken inside the facility. Once inside, I would confiscate a tunnel maker for Ouro, and Callisto would show me the way out. How difficult could it be? I enjoyed the dark, and the mystery of the unknown was calling me.

Suddenly, the overwhelming wave of pleasure coursed in one direction through me, toward my balls. Confused and still lost in thought, I hollered, "I hope this isn't my stupidest plan ever!" My sweaty and trembling body suddenly seized up. Thoughts of Kellan edging me again flashed a *hell-no* in my mind. I snapped into a sitting position, holding his head, forcing him to keep his mouth on me. He didn't resist. He let me have this as he choked.

"Oh, my God!" I finally orgasmed, roaring as my toes curled. I fell back onto the soft fur pillows and let go of his head. Somewhere in the distance, I heard him chuckling. My mind drifted like an old plastic bag in the wind. Cock jerking sounds forced me to crack open my eyes to see him upright on his knees with a hand flying over his cock, shooting thick pearly white cum, landing on my chest and lower belly.

I panted. He kept shooting. I gasped. "You will get both of us killed if you keep doing that. Now, I want to see if I can beat that."

CHAPTER 18
KELLAN

I WATCHED AS TINY SNOWFLAKES BEGAN TO fall, signaling that winter was on its way again. It wasn't cold enough for the snow to stick, and it melted as soon as it hit the hood of the airplane. "Gods, I told you we should hurry. The damn paint isn't dry yet." I pointed to the final touches of camouflage that were now dripping down the side of the nose. We should have painted yesterday, when it wasn't snowing. "Who are we trying to fool with this awful paint job, anyway?" I muttered nervously.

"At least we installed silencers to quiet the motor yesterday. I want to reach the Light Continent before the snow grounds us! The paint is going to smear all over the already cracked windshield! I'm going to wipe it off," I moaned, grabbing a rag, and jumped out to wipe the rivulets of blue, white, and brown paint. When I finished, it didn't look bad. The airplane looked like a shark swimming in thunderclouds.

"Yeah!" The onlookers cheered and gave me thumbs-ups as I jumped back into the plane. I waved at Draxton. "Come on, hurry up!" The whole village had come to see us off for our first long-distance flight. They waved back at me, and I rolled my eyes.

I was the student pilot, proving to Snow that he could trust me with his waterplane, although I would never fly without Draxton. We promised each other to stay close together, in case we find the door. Just like this airplane had seemingly fallen through the sky from what I assumed was around the early 1940s, I was scared that a hole would suddenly open up and suck us back to our time, or worse, to a place where we don't know anyone. I was ready and waiting for Snow to flip the propeller. "No, no, no, smaller, much smaller!" I yelled at Callisto, who froze in his tracks and growled back at me.

"He says he knows, he's not stupid!" Ouro yelled over Draxton's shoulder from atop the walkway. They were engaged in some heated debate, and I didn't want to seem nosy, so I just waved goodbye from a distance. Callisto let out a puff of hot air at me. "He says he can always stay home," Ouro shouted, pointing at Callisto and giving him a don't-try-me look. The bear was not happy, but he leaped into the air, and by the time he entered through the open door, he was about the size of a six-month-old Saint Bernard puppy.

I shook my head. *All this fuss for a test run.* "Okay, ready! Draxton!" I called while giving Snow a thumbs-up to flip-start the engine.

"I'm coming!" Draxton yelled back as he began to jog down the gangplank, carrying a backpack that Ouro had handed him. I wondered what it contained and waved to Ouro, who stood like a Viking ice warrior with his spear raised in the air, shouting safe travels to us.

The engine *zap-zapped*, and the propeller whooped once, but nothing happened. "Jump in!" I laughed as Draxton waved one last time at the entire crowd. They cheered while he clownishly tiptoed on the float like a ballerina for them, before plopping inside to share a seat with Callisto.

"Okay, one more time!" Snow yelled, standing on his toes as he pulled the propeller. With a sputtering roar, the engine came to life.

I'm not sure if it was the people, Draxton, or our unique circumstances in Anzulla, but every shared experience, every moment we touched, seemed to unfold with a miraculous, unexpected twist. The floatplane, having completed a graceful takeoff, was now in the air, gliding above the water. The engine sounded healthy, and the low humming vibrations were exhilarating, much like riding a bicycle. Flying felt natural to me, even without instrumentation.

Six hours later, even after we did a few short test runs, I still couldn't believe we had been airborne for so long. Draxton, sitting in the back, was responsible for refilling the small tank twice during our flight. Snow had given him a crash course on the importance of fueling the tank, and Draxton took his responsibility to keep us in the air very seriously. The horizon glittered as light danced like static electricity over the artificial ozone of the invaders. The further we flew into the light and out of the darkness, the hotter it became.

"There," Snow said, pointing. "That's the coast, fly ten minutes north and then veer inland. I want to see the prison. Stay low," he added cheerfully. They were all making jokes and staying upbeat in the back, but as the air grew hotter and the Light Continent came into view, a feeling of imminent danger settled in the pit of my stomach. I stopped tapping my fingers on the wheel. Snow sat in the passenger seat silently. I was nervous, and a sense of foreboding washed over me. Danger pulsed through me.

I wanted to turn around. "Yup, just over the coastline, and then we're out of here," Snow said, and I was more than happy to turn back and away from this place.

"It's blinding," Draxton said from behind me in the back row. I agreed that the buildings reflecting the light into our eyes created a glare similar to looking straight at the sun.

"Don't look at it directly, the light will cause solar damage to your eyes. It can blind you permanently," Snow warned. Callisto let out a whiny growl from the passenger seat next to Draxton and behind Snow, sounding unhappy. As we crossed the coastline, the uneasiness in my chest grew. I had half a mind to tuck and run when Snow pointed to what looked like an old lighthouse. "When you reach that, turn around and head home." He turned to look back at Draxton and Callisto. I wanted to look back, too, but I felt too nervous, concentrating on not going further than necessary. As we approached the dilapidated white tower, my heart sank when a shadow of a man passed underneath the airplane.

"Motherfucker!" I shouted. "Draxton's fallen out! Fuck!" My heart pounded in my chest, and my grip on the wheel tightened. *This is not happening!* Callisto groaned, and Snow pushed me back in my seat. I don't know what I was thinking. I wanted to jump after him, I guess. *Okay, yeah, I was flying.* "I must land..." Yeah, *and what then?* "He's going to fall to his death!" Checking over my shoulder, Callisto rolled his head between his paws, howling as if he were a crying puppy. Snow was saying something, but I couldn't hear him as I shouted, "We have to save him! I can catch him!" I rolled the airplane into a dive, searching frantically for Draxton.

Callisto roared his disapproval, and Snow yelled, "No!"

Thwack! Snow slapped me hard.

I froze and blinked. "What the hell?"

"Slow down and listen."

I quickly glanced again to see if I could spot Draxton. "There!" I pointed. No! I realized he had a pack on his back. "Is that a fucking parachute? Did he just fucking parachute out of the plane? Why? Why, without saying a word? What the hell is wrong with him? What was he thinking?" Tears of frustration and relief spilled down my face. "How could he do this to himself?" A heavy sense of dread and betrayal settled in my gut. *To me?*

I leaned forward, squinting through the windshield as Snow said, "He didn't want to tell you because you would either not have wanted to come or not brought him."

"You knew! You fucking knew he was going to

pull this crazy stunt! Don't you understand he has impulse control issues? He's different from us. He thinks differently—like he...he...he...he's going to die here." I stammered as panic set in, my breathing quickening. I inhaled and exhaled sharply. "I'm not sure what to do. We have to land the plane. Draxton is...ah, fuck-damn it! He doesn't know that I know he's on the autism spectrum. I never wanted it to be an issue. That's not who he is, but this is insane." I slammed my fists into the dashboard, crying furiously. How will I help him? I bit my fists.

"Listen to me," Snow said calmly. I sniffled and hoped he had something good to say. "I don't know what this spectrum is, but yes, he is different. He is brave. He is smart. It was Draxton's idea to go sightseeing today. He begged both Ouro and me. We even contacted Simon for input. He provided us with the coordinates, and Draxton assured us he could go in and bring Ouroboros his tunnel maker. He claimed that breaking in and out is easy for him because he knows how to crawl through small spaces. Obviously, he *is* a skydiver, so he wasn't *lying* about that." We watched as he deployed his parachute. "Draxton convinced Ouro, saying that instead of putting everyone in danger, he would go alone and bring us the drill. We'll come to collect him. Callisto will bring him back to you. Ouro insisted that Callisto accompany him to help. Fly south. I will show you where to land. Simon is waiting for us. Callisto will go on foot from there to the prison."

"No! I can't believe you hid this from me. How could you agree to something so dangerously risky? Where is he going to get that drill?" I asked Snow, boring into his pale blue eyes.

Snow broke eye contact and let out a long breath. "He is breaking into the working prison. I could tell that Draxton wasn't like us. But he seemed to know his stuff. Yes, he is strangely absent-minded and likes his own space."

"Jesus Christ, Snow, you should've told me."

"Yeah, but I still would have made the same choice. It doesn't change the fact that he thinks he can do it. He knew you would react this way. That's why he did it."

I was upset beyond reason. "Draxton, you idiot!" I shouted, swinging around to yell at Callisto. The bear was considerably smaller, hiding his face and ears under his paws. "Look at me!" I ordered, knowing he understood. "Callisto, look at me," I snarled. "You shouldn't have let him jump. You're supposed to be our guardian, and this is how you protect us?"

Callisto and I locked eyes. "Puppy eyes? Are you

seriously giving me puppy eyes?" I asked, and he whimpered.

Now, I felt guilty for yelling at him as if he were a child. He let out a soft, snorting cry. I pointed a finger at him. "As soon as we land, you go fucking find him, and you protect him. Bring him home. To me. In one piece. Fuck the drill. Who cares about a fucking drill? If he dies and I never see him again, I'm fucking blowing this whole place up, you hear me? Every-fucking-thing!" I was furious with rage and still shaking when Snow showed me where to land near a camouflaged buoy in a small harbor in a horseshoe-shaped alcove.

This can't be happening.

CHAPTER 19
KELLAN

"THERE, THAT'S SIMON'S HIDEOUT!" SNOW pointed out. I turned the plane to align with the small harbor, reduced altitude, landed, and then we floated toward a man standing on a massive mooring buoy, waiting for us.

"This isn't the first time he's done this," I told Snow as the man tied two ropes around the frame, fastening it to another T-shaped floating structure along the shore, surrounded by jagged cliffs stripped of greenery. No grass. No trees. No life.

Since I landed Snow's floatplane, I figured I had free passage as the pilot. I jumped onto the float, careful not to slip on the hollow homemade deck. Now that we were on the surface and out of the wind, the sweltering heat hit me with full force.

"Hello there!" Snow called to the man securing the plane. "Where is Simon? We have an urgent matter to discuss." The young man pointed, and I followed his directions.

Gods, the sunlight is bright—no wonder they call this the Light Continent.

I shaded my eyes and assessed our surroundings. Scattered along the boardwalk, down the beach, and up the zig-zagging stairs, all the way to the top of the cliff, I estimated there were about thirty to fifty men and women busy either loading and unloading a long sailing ship and carrying its cargo up and down the stairs or guarding it with rifles to protect their loot.

"Simon's the only man not carrying a rifle," Snow noted, pointing to a figure watching us from an estimated five-story balcony nestled within the overhanging cliffs, similar to a hidden nuclear test lab I once saw in a Marvel movie.

Urgency and agitation propelled me from the shade of the airplane. I followed Snow while Callisto trailed behind me. Ignoring the men and women standing with weapons strategically spread out along the dock and now pointing directly at us, Snow led the way to meet the lord of Spire City's underbelly. "Thank you, kindly," Snow said over his shoulder. "They are with me," he added, throwing a thumb back at us, and the guns suddenly pointed away. My boots boomed on the rusted steel platform with the bravado of Batman about to save his Robin as I strutted like an MMA fighter to the cage.

"Stop right there!" the one guy up the stairs shouted from afar.

"No! Don't shoot, he's with me!" Snow flailed his arms like a broken windmill. The guard looked up at the dark silhouette watching us from above. He lowered his weapon when the famous Simon, responsible for sending crow mail back and forth to Ouro, waved back. Snow continued up the gangplank while I followed, keeping an eye on his back. We hello-helloed as if we were untouchable and on a critical mission, which I suppose we were.

The three of us made our way through the first line of guards without any trouble. Callisto's paws thudded beside me, and I must admit he moved quickly when he wanted to. He'd better get his butt to work! Snow slowed to let us catch up with him. More guards greeted Snow and stepped back, nodding their chins in my direction. The creaking, rusted walkway wobbled beneath our feet, and Callisto snarled, growing in size. I scanned the area, ensuring it was safe enough to proceed. It wasn't the time to hesitate or feel jittery. I was here to kick ass. The sound of Callisto sniffing the air and the wetness of his snout on my hand caught my attention. I sniffed too. The air was stiflingly hot, with hints of salt and ocean spray from the nearby waves. The bear's fur must make it ten times hotter.

I stopped at the end of the pier and looked down into those blue, apologetic eyes, wondering what was going on in his head. "What? You know what to do. Go do it!" I said shortly. He gave a mewling cry and swung his head as if to show me something.

Snow ran his fingers through his fur. "Are you going now?" he asked the animal in a soft tone, making me feel guilty. Callisto puffed out a few breaths, blinking his eyes. I still couldn't figure out how many blinks meant yes or no.

"Find Draxton immediately. Protect him at all costs. His erratic emotions could get him killed," I demanded, as my gut was churning with fear for Draxton's life. The bear and Snow both raised their eyebrows in question as I continued, my voice trembling with panicked desperation. "You have an hour," I said firmly, jabbing my finger to the ground for emphasis. "One hour, do you understand? Now go!"

"Yes, go and bring him back as soon as you can, as we had discussed with Draxton," Snow said, and

Callisto gave me one last look. Before I could protest, he jumped into a sprint, beach sand flying. With a frustrated sigh, I watched Callisto vanish behind a dune, then glared at Snow with utter disgust before seizing the intensely hot railing of the stairs, a jolt of pain shooting up my arm. "Shit, that's hot!"

"Yeah, don't touch anything metal," Snow whispered before climbing the ungodly steep stairs rising up the cliff. At the first landing, Snow shook the guard's hand and waited for me while he kept talking as if Draxton's life wasn't in danger.

"Hi, Snow," the woman greeted in a friendly tone.

"Hello. Please unload the cargo, then fill the plane. We will return to the Dark Continent in a couple of hours," Snow said, pointing to the waterplane bobbing on the waves.

Her androgynous, tanned skin indicated that she had been standing guard outside all day. "It's good to see you. I can't wait to have a decent meal. We're all looking forward to steak tonight. Thank you." Her voice was gruff, and her hair was shaved down to the scalp. Her friendly dark eyes met mine, and I nodded hello, feeling more lost than ever in this strange time and place. If I lost Draxton, I would be alone. I wouldn't be able to do this without him.

I turned back to Snow. "We are not leaving without Draxton."

"Excuse us, Sarinka," Snow said, grabbing me by the elbow and whispering, "Ouro is waiting for us at home. Simon will send crow mail when it's time. We won't be staying here. It's dangerous."

"Excuse me." I shot him a what-the-hell look and pulled my elbow from his grasp. "It's dangerous here, but you're sending Draxton into a freaking prison! Why?"

Snow jabbed a finger at my face. I had never seen him this close to blowing a fuse. He scowled and spoke through clenched teeth. "For many reasons. First, we didn't send Draxton. He asked to go. And second, we've brought things to trade. The meat, remember?"

I began my ascent. It was hot, so hot that each time I forgot not to grab the railing, it burned my hand. I looked at my red palm in disbelief. This heat was overwhelming. Draxton is in danger. This is just too much. "Fuck the meat! Draxton's life is more important than meat!"

I wanted Draxton out of that mine and in my arms within the hour. With each step, my boots thudded against the worn steel stairs as I ascended the cliff toward the man who had become my target. Simon was undeniably guilty. He was the one who sent the coordinates to Ouro. Yes, he claimed it was risky, but he should have said it was impossible—finished, done, end of conversation. If Simon was as connected as they said, then he ruled the black market and had connections, so he'd better get Draxton right now, and once I had Draxton back, I was going to talk to my brother. Ouroboros wasn't our leader or my boss; he wasn't deciding what I should or shouldn't know.

Simon waved, holding a glass in one hand. "Hello!" he shouted, sounding like a garden gnome. The balcony of his grand clubhouse was a unique structure nestled and camouflaged against the dark-brown cliffs. As we walked toward him, my eyes were drawn to the small red pegs scattered everywhere. They were hammered into the walkway, dotting the rock facing up the cliffs and covering the outside of the building. Even the Viking-like boat below resembled a pincushion on a massive scale.

I pointed to the peculiar red pegs, about four inches long and as thick as my thumb. "What are those?" I asked, waiting for an explanation to see if the red pegs would allow for another way to escape from the invaders.

"They are magnets. I also have them on the airplane to avoid camera detection." He gestured up beyond the clouds to the shimmering artificial ozone layer. "The hoverbots can't detect anything beyond magnetic fields. That's why most structures here are reinforced with magnetized steel plates."

I would have taken a moment to absorb this revelation, but the oppressive heat, causing sweat to trickle down my face, and the cacophony of screeching seagulls fueled my urgency. Spurred on by a head full of tumultuous emotions, with fury being the biggest motivator, I grunted and pressed on toward my target. When we reached the top of the stairs, I realized I wasn't even short of breath. My body was in the best shape it had ever been. I felt twenty-one—like I could climb triple the amount and still hold a conversation. I was ready to knock Simon down and wring his neck.

But as he opened a heavy, reinforced sliding door, I realized it wasn't going to be easy, since Simon was a tall, muscular man. "Welcome!" he called, waving us inside. Once we were inside, he closed the door behind us with a loud bang.

Snow slipped off his boots and his shirt as he stepped inside. "Hello, my friend!" They hugged, and I followed Snow's example by undressing most of my clothing. Simon took my unoffered hand to shake it. I thought the steel must be blazing hot, like the stairs, but it was cool beneath my feet. As we entered Simon's enormous abode, the cool air conditioning hit my face, and I eagerly moved past them to cool off, escaping the desert-like heat. Snow, standing beside Simon, smiled. He was pleased that I was following his lead, as they were both licking their lips and adoring my body.

I took a deep breath. Goosebumps appeared on my arms as the cold air brushed my sweaty skin. I rubbed my arms and tilted my head to the side to look Simon up and down while he and Snow embraced again like old friends. Simon wore a pair of gray shorts, and judging by the outline, he wasn't wearing any underwear. Like us, he wore no shirt, and his toes were the ugliest, shortest, fattest ones I've ever seen. He resembled Moana's Maui. Long black curls sprouted from his head, and more hair covered his sun-kissed copper skin, stretched tight like leather over his muscular frame. It seemed like he had plenty of free time and nothing better to do than let tattoo artists practice on him. He was stocky with an abundance of hair. Too much hair. *How does he tolerate this heat?*

I cleared my throat, surprised by the awkward Hawaiian demigod. "Maui...um...Simon," I said while approaching him.

"Gods, the cool air—it's heaven," Snow interrupted me.

"Yup, it is," I grunted, turning to Simon and

taking a deep breath. "Listen, I need you to go get Draxton for me. He's not safe in a prison or anywhere like it. Not in a mine or a place where they don't understand him. He speaks without thinking, and the more anxious he gets, well, let's say, prison isn't for someone like him."

"Me neither," Simon chuckled. "Unfortunately, I can't. He has to get himself out. He said he could. All he needed were the coordinates. Don't forget that Callisto will help Draxton escape and get back to us. Ouro kept in touch. Crow mail just arrived, stating you're on your way, and here you are!" He threw his arms wide as if performing on stage, like an actual clown. I did not find him amusing.

I sputtered. "But, but, but." I pointed to Snow and somewhere outside. "I told Snow and Callisto we would pick Draxton up in an hour. Take us to your meeting place. Callisto will bring Draxton. He will need help. Please, he reacts differently to stress than we do."

Simon looked at Snow, who shrugged. "That wasn't the plan. If there's one thing I've learned, it's to stick to the plan. There are many players. Draxton is risking his life by going deep inside the prison. He has to infiltrate the penal colony, win their trust, steal the laser drill, break it into pieces, and hand them to Callisto. Once the drill is outside, Callisto will bring Draxton out. This is a long, drawn-out process. At least a week, at most a month. He's probably not even collared yet—"

"What the hell? Collared!" I shouted. The more he spoke, the worse it got, and the look Simon gave Snow told me there was much more to this. "What?"

Simon waved my questions off. "It doesn't matter. It's not important."

"Tell me!"

"Let's drink something. Snow brought us meat. My men and I are looking forward to a steak." Simon clenched his jaw, and Snow's gaze flicked nervously around the room. "Let's talk while having a drink," he said abruptly, gesturing towards a table laden with weapons, books, and maps. His rugged crew eagerly left, nearly rushing down the stairs, most likely to unload the carcasses from the airplane, judging by the open fire for a BBQ in the center of the large room where Simon guided us. Handcrafted couches and tables made from old, rusty scrap parts and pieces of wood filled the area. I could tell that many people lived here. "Have a seat," he said, motioning to the mismatched chairs around the table. "What would you like to drink? Would you prefer water or something with a kick?" he asked, gesturing to a bottle of clear liquid on the counter.

I stood my ground, taking in the scene. It looked sad and rich at the same time. Stacks of scrap and ancient salvaged items, including pipes, mirrors, and industrial-sized fan blades, were neatly sorted. Simon's beachside hovel was a massive warehouse filled with valuable old scrap. My eye caught a rusted toilet and a basin, like the ones you might find in the cramped spaces of a prison cell or an aircraft lavatory.

"I have a plan. I see you like the restroom appliances. Why don't you go home and create a decent place for your man to shit?" Simon smirked at me. You don't get to tell me what to do! You aren't from here, and we—Snow, Ouro, Callisto, Draxton, and I—have gone over this plan again and again, agreeing it's risky, but it's their best bet for getting the rock cutter and getting Draxton back out."

"You jerk!" I lunged at Simon, aiming to wring his thick neck. He dodged to the side but was too slow. I was on him, my hands gripping his throat. Snow's hands gripped my arms. We tumbled onto the dusty floor in a scuffle. Simon wasn't quick, but was as strong and tough as a young ox.

Snow grunted. "Let him go. It's not his fault."

In excruciating agony, I clenched my fist tightly in Simon's bushy, wild hair, desperately trying to kill something to rid myself of my frustrations.

Simon had a firm grip on my balls. The searing pain coursing through my body forced me to release my grip. I crumpled into a mess of profanity-laden vocabulary. Only when rendered completely incapacitated did he let go of me. Gasping for breath, I muttered through clenched teeth, "I'm going to kill Ouro!" I groaned, rocking and clutching my gonads until the blinding pain subsided. I lay there recuperating, wondering what the fuck was happening. As the intense pain gradually vanished, my mind cleared, and I muttered, "What will I do now? I will go mad, wondering and waiting for him?" I rolled onto my back, staring up at the red magnet-pegged ceiling, and let out a long, defeated sigh.

"I told you, go home and keep busy. He did this for you. Show him how much you appreciate him doing it," Simon said, holding out a hand to pull me up. Once I sat down, he offered me homemade alcohol that tasted like jet fuel. Two sips of the stuff, and I relaxed a bit. "Don't worry. The best you can do is stay positive. Don't think negative thoughts."

"Yeah, Callisto will find him. Keep him safe," Snow added.

I nodded and shook my head in disbelief. "Alright, I will try. I'll trust Callisto," I whispered, my voice cracking with emotion.

"Yeah, remember, Callisto fought in the war. He knows these bastards," Snow said.

I love Draxton, and I was sure Snow deducted that from my reaction. "A magical fucking polar bear," I said, disgruntled. But maybe I shouldn't be angry at Callisto. He's the only one who is able and willing to help Draxton. I know nothing about breaking in and out of prison camps. Now that I think of it, just based on that thought alone, I would never have okayed this in the first place. I hardly think Draxton knows anything about labor camps. The depravity would unhinge him. He wouldn't be able to follow orders. I doubt he knows how to steal. *What was he thinking?*

I know what he was thinking. He thought he could prove himself to Ouroboros and Snow, maybe even me. Who was I kidding? In his mind, it made sense to handle it himself and save me the trouble.

I tilted my head back and groaned at the realization. "I can now clearly see how he had concluded that he was the better choice. He can't get lost, even in complete darkness. He possesses a unique talent. He can effortlessly navigate underground tunnels and cave systems simply by crawling through them. Once he's outside, with pen and paper, he can recreate everything from memory as if a machine had scanned and recorded

it. Draxton Dubois is the world's finest cave cartographer."

"Then relax, trust in that, trust him," Simon said.

"Are you sure he would be okay if Callisto were
with him?" I asked Snow, rolling my eyes at myself
for even thinking about going home and making
Draxton something he would appreciate. Maybe
keeping busy was the only way I'd survive the
waiting.

"Callisto has exceptional abilities. He can easily
infiltrate any location. Ouro believed Callisto could
bring Draxton back home. I trust Ouro's words because he is wise and has never lied or been wrong.
Callisto can help Draxton with any injuries and heal
his body and mind if needed. You think Draxton is
not normal, but I believe you underestimate him."
Snow's reassurance overwhelmed me with emotions. My eyes stung like someone was pouring sand
into them, and I bit my quivering bottom lip. His
words made me feel relieved and guilty. My hostile
feelings vanished, replaced by tears and suppressed
fear.

"I can't do much now," I said, wiping my tears.
"I'll drive myself crazy with what-ifs. Once he's back
in my arms, I'll make sure he never does something
so foolish again," I cried.

"I'll have my men pack all the best items for you.

Ouro said to give you whatever you want because Draxton is doing us a huge favor. Ouro wanted a way inside the mountain; the only way through that rock is with a laser drill. My informant, Joseph Malherbe, has promised us a drill since last year. But if Draxton can pull this off, we won't have to risk our cover or the life of our only inside man," Simon said, raising his glass in a toast. "To Draxton, may he return safely with the drill."

CHAPTER 20
DRAXTON

I MADE IT. I WAS TRAPPED IN THE MINING penal colony.

I missed my earbuds. I would have loved to hear some music. People spoke the bare minimum. Our group of new arrivals had tried asking questions earlier, but only received uninterested shrugs and short answers about where to find tools and where to start working. We fell in line with workers of all ages to collect our chisels, hammers, and crates, then followed them into the tunnels.

My fingers traced the cold, rough stone of the mining tunnel, mapping every crevice and imperfection. The thick smell of damp earth reminded me of home, but that's where the comparison ended.

Misery had woven itself into the existence of

these people, wearing it like skin. Beneath that thin layer, thick, oily blood pumped like semi-solid sludge through their capillaries. The prisoners smelled like infected wounds. Like gangrene, it gnawed endlessly, leaving exposed nerves in its wake. Palpable pain seeped into the darkness, filling these tunnels with the suffocating stench of despair, mingling with metallic scents—perhaps from old or discarded machinery, or perhaps I smelled the blood from my wounded feet.

In the distance, water dripped steadily, each drop echoing through the cavernous spaces where rats and cockroaches fought for survival alongside humans, considering them delicacies.

Yesterday morning, I woke in Kellan's arms— free, but not today. My imprisonment was a choice, a deliberate act of my own free will. Unseen, I had landed, folded and hidden my parachute, then slipped into the prison yard as trucks unloaded prisoners, where I joined the line. More workers meant more hands, and overhearing their talk of life inside, I wondered if I, Draxton Dubois, wasn't the only one foolish enough to break in, rather than out.

I missed Kellan and wished he were here. I wanted to show him how much I cared for his brother and his people, a feeling I couldn't express otherwise. Grandfather would have been furious. He taught me to think before promising, to consider whether my actions justified such a commitment. Yet here I was, in a vast, burrowed tunnel system built by people who had evolved—at an accelerated pace—into moles.

Chip, chip, crack! My hammer struck the chisel with a pang, vibrating down my arm. The rock split and shattered into pieces, and I nervously bent down to gather them, filling my crate.

An extremely emaciated, short old man with milky eyes and no teeth halted beside me, whispering in a crackling voice, "After filling your crate, carry it to the back. Fill them with anything resembling shiny, precious stones."

"Th-thank you, sir," I said, but he moved on, shuffling his feet while balancing an entire crate of rocks on his shoulder.

I was relieved to have someone to talk to, *finally*. "Excuse me, sir, how long have you been down here? When's my break? Will I get a chance to eat and sleep? Where can I rest? Which cell is mine?" I asked, trying to avoid looking into his strange, ratty eyes. He ignored me. The hoverbots barked instructions—what, where, and how to work—but no one mentioned when to stop, or what came next.

"Hey, you. Mister," a young person with small, pink eyes approached me. I guessed he was a boy, but I couldn't be certain. His skin was dark brown, covered in dirt. Black rims of exhaustion and mal-nourishment circled his strange, sunken eyeballs, but his hair was long and braided, suggesting someone was caring for him. "Mister, you don't get food if you don't fill your crate. You work until your crate is full. If it's full before eight hours, you return and start on your next crate to ensure you get food next time. Keep an eye on your crates. Someone very hungry might steal it. Then you'll have to work double shifts to fill your stomach or steal someone else's crate."

"Oh, okay, thank you," I whispered, smiling at the young person. A woman approached us, her expression calm and unreadable. She wrapped her arm around the child's bony shoulders, gently guiding the child away from me without a word. I smiled at her. She was barefoot and wore a dirty rag, like most others. She turned, handing the child a chisel. Together, they chipped away, filling their crate. These crates weren't large—about the size of two shoe-boxes—which made sense, given we had to carry them to the sorting tables. I noticed them immediately upon arrival; the clatter of smashing, sifting, and sorting was impossible to miss before it was whisked away on escalator belts.

Human misery had a weight. Though it wasn't

physical, it wore down the bravest and strongest until they became nothing more than husks of flesh and bone—a vile weapon that slavers wielded as the most powerful tool to control the masses.

I realized my impulsive idea might not have been my best. I didn't want Kellan to convince me otherwise. I thought this would be a quick in and out, but what I saw and experienced could not have been predicted, or ever unseen.

The stench of unwashed bodies clung to those working beside me, a smell of old sweat I hoped to grow used to. The constant nausea was overwhelming, and the cloth wrapped around my mouth and nose did little to block the acrid taste and smell of rancid blue cheese and bile—a sour flavor permanently seared into my nose and mouth.

These children grew up seeing their parents' despair, their brokenness a constant reality. We saw no guards or soldiers, only hovering surveillance bots. Most workers wore a silver collar; only those born in the mine were exempt from wearing one. Prisoners were collared and shoved down the chute, vanishing into the mine's depths—never to return to the surface, not even to collar the mine-born ones, and it seemed they preferred living down here.

Yesterday, after we tumbled down the chute and landed in a jumbled pile on top of each other, our fellow prisoners told us that life inside the mine was better than outside and that our next meal depended on how hard we worked. If we maintained our productivity, food would be our payment. They said we were lucky because we were human and that it could have been much worse. That sounded twisted to me, but I held back from saying that nothing could be worse than this place.

Perhaps I should consider befriending this woman and her child. I should stay close to them.

One positive recompense was that Callisto would visit me often, and I was grateful that Ouroboros had insisted. It was my second day, and I needed to see a friendly face. I reminded myself to focus on my reason for being here and that my reward would be seeing Callisto's fluffy face, rescuing me. Stealing a laser drill would undeniably prove my worth to Ouroboros, and especially to Kellan. Hopefully, Ouro could finish his war by the time Kellan and I returned home. I wanted no part in their conflict or getting involved with these prisoners' unsolvable problems.

At least we uncovered proof of an advanced civilization and mythical beings—unexpected, yet sufficient to satisfy my curiosity and ensure Kellan's safe return to his mother—only once I found and borrowed a laser drill.

My hands cramped, and each blow of the hammer and chisel sent jolts of pain through the broken blisters on my palms. "Ugh, I'm bleeding," I muttered, ripping another strip of shirt to bind my hand and the tool's handle. They had made us remove our shoes before shoving us down the chute. My clothes were in shreds; at this rate, I'd be shirtless by tomorrow, having already used strips to pad my feet.

I let out a loud sigh, craving a cool drink of water. "I'm thirsty," I said to the woman behind me. "Where can I get something to drink?" She paused her work, glanced back, and hushed me. "Fine," I muttered. "Thanks for nothing. I'll find a cup myself." I eyed the trickling water on the wall. "Or, even better," I thought out loud, "I'll just drink straight from the source." I started chipping away at the rock, making a little well to collect the dripping water.

Suddenly, a bright light shot down the tunnel, whizzing past me before hovering, its spotlight blinding. "Prisoner, are you distracting the others?" a man's voice boomed from the hoverbot's speaker. My eyes darted to them as I understood their reason for silencing me. They were trying to avoid the hoverbot. *Damn!*

With a sheepish look, I raised my hands and apologized, "Sorry."

"Mom, tell him to get down, face down, and don't look," the child whispered, tugging her hand. She whirled him around, hiding him from the hoverbot and me. I kneeled, silent, hoping to blend in.

"This is your last warning. No talking," the voice echoed disturbingly loud and hurting my ears.

I nodded without looking up at the hoverbot and bent even lower, the tip of my nose scraping the dirt. *Stay calm, remember this is for a tunnel maker.* Moments later, I felt a rush of air as the hoverbot sped away. I waited a few minutes, resting and weighing my options. I needed to ask about that laser drill.

I glanced up as the feet of the mother and her child passed me, each balancing a crate on their shoulders.

"You stole my crate! Hey! That's mine!" I shouted.

Pain, unlike anything I had ever felt, shot through my skull. I toppled over, convulsing, gritting my teeth, thrashing, and spitting foam. Bubbles of snot streamed from my nostrils. "Hm-che-che-che-che-gn-gn!" Choking noises escaped through my locked jaws while the hoverbot's light flickered like lightning.

"Prisoner! I said no talking. No sounds!" The male voice blared from a speaker on the hoverbot.

"B-b-b-b-but!" I stuttered, one eye open and un-focused. "Fuuuck!" My eyes rolled back as another blinding pain shot up my neck and into my brain. Slithers of fear crawled through my veins like inky black snakes, their venom seeping over the blood barrier of my mind. Black fog smothered my thoughts. "Sh-sh-st-stop it!" I cried through clenched teeth. *Help me*, I called from the unfath-omable depths, but no one heard me. I wrapped my fingers around the collar and pulled.

"Go ahead, pull on it, and your head explodes like a balloon right from your shoulders," the voice boomed.

My eyes felt like they'd explode. I twitched vio-lently and released the collar. The agony subsided, but I was left blind, disoriented, and nauseated. Shut up, I told myself. Don't speak. I turned onto my stomach, scraping my chin, chest, and knees on the wet, grimy ground. Staying low, digging my finger-tips raw, I crawled away in search of safety.

"Next time you break the rules, we'll shock you three times. The more you speak, the longer your punishment." The hoverbot's departure plunged me into darkness, like a stage curtain falling. I coughed, my throat tight, the collar suffocating. Panic seized me. Trapped, that's what I was, as the stench of my piss hit me hard.

This was a mistake. How could I *ever* have thought I'd survive down here? I made a mistake, mistake, mistake...I rocked, curling my legs, gripping the collar, and praying it wouldn't shock me again. *Callisto, Kellan, someone, help me!* Please come and get me. I prayed over and over as I lost consciousness, alone and afraid.

My mind was shattered like glass, irreparable, forever broken. Pain. So much pain. Sore muscles. Stiff joints. Thumping headache. I opened my eyes and saw only darkness. Why was I on the ground? I lay still, taking stock of myself. My heart pounded. This wasn't the Star Caves, and my helmet light wasn't just switched off. The damp stench of wet soil and rot jolted my memory. This was as real as the smell of stale urine. It wasn't a dream. This was a working prison.

A distant, soft sound of chains scraping and clanging caught my attention from far away in the dark.

When my strength returned, I pushed myself onto my hands and knees to stay low, hiding from the hoverbots. I remained silent and made my way to the main congregating area. A small waterfall dripped down where they sorted the ore. I shuffled over, waiting in line until it was my turn. Following their example, I drank the liquid, holding my mouth open to let it drop in. I watched as men, women, and children returned with their crates and queued up to dump the contents onto the large sifting tables. Unloading the heavy rocks triggered a lever, opening a gate to an area where hoverbots delivered food bowls. I felt too sick to be hungry. A man tapped me on my shoulder. "Are you done?" he asked. I shook my head, filled my stomach with more water, rinsed my face, and then looked for a place to lie down.

I lay shivering, then my dreams of Callisto visiting me began. He appeared as a small, glowing ball of fur, keeping me warm. Upon waking, I felt stronger and wondered if he had truly visited me. He did because it became my new routine—working while looking forward to seeing him again—whispering in his ear. His visits helped me refocus, reminding me why I was here.

One day, a week or more later, I finally ventured further than anyone else dared. That's when I heard it again—the unmistakable scrape of heavy, rusty chains on rock.

I investigated.

CHAPTER 21
DRAXTON

PITCH-BLACK DARKNESS ENVELOPED ME LIKE the softest baby blanket. Only in darkness like this does my brain illuminate. It overrode the signals from my eyes which made me think I was almost one hundred percent blind. But I wasn't blind. I saw with my hands and all my other senses. I strained my ears, listening for any sign of movement behind me, but there was nothing beyond the dripping water and my shallow breaths. With my arms outstretched, touching and feeling, I continued my exploration. I knew that somewhere ahead, someone or something was waiting. *I wasn't alone.*

My bare feet slid carefully along the wet stone, slick and slippery with water. It wasn't safe, but I had to know. I used my gift to override my perception of the darkness. My shaky breath felt deafening as I moved slowly, straining to hear the faintest noises, especially from hoverbots, but more importantly, those unnatural clanking sounds.

It felt as though they were beckoning me, yet they didn't want me to listen. It was as if they were hiding but still wanted to be found, and that thought alone intrigued me because I loved discovering things in the dark. The air was cold and damp, and from the echoes of the rocks I occasionally kicked, I sensed the vastness of the space spreading in all directions, but mostly down, down, down, deeper into the ground.

Apart from the occasional cockroach and rat scurrying, there were no other signs of life. They had become a rarity, much like escargot, that one had to know how to prepare for consumption. So, whoever was down here had access to that, at least —cockroaches and rats.

Yesterday, I learned something interesting. The prison population doesn't track days and months through lunar cycles. Instead, they count numerically—365 days, then start again at one on the 366th. Nobody knew how many years had passed since the invasion or how long they'd been underground.

A strange voice called to me. Inviting me to

come deeper. *To look and see.* It wasn't a voice or noise I was accustomed to. This was something— someone else.

My grandfather always said I was lucky to be born this way. He often mentioned that he wouldn't have minded having gifts like mine. Not only did I get to do what I loved, but I felt destined for speleology. I could map caves or tunnel systems with my eyes closed, simply by walking and running my hands over the surface. My mind lit up with visuals as far as I roamed. I never got lost, whether down here or inside a maze. I was wired for this; it's woven into me, and as far as I knew, I was the only person with this kind of talent. I felt so grateful for it because if I hadn't had this gift, I wouldn't have been able to do this. Those memories of my grandfather and our conversations pushed me further to leave the hardships of prison life behind, even if just for a little while. In the name of research, of course, and for Ouro's tunnel maker too.

My sensitive fingers glided gently over the smooth walls, revealing areas that had been gnawed out. I thought the smooth patches were likely where the laser drill had melted the rock. Maybe the hollowed-out sections were spots where the miners searched for veins of gold and diamonds. It seemed they must have found none, as my tunnel made a ninety-degree turn to the right. I spread my arms wide to feel the tunnel's width, and it felt just right, matching the size I worked in daily with my fellow miners. I felt certain I was heading in the right direction. A new scent wafted toward me. It was the unmistakable scent of a person's sweat, and I knew I was getting closer!

The vapor cloud I exhaled carried the noxious smells of my unbrushed teeth and starving ketone breath. I closed my mouth and sniffed a slow lungful. A reactive stirring came from ahead. I rolled my foot over loose rocks. Someone inhaled sharply. They were aware of me, just as I sensed them in the dark nearby. Despite the flickering in my mind, I couldn't see what lay ahead. I could only visualize where I had been and what I had scanned with my senses.

We were alone. The pitch-black darkness confirmed that no hoverbots were nearby because whoever was remotely controlling them needed light to see where they were going.

A loud nasal indrawn breath, then silence, told me they were listening to me, getting closer. The atmosphere felt friendly. I should say something and stop skulking like a weirdo. "Hey, it's okay, it's just me, Draxton. I'm just coming to see why it sounds like you're chained up, all alone, in the dark. Yes, I have a collar, and yes, the hoverbots are probably coming because I'm talking too loudly. They might either turn our brains into soup or splatter them all over you—"

"So, shut up and stay quiet," a male voice croaked hoarsely. I jumped in surprise, but soft chuckles reached me, and I relaxed. The sound echoed back from about twenty to thirty feet ahead, but not directly down the tunnel. No, he was somewhere hollow, perhaps in an alcove or maybe in a cell. A vision of a middle-aged cellar in an old castle sprang to mind as the odor of sweat and human excrement hit me like a red light after driving absentmindedly. A strange rustling noise followed. Maybe he was sleeping on straw, I thought. He chuckled to himself before breaking into a coughing fit. Now, I was certain he was indeed in a hollowed-out area. I patted the wall and suddenly found its end, and I stopped. This was an opening. I turned toward the sound of movement.

"Don't fall and break your arm, or worse, your leg." He sounded mature and had an accent reminiscent of Ouroboros's dialect, but his voice was scratchy as if his vocal cords were damaged. Maybe he was one of Ouro's men. Slowly, I felt around, careful not to poke the guy's eye out while keeping one hand on the wall. A trickle of sweat ran down my temple. The nervous anticipation of meeting this person urged me to tread carefully. I worried that I might be missed, but I didn't know if the authorities even cared if someone got lost down here. My fingers slid around a smooth corner. I was right. This was a hollowed-out area, much like the hovel I had chosen for myself the night before.

He was close to me and very quiet.

I felt his warm breath on my cheek for a few seconds. Then came the unmistakable sound of chains and shackles.

"Who the hell are you, and how the fuck did you find me?" the voice rasped flimsily at me.

I sprang back, searching for something solid behind me. "Good grief, you're going to give me a heart attack!"

The man chuckled again, his voice rich and deep. "Then don't creep around in the dark. Like a creeping creeper."

"You sound oddly cheerful for someone locked away like Lucifer in the bowels of Hell."

The man scoffed. Strange snorting noises escaped him as if he were holding back, cracking up at me while air exploded through pursed lips anyway. I smiled. The sound was infectious.

He was doing a piss poor job of making me feel like a hero saving him. "I'm not going to ask, because it probably won't make sense why you are laughing at the only person who found you. By the way, how long have you been chained up down here?"

"Oh, you have no idea," he said, his heavy-sounding chains grated on the rock as he shifted. "I've been down here so long, I've started naming the rocks. That one shaped like a horse over there? I call him Mr. Chattermouth. He's my favorite. He never sits still or shuts up, teasing me about not being able to pay the Ferryman. I have but one coin and I need two."

What the fuck was he talking about? I squinted into the darkness, trying to make out any shapes. "I don't see any horse-shaped rocks. It's darker than the inside of Lucifer's asshole down here."

He burst out laughing again. "Of course you don't. They're imaginary, just like my sanity and love life at this point." He chuckled again, a sound so melodically smooth it sent shivers down my spine.

"But seriously, who are you? You're not one of Ouroboros's warriors, are you?" I asked.

He inhaled loudly, and then I heard the snapping of stiff joints and the popping of vertebrae. He was moving, grumbling like an old man getting out of bed. His voice rose with his height, and I could tell he was enormously tall—taller than Ouroboros. The air moved around us. Tornado strength, and then it was gone as fast as it had happened. *How did he do that?*

"No, not a warrior. Yes, maybe I was a warrior, but not one of the San warriors...maybe...I can't remember. Don't want to remember. Wait, why do you talk about Lucifer as if you know him?" he asked.

Now it was my turn to titter.

"Have you met him, and who are you?" the stranger asked insistently.

It felt good to chuckle. Shaking my head, I hesitated, uncertain about how much to reveal. I was convinced that telling him I fell through a door in the sky would likely cause severe breathing problems, judging by how he was laughing and coughing at the silliest things. "No, I'm not discussing Lucifer as if I know him. It's merely a reference to a mythological being that guards the wicked souls of wrongdoers in the underworld. Also known as 'the torchbearer.' The master of hell. You know?"

He exclaimed voicelessly, stifling, puffing, and

snorting, "No, I don't know!" *Brrrrp!* More ridiculous noises...*and was that a fart?*

Scrunching my face, I whispered, "Calm down, man. My name is Draxton, but that's not important right now. I'm here to help. Can you tell me why you're locked up?" I asked, making sure we were on the same team in the same situation. Judging by his unnatural height and the metal chains, he might be some psychopathic monster refusing to die, a murderer, or something. He fell silent for a moment, and I heard that rustling noise and felt that wind again. *What a strange sound to hear down here.* I shifted my feet, patting the floor to search for straw or bedding, but found nothing—only small rocks and filth I refused to identify.

"Well, prince charming, if you're here to rescue me, you're doing a terrible job," he said, the chains rattling as he shifted. "Got any tools or spare change? Or were you just passing by?"

I bristled at his tone but kept my voice low. "I'm not exactly equipped for a jailbreak. I'm just as trapped down here as you are. Only I'm not in chains, and I have someone who is going to help me escape once I find a tunnel maker—"

"Fantastic," he drawled. "Who?"

"Callisto," I whispered.

"Ca-callisto?" he parroted.

"Yes."

Silence.

"So you're a lost prisoner, hoping to be rescued, and I'm still chained. What a pair we make." Despite his sarcasm, I felt a twinge of sympathy. How long had he been down here? The stench of his cell told me it had been a very long time. "Look, I can try to find something to pick the lock. There must be some loose metal scraps or pins lying around."

"Oh, of course. Take your time. I've only been waiting for...how long has it been?" His tone expressed disbelief.

I cleared my throat. "On which side did you fight in the war during the invasion?" There was a long pause. I waited, listening for more clues about him.

"I tried to fight. Everyone tried to. But we all failed." His voice dropped to a disappointed whisper. I never liked reaching out and touching strangers, but I felt compelled to touch this one for some reason. My instinct told me this guy was on Ouro's side and was in trouble.

"I'm going to help you. Do you have any food? I can bring you some."

He laughed with bitterness. "Food? Luxuries I've forgotten long ago. But please, don't worry about me. I've managed to survive this long. Just ask Mr. Chattermouth."

I frowned, torn between frustration at his attitude and a growing determination to help him. "I totally understand if you don't trust me right now, but please know I won't just leave you here, chained up in the dark. I'm here to help you get free. You can come back to my hovel, we can work together for food, and maybe even find a way out together."

If only I could see what he was doing. There was a scraping of chains as he shifted. His voice softened, becoming less cynical as he asked, "And why would you do that? What could you possibly gain from freeing a nameless prisoner? But most of all, why me and not someone else?"

He had a point. I hesitated, unsure why I felt so compelled to help him. "Because...because it's the right thing to do," I said. I rubbed my eyes as if that would help me see better. "And because maybe together we stand a better chance of saving these people and escaping this place."

He was silent for a moment, then sighed. "Very well. If you're foolish enough to try, I won't stop you. It's better than waiting to die, like me. You sound like you have a plan. If it helps you to keep going while you come to my rescue, then why not? It would be my pleasure to help you help me. Perhaps you can encourage your coworkers to understand that I wanted to help them, just as you are helping me. Then, we all help each other. That is, if they want me to help them to help you. They are my flock, after all. Together, all of us can help each other die by electrocution."

"In the meantime, you win the prize for the best sarcastic answer. Maybe before we all sizzle together, we can have a ceremony and hand you a medal," I retorted. This man needed at least three psychiatrists, I thought, as I made a face. Why was he chained up in the first place? It sounded like he was one of the first prisoners of war. "Why are you down here? Were you captured?" I asked.

"Is the war still ongoing? Are you a warrior? Is Ouroboros your leader? Where is Callisto?" he asked without answering me.

"No, not a warrior. It's a long story to tell you, and we don't have time...my coworkers might report me missing, and I'm worried those hoverbots will come looking." I clucked my tongue. "Now you have me speaking of my fellow slaves as if we were white-collar office workers."

"Well, we were all collared, after all," he snickered.

"Gods, you are incorrigible. Is this why they chained you up?"

"I'm chained up and being punished, probably forgotten because I dug, I hauled, faster than the humans. I've made many attempts to escape, trying to free them until your coworkers decided to chain me down. It's my fault that no one is speaking. I'm here because nobody wants my help. They might have mentioned that I should shut up, but that's Mr. Chattermouth's fault. Not mine. It's not our conquerors who are making me rot here," he whispered, and I shockingly believed him. "So, you see, I can't go with you. I'll stand out, and I don't know if enough time has passed for them to forgive me, or even if they want to escape. When they chained me to this wall, they told me they were alive, that they were human, and that it's safer down here than surviving on the surface. They asked me where I would take them once we were outside, and I didn't know the answer. I still don't have an answer. It's safer for them if I stay with them. Perhaps, once I find an exit and have an answer, I can convince them to leave."

I shook my head in disbelief. "Are you saying the prisoners chained you, and you chose to sit here until they changed their minds?"

"Yes, what else can I do? They want to live down here. They don't know better. If you free me, I could try to dig my way out of this place one day. They can choose to follow, but I have to admit, trying to get them to follow is like arguing with Mr. Chattermouth."

As he explained his predicament, I understood because I had already gotten to know these people. "I'm here to get the laser drill for Ouro. Maybe we should use it to blast our way out to the surface." I nervously checked repeatedly over my shoulder for oncoming hoverbots.

"You don't sound like you're from around here," he said.

"We can talk more later. Let me quickly feel the lock and chain, so I can plan which tools to bring." I didn't reach out. I waited for his response and flinched in surprise when he grabbed my wrist and guided me to the wall. He helped me feel around, leading me as if I were blind, which I was.

"Here, feel this," he said, placing my hand on a metal box with screw heads as big as my fist. It's going to be impossible to unscrew. I ran my hands from the four gigantic screws to the enormous links in the chain, which were as large as a sailboat anchor chain.

"Holy crap, how do you move around?" I asked, stunned by its weight. I couldn't lift it—not the way he was moving around, sounding like he was dragging it behind him. "How did they chain you if I can't even lift it?"

He grumbled.

"Don't tell me you did it yourself," I blurted.

"No, a laser drill, a sledgehammer, and very eager humans operating machines did this."

"But you allowed it?"

"I might have."

How big and strong was this person? Was it even a person? His size, the size of the links in this chain. All this time. What was he even eating or drinking? The horror these prisoners had done to him, and still, he wanted to save them. I looked up. "You aren't human, are you? You've been locked up here for a hundred years, haven't you?"

He chuckled, and his hand rested on my shoulder. I winced as he touched the side of my face. Like a friend, he patted me on the arm. "You are one of the smart ones. A stranger. But you knew my name before meeting me?"

"Yes, I think of myself as smarter than the average human, but I really don't know your name."

"You do. You said it twice."

"Not a clue what you are saying," I said as I ran my hands over the links until I reached the end, shackled to his ankles. I had to know what he was. "May I touch you?" I asked and waited.

"You may," he said softly. I felt his feet—they were at least a size sixteen or seventeen, I guess. His toes were human—five on a foot, as I ran my hands over him, a picture formed in my mind. Above the shackles, I felt hairy calves, so I ran my hands over his kneecaps. His pants were shredded. I stopped halfway up his upper leg, not wanting to run my hands over his crotch. "So, are you human or not?" I asked.

His breath hitched. "Not quite. I'm something more, something else," he breathed, and the wind moved around us again. This time, I was sure it came from him. The sound, that sound, the sound of linen in the wind.

I gasped. "You have wings?"

He sounded amused again. "Yes, I do have wings. How do you not know my kind? You know my name, but you are surprised by my wings?" he asked, sounding very interested in my answer. There, he said it again, that I knew his name.

"What is your name, because I promise you I do not know you."

"It's Luci, short for Lucifer," he said, and I froze, blinking as if it would make me understand better in the dark. What in the ever-loving fuck, Grandfather? The Dubois map and secret codes flashed in my mind. The angel wings.

"Angels are real! Okay, this shouldn't be a shock. I apologize. I truly didn't know I was down here in the guts of Hades with the famous Lucifer." Now I was sounding silly, as a girly giggle escaped my mouth. I slapped a hand over it.

"Luci, please. I've not used Lucifer in a very long time. I am a birdman. A sable birdman, not an angel. There is a big difference."

"I know!" I clapped my hands over my mouth again, but I muttered between my fingers. "Angels have white wings, and sables have black wings. It's common sense, isn't it?" I whispered excitedly. "Luci?"

"So, nice to meet you. I'm Luci," he said, sounding pleased with himself. I reached out my hand, found his right hand, and shook it. What a discovery! It was the best. My grandfather was right, I was born to find things in the dark.

Just then, far away, a loud announcement from a hoverbot echoed that there would be no food if the crates weren't filled to the brim. "I'll bring something to eat, okay? It makes sense now that I know you have wings."

"You're so kind," he replied, "No one else has ever come to me in all this time."

I stood awkwardly for a moment, allowing the wonder of my discovery to sink in. Images of all the maps and research lit my mind. I rearranged them until they began to resemble a puzzle. He waited patiently, not asking what I was doing, which I appreciated. When I was ready, I said, "Okay, I'll bring back food and something to unlock or break your chains."

"I'm not going anywhere," he said. The sounds of him shifting told me he was sitting back down. So, I turned to make my way back to my hovel, thinking that I should have asked if I could touch his wings.

CHAPTER 22
DRAXTON

TWO WEEKS HAD PASSED, AND MY ONLY source of hope and motivation was freeing Luci and the belief that Callisto would eventually rescue us. I maintained a monotonous routine, surviving by completing my assigned tasks, keeping a watchful eye on my crate, and sneaking off into the darkness to bring Luci things while entertaining him by explaining what was happening on the Dark Continent. I told him about Ouro and their plans, how they were living in manmade caves carved into the mountainside and the huts we taught them to build. I shared stories about Callisto, and that had brought us here, to Anzulla, apparently to help the survivors. I explained that if we could open the mountain to free their protector, they would be able to fight back against the invaders. These were quick, short visits, and I focused only on the most important in-formation.

Luci's mood grew darker, and he refused the food I brought him. We debated who, between us, should eat the disgusting stuff. He offered to share his tunnel rats and cockroaches, claiming they were plenty, but I politely declined, enjoying my chalky prison stew.

As time crept by, I collected forgotten and dis-carded items like a handsaw, a hammer, ten-inch spikes, and even a chisel for him. He didn't sound optimistic but said he would begin to loosen the rock to which the chain was anchored.

I mimicked the prisoners' behavior, but no one looked me in the eye to reveal what they were think-ing. Why they didn't use sign language remained a mystery, and I wasn't here to figure that out. My first job was to steal a laser drill for Ouro, and to do that, I had to stay alive. The food we received in exchange for a whole crate was nothing more than bland, un-appetizing chunks of slop delivered by hoverbots.

Talking to Luci and waiting for Callisto in my dreams helped me survive this hopeless place. These people's minds were so twisted that they chained and locked away their only hope for freedom and the chance to escape. To make matters worse, I sensed that Luci only indulged me to give me something to look forward to after my shifts. He had a heart of gold with not an ounce of selfishness in his bones. Confirming yet another theory that Lucifer was a made-up story to scare people into following the rules.

A century after the invasion, most prisoners went kaput. Those remaining were born here, knowing no other life. They believe death lies beyond the surface, their survival prospects so bleak they find comfort in this grim reality.

My thoughts often wandered to Kellan. I missed him and worried he might be upset with me, possibly never wanting to speak to me again because we had lied to him. In the back of my mind, I knew Kellan's anger would be worth it if I managed to escape this ordeal with the drill and a backup advantage—Lucifer himself.

Today, my visit to Luci went bitterly tits up in the mud. He was in a foul mood.

"Get out! Let me die in peace and quiet. Your yapping irritates me!"

"No!"

"Get out of here, or you'll die!" he hissed, his voice low enough to avoid attention. I stayed as far away as possible, but I wouldn't leave. The stench of feces and blood repelled me, forcing me back into the short tunnel leading to his cell. Damn it! I'd expected him to be free by now. I'd finished mapping the forgotten tunnels and hoped Luci would help me find a laser drill and a way out.

I waited until the swearing and rustling of his wings quieted before I spoke. "I discovered a long tunnel with a steep upward slope. We could talk more than usual there since we'd be far from the main section, away from sensitive ears and patrolling hoverbots. We could blast an escape route to the outside with a laser drill. That way, people can come and go as they please. That's freedom. They could choose to stay or leave on their own," I explained, whispering. He remained silent, and I hoped he was considering what I was saying. "We should also get rid of these collars." I tapped a finger against my neck. We were both still wearing our collars, and I was afraid to fiddle with them, fearing we might risk having our heads blown off.

"It's not just our collars that are the fucking problem," he growled. I smiled. That was a good sign. At least he wasn't ignoring me or, worse, dead, while I stood here talking to myself.

I kept the conversation flowing. "Yeah, I'm worried I'll do something in my sleep while scratching my itchy skin. It's so bloody tight. As for blasting our way out, we should steal two tunnel makers—

one for you and one for Ouroboros," I said excitedly.

But then, the devil himself ruined my only bright idea. "I'm sorry, Draxton. There's only one drill, and if you take it, the prisoners won't be able to drill deeper, to produce enough rock. They will be punished severely. They will starve to death. I don't think we can even borrow it for a few minutes, they would notice it right away," Luci said, crushing all my hopes and brave promises like pissing on already dying coals in a fire.

"Fuck!" I bit my lip in frustration. "How are we going to free their protector?" I punched and kicked the smooth wall of the tunnel.

"I don't understand why Ouroboros refers to them as their protectors. They are young boys just trying to survive. Their fathers and everyone they loved have been killed. They don't deserve that responsibility. I know Callisto, and I witnessed how Atlas set everything ablaze before retreating. I lost both my lovers. We were falling like flies from the sky," Luci said. I didn't know how to respond. A moment of silence passed. "Fifty-three, you say? Just fifty-three people?"

My head dropped as I rolled it between my hunched shoulders. All my plans lay in ruins. "Yes, Ouro says he was the last of his kind, still alive. The others are the descendants of the survivors. There are also more people, either captured, enslaved, or willingly becoming Zelk, like the invaders. Some serve as informants, to Ouro, while others are turn-coats siding with the enemy." I clucked my tongue, rubbing the back of my neck where the collar was pinching me. "Ouro would be so disappointed. Kellan is going to be upset with me," I murmured under my breath. I kept rubbing the back of my neck, wondering what I was supposed to do now. Luci grunted, and I heard feathers rustling. I longed to touch them, again wondering what he looked like —probably hairy, with a thick beard. He must have been scratching that. No baths, I imagined...his wings...his feathers...While I complained about an itchy neck.

"Atlas will probably be sleeping...if he is alive. Ever since the boys were born, wherever Atlas went, Callisto followed in his shadow. They are brothers."

"I know as much. It sounds like what Ouro told us."

"Yes, Ouro, Gu's boy. I had a lot of time to sit and think in the dark, and I believe—"

"But what about your kind, the Birdmen? Are you brothers of Callisto and Atlas?" I asked, seeking to uncover the origins of angels and all the paranormal creatures that existed only in myths but were living and breathing in this time period.

"Yes, we have the same fathers. We are the first children of Anzulla," he whispered.

I grinned and stood. "So, Birdmen, like magical polar bears and dragons, are the first children? But who are the fathers?" I asked for clarification because if this were the birthplace of winged creatures, I would have solved yet another riddle for my grandfather. That's why naledi brought their dead to the Star Cave System. Heaven or Hell, depending on the time of arrival, was, after all, beyond that door.

"We are the children of gods and kings," Luci said in the dark, but I knew he was smiling because I could hear the fondness in his voice.

"But that makes little sense because Ouro and Kellan told me their father saw their arrival. That Atlas and Callisto were born after their arrival. And now you say you were also here before their arrival, before Callisto and Atlas were born. How could you have been born and lived with the San if the kings and gods only arrived after the fact and had children after their arrival?"

A long grunt rumbled from Luci's cell. "Because...under the mountain, time is stuck in a loop. Things happen differently, sometimes over and over, sometimes differently." Luci confirmed succinctly.

"Our fathers have been coming and going for hundreds of years. We are their children. We were born here in Anzulla. Our fathers have been fighting the Zelk forever. Sometimes we wake up, and we know evil was there and gone again, but small things are different, like people, buildings, animals, and even the mountain."

"Because they kept traveling back in time, changing the future?" I asked, whispering and oddly imagining it.

"Yes, all the time. We thought it was over, that everything was put back into place. For hundreds of years, things were good until the Zelk began attacking one day. Some said, '*One last time,*' while others said no."

"Holy shit, so it's like a never-ending eternal time loop?"

"Not never-ending, because the Zelk knew exactly when to invade and cloak Anzulla."

I rubbed my neck, easing the tension. "Hmmm," I mused. I needed a moment. My brain felt like scrambled eggs. "Now it makes sense. The Zelk knew, but their fathers didn't, and that's why Callisto tried to warn them, but couldn't because Kellan and I brought him here, to this time."

Luci let out a long, tired sigh. "Uh-huh." Iron clanged on iron—Luci was changing position.

"Thank you for sharing and for telling me this." I couldn't wait to relay this to Kellan, I thought. "One last question. How did your kings and gods travel through time?"

"First, they came with a small ship carrying two gods, then they went home and brought the entire city—they brought the magic to make the babies, us, their children."

Scratching my chin, I muttered to myself. "So they had advanced technology even before the invaders came?"

"Yes, and it was because of them that so many fell from the sky. They left, and days later, I had to claw myself out from the red blood mixed with ash and mud that swallowed us. We were desperate to save Anzulla, and Birdmen soared high with explosives, aiming to destroy the cloak. We were blasted to bits—feathers, flesh, and shattered wings. Atlas fell with us. He was insane with rage. We couldn't find anyone alive. Only bloodless, broken pieces of bodies. He fought the invaders with fire, and at the sight of them retreating, I believed there might be hope. But Atlas couldn't win a war alone...they'd injured him...and he'd retreated..." Luci said with a cracking voice. "I'm so tired, and now I feel so very old. Leave me. I wish I had another coin to pay the Ferryman. It doesn't matter if I ever see the blue sky again or not. My lovers, my life, dried to crumbling dust, blowing away from this plane to another life, without me." He cried softly. "Please, just go," Luci pleaded—some of the things he said made little sense. I couldn't tell which was fact or fiction.

"The city! What happened to the city?" I interrupted. "I want to know about the advanced race, damn it."

I heard Luci rolling his eyes at me. He coughed weakly, then answered in a raspy whisper. "The city that came down from the sky vanished with a thunderous crack. It's their fault the Birdmen were wiped out. Atlas was wounded. Our last hope was to send Callisto to warn them. I've lived here in the dark, feeling a hollowness in my chest, hoping he'd succeeded, but he brought you. I give up. I'd hoped to wake up one day in a land that had once been filled with laughter, but now you say you want to wake Atlas to win a war. You will fail. You will only see a mountain filled with the stench of burned bodies. Like us, you will be taken prisoners, covered in the dried blood of the last living. You will also be covered with flies, worms, and rodents that grow fat on decaying flesh. Not that it matters now. I lost my lovers, my friends, and my family. Now I eat the rodents to stay alive for what?" He chuckled cynically.

Goosebumps rose all over my body as shivers ran

down my spine. Luci's voice was heart-wrenchingly sad, yet still enchanting with its melody. I felt the urge to either cry or hit something, so I just sagged against the cool, wet wall with my back.

"Ouro showed and told us about the crystals, but they can't enter or get to them. The entrance is covered with hardened lava rock. That's why they need the drill."

His words sounded drowned in emotion as he said, "I know...I witnessed it. But Mr. Chattermouth and these miners are now my people. I can't let you take away their only way to stay alive down here. If you take it, they will notice, and everyone's lives will be in danger."

I felt the unwelcome tension building in his prison cell. "I'll come up with another plan. I won't take the drill. I promise." I got up and left him alone in the dark, just as I had found him.

I stopped visiting Luci after that. He can talk to Mr. Chattermouth—his imaginary friend.

It's pointless. This is about survival. My survival. He could free himself if he wanted; he has the means. If he chooses to end it, that's his decision.

We had different missions.

I was going to leave empty-handed.

By the end of my third week, I had learned to

stay away from the prisoners. Staying alive became my only mission.

Days dragged on in monotony. The relentless labor made my hands rough and calloused. My back ached from stooping, and my eyes no longer stung from the harsh fumes of body odor, which merged into a haze of drudgery and despair.

By isolating myself and avoiding unnecessary interactions, I found it easier to endure, conserve my energy, and outlast this harrowing experience with less emotional and physical exhaustion weighing me down.

The darkness, once a refuge, a sanctuary of safety and potential, had transformed into a constricting thing, squeezing the life out of me. Only my thoughts and memories of Kellan kept me company during my shifts, and at night, I waited to see Callisto in my dreams.

I sank into a restless sleep, drifting through fleeting dreams while hearing fragments of Kellan's familiar voice calling my name. I stirred, blinking awake to find Callisto staring at me, his white fur almost glowing in the dark.

"It's time," I faintly heard a boyish voice in my mind. I nodded, blinking back sudden tears, and rose, ready to follow him out of the mine.

CHAPTER 23
CALLISTO

I GUESS IT'S COMMON SENSE THAT GETTING imprisoned was the easiest part. The breakout was the hard part. Today will show how tough it really was.

Late last night, Simon's message reached Ouroboros. Our informant, Joseph Malherbe, had been discovered and was being publicly executed today. Mandatory attendance for all citizens meant most guards and hoverbot crews would not be on the premises, providing the perfect chance to extract Draxton. To protect Kellan, he'd taken a risky shortcut—stealing a laser drill for Ouro, lying to Kellan, and parachuting from the plane to infiltrate the underground penal colony, one of the invaders' mining operations.

Kellan and Snow waited at the inlet below while I climbed the dirt road branching from the old coastal highway, past a crumbling lighthouse and the shiny mining prison's outbuildings. Approaching, I ducked out of sight, seeing no one. The place felt deserted—good. I slipped through and under the scanners, then hopped inside.

I was a murderous, magical polar bear. A Titan!

I looked ridiculous, being adorable.

Lifting my paws high, imagining myself extra cute with a *hop-hop-hop-hop*, I pretended to be a small and innocent lost puppy. Nothing dangerous or intimidating here, I said to myself as I approached the guards in the security office, swinging my head from side to side, and sneezed playfully.

I sighed mentally—*the things I do for humans.*

The first few days after Kellan, highly upset, had sent me to follow Draxton, I hung around and pretended to whine and pine for my supposedly gone owner. Eventually, Felix and most of the regular guards got used to me and allowed me to come and go as I pleased.

Standing on my hind legs, I sniffed the ugly guard's leg while humping it. "What the fuck?" he asked, and I jumped to chase my tail, playing eager for praise and stupid as wool. His horrid, soapy smell turned my eyes askew.

"Go away! Shoo, dog!" Mr. Stinky Soap in the crotch said.

"Leave him. He's only saying hello. He's harmless."

I growled at the ugly fucker when he hit me on the snout. "Where is his owner?" he asked.

"Don't know. Probably arrested and dying inside the mine. The puppy's been coming and going. He's not hurting anyone. He's lost and alone."

"Get out!" He kicked me. "He's the ugliest dog I've ever seen," said the ugliest man *I've* ever seen.

"No, don't chase him away!"

I growled again. Warning the nasty one that I wasn't going to take his abuse.

"The poor thing is probably also about to die. But watch, he is the smartest little puppy. He talks to me," Felix said to the ugly, abusive one, whose name I was unfamiliar with and didn't want to know.

I lifted my snout and huffed, "Hello," as I approached Felix, then let my head fall like a sad, harmless puppy, a tame, miserable creature, and not one who loves shredding men like him to pieces. I guessed in a way I was miserable, but not for long, once we opened the mountain. To do that, I'm freeing Draxton today. I wagged my short tail. Felix picked me up, patted my lower back, scratching those spots I never seemed to reach and was too proud to beg for.

Cooing and whining noises escaped me. "Aww, thank you, thank you," I puffed twice through my nose.

"The prisoners will eat him," the stinky, ugly face said.

Felix scoffed, putting me back down. "Well, then he won't be bothering you anymore." Both guards were still human, but like so many others, they traded comfort for freedom.

I'd befriended Felix and even liked him until he started being too touchy and baby-talking to me. I had to create some distance between us and set boundaries, but not before I snagged a set of keys for Draxton's collar for his breakout. First off, I'm not a dog, and second, I don't do sleepovers. *Brrrrr*. I still cringe thinking about all that unwanted attention. However, he did give me good scratches.

I slid down the rusty steel staircase to the change room, where one guard was sanitizing before heading home. "Boss says everyone needs to be there—only one guard needed on each level," a new guard coming on duty told the tired one.

"I don't care, I'm going home to bed. I'm not going to the auditorium to watch."

"Suit yourself. I have an excuse not to go."

"I could stay and say we had trouble," the tired one said.

The new guard waved a hand. "No, go. I'll cover for you if anyone asks."

"Thanks, I owe you one," the tired-looking one muttered.

"No problem," the new guard said as he sauntered off.

No one saw me, so I relaxed a bit and waited until I was alone. Quickly, I zipped across the room, grabbed the keys I had stolen from Felix and had hidden behind the locker until today. The guards were usually lazy and complacent. That new scarecrow at the front security could be a problem, though. He seemed like one of those annoying try-hards. He'd better stay put and not wander, because my teeth itched for him. Luckily for him, I don't plan to come back this way.

My long black toenails tap-tapped as I trotted across the steel floor. Above ground, everything had been cleaned and polished by their electric machines. On this level, they sorted the strong from the weak. Only the strong, like Draxton, were classified as miners, while the weak ones got to decide if they wanted to be hybrid or not. Their incentive was being allowed to move freely around the city. They were then sterilized, processed, and transported to work for the invaders in the electronics manufacturing hub, including the computer parts assembly center. The leftovers, who did not conform, were sorted to extract precious stones and minerals, such as gold, diamonds, and crystals, at the ore processing industrial plant. Simon said the diamonds were crushed into diamond dust, which served as the building block for their nano-diamond technology. The gold was melted and used for wiring in their thinking machines.

I had heard stories that humans who died or misbehaved were thrown into industrial-sized meat grinders and ground into an oily sap used as battery fluid.

Yuck. I shivered and slipped into a narrow air duct. My ears popped the deeper I went, a sign that I was descending into the murky underworld, which contrasted sharply with the pristine world above. The pungent mix of sweat and blood, of unwashed bodies, pulled me further underground. I jumped out of the air duct into a cooler, damper area where prisoners had to step into a machine, be collared, and then step out, to be divided into working crews, ready to go down to their final destination.

It was noisy and reeked of mold and despair. I

rolled over to hide my natural shine, rubbing my shoulder and back for good measure in the filth.

I had memorized the layout and was now familiar with it. No guards, except for hoverbots, ever went further into the tunnels. The Zelk knew that human slaves needed food above all else. As long as the ore kept coming out, only food and hoverbots followed them inside. That's why the guards weren't bothered by the horridness of their living conditions. All they did was sit in front of screens, watching them from a distance with their flying cameras.

Felix claimed no one had ever escaped, which is why he wanted me as a pet—my owner wasn't coming back.

There were many ways in, but only two ways out —and neither was for prisoners. Only the hoverbot tunnel and the ore conveyor belt led to the surface. The bot tunnel was out of the question, leaving only the ore belt.

Draxton has been assigned to the ore collection section. A few days ago, he was optimistic; he told me that a fellow prisoner would help him access the tunneling section to steal a drill. Carrying a large laser drill in my miniature form was impossible; otherwise, I would have gotten one a long time ago. But if the three of us teamed up, I might be able to rescue Draxton, the drill, and the prisoner.

No sound came from the openings, where prisoners were sent to their assigned sections via a one-way slide. Next to the drop chutes, the conveyor belt unloaded its contents into a smasher and grinder, which washed and then pumped the contents up inside a closed tube. This is where we should get off. Otherwise, we will find ourselves smashed and dumped into trucks, ready to be transported to the factories. From here, we would have to sneak the way the guards exited. And that's why today is the best day to get Draxton, because there are fewer guards than usual.

I bit the keys tightly between my teeth and jumped inside the sliding tunnel. Down I went, landing feet first. After that, three more trapdoors.

My tummy burned scraping down the last chute, and I ricocheted like a bullet upon landing.

Zing-zing-zoom!

A hoverbot whizzed past. I ducked into a dark corner, waiting a few minutes before it sped from one tunnel into another. Soon, prisoners emerged, carrying crates. Years of dirt, silence, and exhaustion etched their deformed faces. They moved with apathy, dead on their feet. I longed to save them all, but not today. Winning the war came first; freeing the prisoners would follow.

I sighed and blew out a desperate plea. *Please let Draxton be safe. I'd rather let him be safe than have the drill.*

Some retreated to their tiny rooms—the doors left open, and never locked because the prisoners couldn't escape if they wanted to. Others gathered in the common area, women and children taking turns drinking and washing at the trickle of a small waterfall. It was utterly depressing. The tiny lights on their silver collars flickered, a constant reminder of their confinement. One wrong word or step, and the guards would activate the execution button, their heads exploding instantly.

I lay down on the floor and pressed back into the corner. I'd wait an hour after the last movement before I snuck from my hiding spot.

Zoom!

Struck by the light of a passing bot, I heard a voice calling out that the next shift was beginning. I suppressed a growl. Witnessing this suffering and doing nothing felt unbearable. My heart ached. I closed my eyes, gathering my thoughts. Stay calm, free Draxton so that he can liberate all these people later. When my fury subsided, I opened my eyes. Scanning the area, I stayed low and slowly crawled forward from the safety of the dark corner where I'd been hiding. I crept down the long, unlit tunnel to the cell where I knew from previous visits Draxton had slept—a room close to the equipment room.

When I smelled Draxton, I knew I was near his small cubicle. I kept my head down, following my nose, staying close to the floor like a rat.

Once inside his small cell, I found him crammed into the corner underneath the pieces of rotten wood he'd screwed together for a heat.

"It's time," I whispered into his mind.

Big, unbelieving eyes stared at me through the gaps. He lay still, not moving. "Callisto, you came for me!"

I sat back, waving my paws and hopping for emphasis. I blinked, silently saying, "Yes, yes, it's me! Come to me!"

Hope sparked in Draxton's haunted eyes as my faintly glowing blue ones beckoned him from his shadowy hiding place. Gaunt and ravaged, he looked near death. "Come, Draxton, it's time. Let's get you out of here." He nodded, and as a glimmer of relief flickered in his dark, sunken eyes, framed by muddy, matted hair. *Oh, Draxton, you foolish, brave soul.*

He scooped me up, his long fingers wrapping around my small, fragile ribcage, and he hugged me with his nose buried in my fur. I smelled his salty tears silently falling. The magic faded when I realized he was using me as a tissue. Feeling sorry for him, I stayed still. Breathing could wait. I let him sniff and nuzzle me. My chest tightened, my eyes bulged. A soft cough escaped from my strained lungs. I was being smothered with joy.

Finally, just as I started to see stars and thought maybe I should grow in size to save myself, he released me, and I gasped to get air into my tiny lungs.

During our reunion, the keys had fallen into his lap. He spoke again, so softly that I thought his vocal cords might be missing. "Thank you, thank you, thank you," he repeated.

Then I remembered that sound was prohibited down here. The only noise permitted was the tools carving the rocks. Draxton carefully fiddled with the keys, looking as if he were pondering their significance. Maybe he had brain damage. He showed them to me as if asking, "What is this?"

I gave a soft growl, lifting my paw to point at his neck, indicating it was the key to the collar. I panted, hoping he could hear and understand me like Ouro and the others did. He shook his head and placed his finger in front of his lips, pointing to his ears to suggest we should be quiet. "Okay, okay, I can be quietly silent," I said wordlessly, mind to mind.

Draxton picked me up, pressing my ear to his lips. "It's for unlocking the collar, isn't it?" he whispered. "Thank you, Callisto. Please, get me out of here. But I have bad news. I can't bring the drill. If I take it, all these people will starve."

I wiggled my hips. My tail signaled that I was okay with it and that I understood.

"Good?" Draxton whispered.

Nodding my head, I replied, "Yes, understood."

"Okay, give me a second." Draxton unlocked the collar. There was a zipping sound, and then he unsnapped the decapitation contraption. He picked me up, and once again, his stinky breath warmed my ear. "I will bring the keys to Luci. I trust him. He will help the others escape."

My head snapped up. "Luci? Our Luci, is he here?" I asked, but Draxton wasn't listening. "Stay here." He pointed down, indicating that I should stay put. "I will be back in a few minutes," he said excitedly, so I communicated with my eyes by blinking several times that I would wait for him.

He slipped into the darkness, and I hid behind the pile of wood he'd used as a blanket. I waited and waited. It felt longer than a few minutes, I thought, and I waited a little longer.

"Okay, ready." He waved for me to come out. I bounced ahead, checking if we were alone. He followed as I led him to the area where they dumped the ores onto the sifting tables to be sorted and taken outside.

The air was thick with dust. Two shaking rectangular tables with rippled surfaces stood tilted at an angle while a large drum sloshed and banged.

"We must hurry," he whispered as the tables rocked, water pouring over them and flowing along their long axis, causing low-density particles to move faster and fall into the scooping hands feeding the conveyor belt, while high-density particles tumbled into the muddy heaps below. Draxton dropped to his hands and knees. "Do you want me to get onto this?" he asked, pointing from his chest to the belt. I nodded yes, nudging him with my snout. The constant vibrations created enough noise for us to escape without being heard, but we had seconds.

"Okay," he mouthed as he crawled like an eight-legged spider onto the table. We had to act fast. I lifted my paw, pushing the lever that controlled the large sift and precious stone scooping arms. The machine stopped vibrating. Draxton rolled and wormed himself between the already filled belt, burying himself. Smart.

Once he was ready, I lifted my paw, turned on the sifting table, and leaped to where his feet were, following him. As soon as the multiple arms started scooping, covering me, the belt began moving.

"Gods, help us," Draxton croaked as we inched away. He didn't seem to mind tight spaces. Seconds later, a hoverbot approached, zooming up and down, searching for movement. We waited, not moving while the belt carried us to freedom. Not even breathing, out of fear of being noticed, we slowly left the hoverbot behind, traveling hundreds of feet up inside the narrow shaft.

Far below, the bot's light stopped sweeping the sorting area. The conveyor lurched and sped up.

"Phew," we sighed with relief. Draxton had lost weight, which was a good thing; otherwise, he could have been badly scraped getting out. His unwashed smell was overpowering, and I breathed through my mouth as my eyes watered.

We lay still, rising slowly inside the chicken-wire tube, leaving the prison below. I turned my head to avoid more of those overripe smells stinging the insides of my snout. When the conveyor belt reached the crushers, we scooted, rolled, and crawled out of the small opening, then made our way to the exit. Luckily, there were no guards, and Draxton kept up with me as we scaled the rusted stairs I had taken to come inside.

It felt as though we had done this many times

before as we slipped outside into the bright sunlight. Draxton covered his eyes with one hand, weaving his finger into my growing fur as I transformed into a larger version to protect him. I led him through the parked trucks, waiting to be filled with the precious stones. Finally, the back gate came into view. We ran with Draxton moving in a low crouch, next to me.

"Gods, the scent of freedom and fresh air! I was so glad to see you," he said a little louder once we were outside the complex and our feet sank into the hot desert sand. I expanded, hoping to scoop him onto my back so I could carry him down the hill to where Snow and Kellan were waiting.

"That was easy. Where are the security? Why was this so simple?" He was right. It was the perfect day to come and get him.

"Something is going on," Draxton said. I agreed, something stranger than usual was happening—the execution of our inside man. I pushed my snout between his knees, urging him to climb onto me.

Draxton tensed, then I heard it too—the rhythmic *puff-puff-puff* of boots behind us. I spun around, letting out a battle cry. Leaping in front of Draxton, I scanned the gate. There he was—that bloody guard from before, jogging toward us. What was he doing at the back gate?

"Halt!" he yelled. Draxton froze, hands raised in surrender. I continued to grow larger, my four legs surrounding him protectively, ready to shield him from the enemy's fire. Barefoot, naked, unshaven, and reeking of a fugitive, he would have been shot on sight. I growled a warning, and Draxton remained still, clinging to my hind legs.

"The guard's shouting is going to attract the hoverbots. Stand still, don't move, Callisto," Draxton cautioned as I went down on my front legs, blocking Draxton from the danger and preparing to pounce on the ugly fucker.

"Callisto!" Draxton cried, fear lacing his voice, but I was already reacting. I'm not a dog! I'm his guardian, his protector.

The guard swore, and I leaped before he could fire. A bullet zipped past; another thudded into his chest. His knees buckled, his face a mask of astonished disbelief. He crumpled. I glared, disgruntled. He stared back, accusingly, sputtering, "You shot me?" he said disbelievingly. Wide-eyed, and blood dripped from the corners of his mouth.

Do I look like I'm carrying a gun?

The answer to that foolish question would forever elude him. He let out a pained moan, then expired. I grunted throatily, sniffing him and making sure he was really dead.

"Come!" Draxton patted his leg. "We have to go..." he said, as his eyes rolled back and he sank to his knees.

"Oh, no you don't!" I huffed—I'm no dog. Swinging my massive frame, I hoisted Draxton onto my shoulders. "Hold on!" and thundered down to the beach, where Snow was stowing his long-range rifle in the boat.

"Kellan and Snow!" Draxton cried weakly. I slowed, gently setting him down before them. Tears of relief were streaming down his face.

"No drill?" Snow asked. Kellan gasped at the horrid sight of Draxton—only bone and dark shadows.

"N-no drill." Draxton whimpered.

"I don't care about the drill!" Kellan yelled. "Look at you!" He scrambled for warm blankets, hastily covering Draxton's failing body.

"I-I'm so sorry, Professor. Ah-hum...please take me home. Please." Draxton sounded broken and horrible. Tears streamed like rivers down his cheeks. Kellan helped him into the small motorboat and began to give him fluids.

Draxton suckled on the bottle like a starved baby. "Slowly!" Kellan cautioned.

"Don't worry, Kellan. We'll take care of him at Simon's," Snow said reassuringly. "Simon has medical training and a full surgery with equipment. We'll stabilize him there."

"Please, hurry," Kellan said, panicking, as I had never seen him before.

Draxton didn't protest. He hung his head and melted into Kellan's embrace.

With Snow's help, I pushed the boat farther from shore. Before I went in too deep, I shrank my bulky guardian form to avoid sinking the rescue boat as I jumped aboard.

CHAPTER 24
KELLAN

WHEN I SCOOPED DRAXTON UP AND LOADED him onto the speedboat, I held him as tightly as I could, vowing never to let him go. I fed him electrolytes, praying that his limp body, barefoot and dressed in scraps of tattered clothes, would hang on. Although half unconscious, Draxton was alive and breathing, ice-cold and shivering, but he was the most beautiful sight.

Back at Simon's, we fed and patched Draxton up before heading home to the Dark Continent. Many helping hands carried him from the floatplane to our hut. He slept for forty-eight hours straight after we put him to bed, exhausted. Holding him safe at home was wonderful. Despite severe malnutrition, dehydration, and trauma, his spirit remained strong.

Now that his body was almost fully healed, I took off my clothes and stayed in bed, keeping him warm while I watched him sleep. Emotions washed over me in waves, and when he woke up, he still radiated that cheeky confidence and shining brilliance. His long black eyelashes fluttered before his eyes opened. He looked right into mine. He groaned, "Hmmm," wiggling slowly. Stretching overhead, he smiled crookedly, revealing a cute dimple on his right cheek.

I had to have him.

I wanted to be inside his body, reconnecting and reaffirming our connection by showing him how happy I was with his safe return. I tried to wipe away my anger toward those who had hurt him, my fear of what might have been. But most of all, I needed him to feel my overwhelming love because he had captured my heart and soul.

I knew we still had a long journey ahead of us before we could go back to our real homes, to our time. But as I held his face and slowly pressed into him, I realized we could face anything together.

He pushed my shoulders up and positioned himself beneath me. "Cover me," he said. "I want your full weight on me. I need to feel you're here." I complied, and he moaned in satisfaction.

"I thought you'd be mortified after that mess, but

you're even more dedicated to helping Ouro," I murmured, kissing Draxton's sweaty chest. Ouro had given Sopora two tiny crystals. She made pendants for us both. He couldn't wear his in prison, but it was around his neck the moment I had held him. His deep, infected wounds healed remarkably fast—I suspected the crystals and Callisto helped.

Draxton lay on his back while I kneeled between his trembling thighs. "The braver you are, the more I worry about you. The more I worry, the more I want to show you how much I care about you. The more I care about you, the more I lust after you," I said honestly in a low, serious tone. I didn't mention that his foolish bravery made me fall a little more in love with him or that his absence had made my heart grow fonder and turned me into a broody househusband—I would never admit that to him. Not yet. I grinned at the thought. The more I got to know him, the deeper my connection to him became, and the more I want him to be mine.

He exhaled deeply and wrapped his arms around my neck, pulling me closer until his ankles pinned me around my lower back. "I promised myself I would listen when someone tells me my plan is risky and I might not make it out alive. I've learned my lesson, Professor. There's no need to feel inferior or pity myself. If anything, I'm more confident than ever. I take pride in my ability to persist and persevere. My grandfather would have had an epileptic fit and scolded me for weeks. Thank you for not doing that."

Our eyes locked. I felt as if I might tip over, drowning in the bottomless depths of his dark, cenote eyes. "I'm proud of you," I whispered. He smiled and then squeezed my hips with his thighs, kissing me.

"You are like an octopus devouring me," I joked as he finally released my mouth to breathe. My instincts screamed to possess him, to tell him I'm only his and want him to be mine. I was frantic and worried because I loved him. But I was terrified that the moment I uttered those words, the moment I looked and sounded like I wanted to cage and keep him like a pretty bird, he would tear whatever strings kept us attached and distance himself from me.

We rhythmically rocked, sharing each other's breaths, gradually increasing the pace but not rushing to climax. But rather a steady, steamy seduction of our minds and our bodies. We held each other's gaze, transcending into a spiritual connection as we worked together, pushing, pulling, grinding, slipping, and gripping tightly, enjoying the climb to the apex of simultaneous pleasure. We grunted. We moaned. We sang the crescendo of men making love, then sudden silence followed as we exploded into stardust. Drifting somewhere far beyond the universe until all that was left was the here and now.

When we caught our breaths, I wordlessly withdrew myself from him and fell to his side, leaving my leg and wet, limp cock draped over his hip. "Hm, this feels nice. I'm relaxed now that you are in my arms," I said and closed my eyes.

"I missed you. You make me feel that way too. I was worried that you would hate me."

I pushed myself back up onto my elbow. Looking down at him while scowling, I said, "Hate you? Never!" I made eye contact with him to make sure he had heard me.

"Yes, for lying and deceiving you."

"Never. I could never-ever hate you. I was upset, yes. But, after the initial shock had worn off, and I thought about it, I was not surprised. I'm getting to know you, Draxton Dubois." *I know you very well because I see your magnificence.*

He closed his eyes. "Hm, that's good. You are good to me." I enjoyed watching his contentment. His face was so expressive, and I could now see his clear mind. Nothing seemed to bother him.

"You know, it wasn't all for nothing. You could create a map of those tunnels. Ouro and even Simon would appreciate that," I suggested.

His eyes widened. "Yes! I can do that! You're so smart, Professor," he said with the broadest grin. "I almost forgot!" Draxton burst into laughter. "You won't believe who I found in shackles...deep inside...hell!" His shoulders shook with mirth as he stammered through snorts and giggles. "I...I'll give you ten guesses...because three won't be enough."

"Hm, a challenge." I made a face and asked, "Ten?" His excitement triggered a million flutters of happy synapses inside me.

"Yes, yes, ten, and I bet you still won't guess it." He laughed, his eyes glinting with mischief.

My brows furrowed in concentration as I racked my brain for potential answers. "If you know I won't be able to guess, why don't I just admit defeat so you can tell me, anyway?" I said, wiping the tears of laughter from the corners of his eyes.

Draxton stared at me, waiting for me to guess. "Only the devil knows," I said, bemused.

Draxton's face shifted from wonder to disgust, and then his head drooped as he said, "I must have been talking in my sleep because you can't be that smart." He chuckled.

"What? I was picking the most random answer."

I shrugged, not understanding that the "devil only knows," the most ambiguous answer, elicited this disappointed reaction from Draxton.

I threw my hand up. "I knew you'd be disappointed if I guessed correctly. The answer is still not clear to me, I swear, I promise. I'm really sorry." I laughed. "So, what's the answer?" I asked.

Draxton smiled. He nodded vigorously with wide eyes. "It's Luci, short for Lucifer."

"No!"

"Oh yes!"

"No!"

"Yes," he said with a big grin.

"I can't believe this! So this is some weird coincidence," I said, to see him light up again. It was so refreshing.

"I didn't see him. I couldn't, it was dark, but he was literally shackled to the wall in the deepest, farthest tunnel down there. By pure accident, I heard the faint, unnatural sounds of metal clanging against the rock. So, one day, when no one was watching, I slipped away to explore."

I stroked his cheek. "Of course you did. Only you would explore the scariest places to go find Satan himself."

Draxton puffed up proudly. "He said he's not Satan. He's Luci, and I could tell he was tall, and he had wings."

I gasped. "You're shitting me!"

"No, I'm not," he said, and inwardly, I shook with delighted laughter. He looked so pleased with himself.

I let him have the spotlight. He enjoyed it so much. "Tell me everything," I said, and he did. He told me every detail his mind had recorded from inside the mine, from the number of tunnels and their measurements to how many toes and fingers Luci had had.

"We have to tell Ouroboros," he said. I sighed, knowing that doing so would only stoke the urgency to get a bloody laser drill for him.

His gaze pierced mine. I waited, giving him time to process everything. I saw his mind wander, but after staring for a few minutes, he said, "Thank you," with a shaky, emotional crack.

I traced small circles around his nipples while resting my head on his chest, feeling his heartbeat and hearing his voice rumble. "There's no need to thank me. Tomorrow, we'll tackle this tunnel maker issue together. No more diving half-cocked into trouble alone and making me sick with worry." I flicked out my tongue, licking and biting his pectoral. "If it weren't for Snow and Callisto, I would have fallen apart trying to come and help you."

Draxton sighed. "That bear is something special. He saved my life. I thought I dreamed about him, but I have a feeling he was with me most of the time."

I chuckled. "He doesn't enjoy flying. When he discovered Simon had a ship, he refused to fly. Snow had to beg him, and he still refused. Can you believe that? You should have seen Snow trying to push Callisto's fat behind and not budging. Snow bickered as Callisto grunted his protests. It was so funny."

"Do they have a ship? Maybe I should take the ship to Spire?"

I bit into Draxton's underarm. Hard.

"Ouch!"

"You're done doing shit on your—"

"Alright, alright. Stop biting me!" Draxton chortled. "I was just teasing."

"No, you weren't. If I lost you, I'd be all alone here. Please don't do that to me." *Please don't break my heart.*

I let out a surprised grunt as Draxton rolled me onto my back to plaster himself against my front.

"Hm, feels slippery between us." He smiled, licked between my lips, gently nibbled my bottom lip, and slid his warm tongue into my mouth. He made love to my mouth slowly and with immense passion. I felt like bursting into tears. I rocked my hips, rubbing my cock against his hardness. I didn't close my eyes. I savored every second I had with him. He's perfect, I thought. He did it unselfishly, whatever he tackled, whatever he set his mind to.

Grinding his hips, pumping life into my spent cock, he said, "I won't, I promise. I just thought I'd save everyone the trouble."

"Hm. Promise?" I hummed into his open mouth, closing my eyes. I lost myself in the heat building between us.

"I promise I won't jump out of the airplane and get myself arrested again."

My eyes snapped open. "Oh, that. Yes, please. I would have followed you if I weren't flying, but Snow stopped me."

"That's why I didn't tell you about my plan. I was worried that you might do something foolish, Professor," he said softly.

My eyes enlarged. "I didn't expect it at that moment. I freaked out and almost crashed the airplane, thinking you fell out," I said with reverence. "I am happy to have you back home in my arms. Try to suppress that wild instinct, that Indiana-fucking-Jones shit."

He gave me that charming smile. I knew he was

aware of how gorgeous he looked when he smiled at me like that. "You like that about me, but I promise I'll listen to reason next time. Indiana Jones, right?" He joked as he reversed down between my legs to align with my entrance. He slid his hands up my arms and intertwined his fingers with mine. "You're slick and ready for me, Professor."

"I am. That's what happens if you don't use condoms."

"That's one positive thing about this place. I don't even feel a tiny bitt of remorse for filling you up."

"Me neither." I groaned and threw my head back as my body arched up into his.

"Gods, the pleasure of entering you is something else." The low rumble of delight as he pushed inside me was the most sincere and vulnerable thing about him. He rubbed his beard against mine. The scratching noise was all male, and I melted under him. Opening my legs wider, he slid up and down, the sweat between our bodies providing the most delicious, slippery movements.

"Oh, my God!"

"I know. I feel the same. Hm," he moaned.

I watched as his eyes slid shut and his face screwed up in pleasure with every stroke. This love I had for him was genuine and powerful. Having him on top of me and in me while I was begging him to fuck me harder cemented my love for him. I was hot chakalaka inside. I wanted to burst into tears. Draxton heaved, and I panted. As my orgasm built, I clamped my fingers into his, lifting my knees, opening myself as far as possible for him as my mind blanked out from the sensations. Draxton's hips furiously rocked against me.

"Fuck, Kellan," Draxton cursed and jerked, pushing himself fully into me.

My thighs trembled from exertion as my orgasm built with the friction of his lower belly on my cock. The sweet desire between us bloomed, and I groaned as his last deep thrust into me pulled me to the brink, to that fine edge, the pinnacle, and with a snap, I couldn't hold back my climax. With our fingers still locked and gripped so tight, I came hard, feeling him throbbing inside me. Burying his face in the crook of my neck, we hummed, nuzzled, and gasped for air. Riding, twitching, and then relaxing as our orgasms faded.

He lifted his head. Sweat ran down his temples. His dark gaze searched my soul. For a moment, I thought he might say he loved me, but breathlessly he said, "You are amazing. I'm sorry I deceived you, Kellan."

I blinked to clear my eyes and refocus my

thoughts. Never had I heard such sincerity. This man was exceptional.

"You too. I missed you, and I'm glad you are safe. There is no need to apologize. You have already."

Draxton let go of my hands, supported himself with his arms at my sides, and then sat up while slipping out of my ass. I clenched my sore, stretched sphincter, joining him in getting up. "We need a shower."

"Yes, we do," I said excitedly, eager to show him his surprise. Draxton led the way. I appreciated his muscled, although significantly skinnier, naked body as I followed him around the corner to our new modest washroom.

His eyes widened. "Oh, my goodness, Professor, where did you find everything? I know for certain there is no Home Depot here?"

I smiled, enjoying the surprised look of wonder on his face. "That's all Snow and Simon. They felt shitty after I yelled at them and asked them what I should do with myself waiting like a maiden for the local hero to come home," I said. "I'm chuckling now, but I was enraged at the time."

"I can only imagine the drama."

"Not all the people living on the Light Continent are Zelk supporters. They live there because they have no other option. There's an illegal black market. Our washroom amenities were traded for meat and potatoes."

"I'd trade my toilet for meat and potatoes any day. That prison food was awful; it barely kept the inmates alive. Without the rat meat, I think they'd have starved to death." Draxton walked over to the toilet and flushed it. It was old and patched up, but it worked. "And it flushes too," he added.

"Rat meat? You don't look like you ate any?"

"Oh, I did," he said casually. "Ugh, just the thought makes me nauseous. It was awful—ground bone, chalk, and water, topped with a rat. Initially, I was terrified, convinced it was human remains. But after a week of starvation, I didn't care. My mission depended on it; if the others could survive it, so could I. I had to eat it...to see you again."

My face puckered. "Draxton, you've endured so much," I said, leading him into our new walk-in shower and opening the tap. "I'm sorry. I don't have a hot shower for you. The water is ice cold. There wasn't enough time—"

Draxton looked up, inspecting the piping. "Shut up," he whispered, his voice hinting at exhaustion. The frigid water glimmered under the soft light of the crystal around his neck. The village was quiet, the ocean calm, and I could only hear the distant calls of nocturnal creatures. Goosebumps formed on my skin as I shivered, anticipating the icy touch of the stream.

"You've done a lot already. I'm not frightened of cold water. Not after surviving an apocalyptic winter or washing out of a little bowl. This is amazing." His words and the water were chilling. A shiver ran down my spine. With a firm grip on my hand, he pulled me forward, the sensation of his touch sending a jolt of anticipation through me. My breath caught in my throat as we stepped into the freezing water, the numbing cold dampening my arousal instantly.

He looked so happy, smiling as the water ran over his face and into his mouth. "Thank you for getting our house ready."

Silently, I was freaking out. The hunger he had endured was evident. Not wanting to draw attention to his more petite frame, I rolled my eyes while lathering soap over his chest. I felt his pronounced clavicles, then his skinny shoulders and bony ribs. "*Pfft.* Honestly, I just needed something to keep me occupied and sane until Ouro got Simon's message," I said, hiding my real feelings. I desperately wanted to cry and strangle him for doing this to himself. He'd become so thin.

Draxton threw his head back, revealing a mischievous grin. "Professor Productive!" He pulled me closer, rubbing his lower half against mine.

My teeth chattered. "I'm going to wash you, then feed you, and then feed you some more after we're done with this. You've lost so much weight."

He took the soap from me. "Hm, I hope it's your cock and balls." He purred monotonously in his best imitation of a seductive tone, and I couldn't help but laugh.

CHAPTER 25
DRAXTON

CHEERS ERUPTED AS WE STEPPED OUTSIDE our home for the first time since I had escaped from prison. The sun peeking through the bulbous clouds cut like knives, and I shielded my eyes to see the wide-eyed faces of my friends waving and waiting to touch and talk to me. Kellan's hand rested on the small of my back while the scent of the sea and ice filled my nose, and I felt safe. I was home.

"Welcome back, Draxton!" Sopora approached me first. She smiled, and I allowed her to give me a motherly hug. She was warm and smelled like lavender and wood smoke.

Out of nowhere, Rocket rammed into us, almost knocking me over. Kellan caught me, and Rocket's strong arms enveloped Kellan and me both while he kissed the side of my head repeatedly. "Draxton, Kellan!" he said, "My favorite men of the hour!"

I laughed, finding my footing. It felt good to be back.

"You've lost weight. Don't worry, I'll fatten you up in no time," Sopora said as Rocket broke his embrace, and I could breathe again.

Libre and the younger ones chimed in, handing me a bouquet of purple wildflowers. "Yeah, welcome back!" Now I understood why Sopora smelled like lavender.

I gasped in surprise at them and checked in with Kellan. He beamed at me. "Thank you," I said, inhaling their fragrance.

"I'll put them in water for you," Kellan said, quickly disappearing back into our hut as I continued to greet everyone.

After all the patting and hugging were done, Rocket said, "Ouroboros and Snow are waiting for you. They asked that you meet them at Snow's hut."

I've never had so many hands on me at once or been touched so much. They were respectful, and I didn't mind because they stepped back at least three feet to give me space to breathe.

Kellan took my hand, and I grinned at him. "Ready?" he asked.

"Never been more ready," I said, meaning I was

ready to trust him. I was prepared to tackle our next quest together as a team.

Before entering Snow's home, Kellan turned to me and pulled me close. He took my breath away, just like he had that day before we entered the Star Caves. He held me so tightly that I couldn't go anywhere and could only look into his eyes. I thought he was the only person able to touch and keep me this tightly without freaking me out. Despite everything that had happened, he appeared so cheerful, and I realized he hadn't said much about returning home to our time, or about his mother worrying and waiting.

"No matter what Ouro or Snow says, remember you don't owe anyone anything. Whatever you say and decide, I will stand by you. If you choose not to go ahead, let me or someone else do it, say so," Kellan said.

I knew he meant well, but I wanted to hear what Ouro and Snow wished to discuss, so I agreed and kissed him to show him. I broke the kiss when Callisto impatiently nudged us to move inside. I laughed. "Yes-yes, we know," I told Callisto.

Inside Snow's modest hut, we found Ouroboros, Snow, and three other men. "Welcome back, Draxton!" they greeted loudly, raising their cups. A sudden jolt of shame coursed through me. I glanced about, lost. Kellan tugged at my hand, and I followed him. We joined the men, each of us grabbing a pillow and plopping down in the widening half-circle in front of the fire in the hearth. Ouro was to my left, while Kellan sat on my right, between me and the newcomers. Callisto guarded the door.

Snow poured us each a cup of their fermented berry wine. "Thank you," I said.

"What do you see and smell?" someone asked as I stared into my cup.

I lifted my gaze. "The bitter-sweet aroma alone makes my mouth water," I whispered, peering back into the cup of deep red-purple liquid, and chuckled. "I see I'm going to get tipsy today."

Relaxing banter about fermented berries and their headache-inducing properties eased my tension. "It's a secret grounding technique," a friendly, stocky man with a head of bushy curls explained. "We used to teach it to parents of children with busy minds. The taste and smell are sensory tools, bringing the mind back to the present."

"Draxton, this is Simon." Kellan pointed to him, making it known that this was the formidable Simon. "But what about the others?" Kellan asked Ouroboros, giving him a pointed stare.

"Oh, excuse me, we've had a few too many drinks while waiting for you. I'm a bit slow." He pointed, cup in hand. "That's Simon's two brothers and associates, Donali and Kawa." Ouroboros introduced us while I struggled to look him in the eye.

"Hello, nice to meet you." I waved awkwardly at the men. They set their drinks down, wiped their hands, and offered to shake mine.

"It's good to see you awake and upright. I'm the oldest and the most handsome brother, which makes me the leader of our small rebellion," Simon said, throwing his head full of thick brown curls to the side, revealing tribal tattoos running down his neck. His smile was wide, showing more teeth than I was comfortable with, but he'd helped us and was very resourceful. So, I trusted him, met his gaze, and shook his hand.

"Thank you for my toilet and the other state-of-the-art amenities," I said, causing him to smile even wider. I shivered and unintentionally pulled back slightly. As if reading my mind, Kellan signaled for everyone to widen the circle. No one spoke as they quickly scooted back two feet. I loved that about Kellan. Just by doing that, I could breathe and confront them.

One of Simon's brothers knee-walked over to me

and extended his hand. "Hi, glad to meet you, Draxton. I'm Donali, and that's my twin, Kawa. Happy to see you on your feet again."

"They helped me stabilize you before Snow and I brought you to the Dark Continent," Kellan noted.

I gave Kellan a nod. "Yes, I remember small bits and pieces. Thank you," I said to them.

Kawa waved, then offered his gloved hand. "No problem," he said. "We're Simon's seconds. Simon's word is law. If he says jump, we ask how high," he joked. I instantly liked the twins. Posh and taller than Simon, they both shared his dark brown eyes and shaved heads. Kawa's handshake was firm, his eyes intelligent.

These three weren't San; their looks and speech were different. Their origins puzzled me. They are not San, Zelk, or Birdmen. I finally got to ask some questions. The miners wouldn't talk, but these men were more forthcoming.

"Now that we're all acquainted, Draxton, there's no need for embarrassment. It wasn't a complete failure, but after speaking with Callisto, we all agree it's best if you don't try that again." Ouro raised a hand, cutting off my questions. "Wait, let me finish." I sighed, rolling my eyes. He glared, so I sighed again, forcing myself to relax. Kellan's hand rested on my thigh. I glanced at his hand, then at him. He offered a reassuring smile, gently rubbing my leg.

"Kellan was beside himself with worry," Ouro said. "I apologized, admitting we should have included him from the start." I glanced at Kellan; I should never have left him out. "Simon and his men are innocent, despite Kellan's accusations. They even provided Kellan with furniture to keep him occupied while he waited for you. I'm overruling your command. Not because it was wrong, but because it was too risky for you and everyone. Do you agree?" Ouro's voice, though calm, was firm. His yellow-green eyes met mine, silencing any protest. "Let me be clear," he said, "the mission wasn't a failure, just dangerous. Your reckless actions endangered not only yourself but all of humanity."

I hung my head in shame, nodding in agreement. I knew he was right. "I promise I will never act on my own again," I said in a remorseful tone.

Ouro's expression softened as he placed a hand on my shoulder. "We all made mistakes, my friend. It wasn't only your fault. Snow, Simon, and I are all guilty. The important thing is that we learn from them. Remember, it was not a failed mission."

I lifted my head and emptied my cup to combat the noisy buildup of emotions inside me. They waited a moment while I wiped the tears from my eyes. Once I had regained my composure, I began to share what I had witnessed. I recounted my entire experience with the prisoners. "Their stubborn refusal to escape meant I couldn't bring a tunnel maker. I'd hoped Lucifer and I could blast open the mine, but he's chained up and won't leave the others."

"No way!" our three visitors exclaimed. I shared what Luci said while their eyes filled with tears. Later, their interest grew at the mention of drawing a map of the tunnels. Donali and Kawa were practically bouncing on their pillow seats at the thought of blowing the mine wide open to free Luci. Explosions and blowing Zelk up were their specialty.

"Man, it would be great to see Luci again!" Kawa said excitedly. Donali and Simon nodded their agreement.

"So, you knew him?" I asked, my inquisitive nature igniting within me. These men were present before the invasion. So, as I deduced earlier, they weren't San, but rather the ones with advanced technology that arrived before the Zelk. They came with the city of gods that had descended from the sky and hid beneath the water, as Luci and Ouro had mentioned.

Simon answered. "Even before the Phoenicians jumped from the ocean floor to ocean floor, hundreds of years ago, the San tribe and the Birdmen were already in Anzulla—"

I lifted my hand. "Wait, wait, wait. What do you mean by ocean floor to ocean floor?" I asked.

Kawa chipped in. "We time-jumped, bringing the City of Phoenix here from 2148 A.D. because the whole globe was flooded. Phoenix was the last city, and it contained the last of the humans in existence."

"How did that happen?" Kellan asked.

"Really?" I wondered too. That meant disaster loomed in our future back home—if we ever went back.

"Global warming and other catastrophes, then global winter and a string of global volcanic eruptions, that led to the almost instantaneous melting of the polar ice caps. Phoenix was covered in a protective layer and able to sustain life underwater," Kawa said as if it were just another thing that happened. Like, oops, my ice cream fell off the cone.

"2148 A.D," I repeated. My mouth was hanging open. Kellan didn't make a sound. Ouro lifted one eyebrow. Simon, Donali, and Kawa nodded like parrots' head banging to AC/DC's "Highway to Hell." *Which I thought was fitting.*

No wonder they needed us, I thought. Callisto

nodded his head, grunted, and huffed a yes, much like a dog barking.

I blinked a few times. "Go on, please," I said sarcastically. More and more, I felt like history had tricked me. "No wonder no one recorded this shit. It's shamefully disorientating. At least now I know where Atlantis went," I said sarcastically.

"From which year did you arrive?" Donali asked.

"2025," Kellan answered. Disbelieving wolf whistles followed.

Simon scowled. "Are you saying no one recorded our history anywhere? No Phoenix?"

I glanced at Kellan, hinting that he answered them. "Uhm, aside from Plato's Atlantis, a hieroglyphic text found at the Ziggurat structure in North Africa described the Gate of Judgment to the city of the gods that rose like a watery phoenix. Scholars assumed it was either Heaven or Atlantis. That's the one connection to the door in the Cradle of Mankind and the tomb of King Solomon. I'm a paleontologist, and Draxton is a world-renowned cartographer. I can assure you, he has the schematics and every inscription of every cave he has studied stored away and deciphered in his mind. It's the only clue about the door to Heaven or Atlantis we know about." Kellan winked at me. My tummy made flip-flops, rendering me a blushing, blinking man. "My

father was a historian, comparing what had tran-
spired here and what was recorded about it. Very
little, if any, was mentioned about the real name of
Earth or its invasion," Kellan added.

"I heard that you share Gugusan as a father.
That's incredible!" Donali noted and gave him a sexy
wink. *What the fuck?*

I cut off their silent exchange with a wave of my
hand. "Alright, alright, tell us your story. I've been
waiting to hear your side. We've all heard Kellan's,
and I know Ouroboros and Luci's versions. Now,
let's hear yours." I pointed skyward. "We traveled all
this way to meet an advanced race and see mythical
creatures. Luci and Callisto proved the latter. So, if
it's not the Zelk, then you are." I gestured between
them. "I don't care which brother speaks first."

Simon cleared his throat and shuffled closer. "I'll
give you the short version. Phoenix was the last
human civilization to survive on the ocean floor for
over a hundred years before it was relocated in time,
as Ishtar and Lasitor had warned that Phoenix
would cease to exist if they didn't transport it to another ocean floor and time. So they parked Ishtar's
time machine inside the underwater city and
jumped almost thirty thousand years into the past.
Two weeks after our arrival, the first attack of Apsu
happened."

"Apsu?" Kellan asked.

"Yes, Ishtar's wicked father, leader of the Zelk."

I turned my head up and said, "The plot thickens." Kellan sipped his drink, giving me a look over the brim. I pursed my lips.

"Things just got weirder and weirder until the day the Phoenicians voted to jump back. Now we sit with the Zelk, and everyone is either stuck in the future, lost in time, or dead," Simon said.

"Tell us, when you arrived here, what did you find?" Kellan asked.

"One peculiar fact was that Luci had a coin like mine. He said his grandfather gave it to him and had told him that the king would arrive through the sky with the blood moon." Simon stuck his hand in his pants pocket and handed us an American quarter. "I've had this coin before Doomsday, before Phoenix." Kellan and I sat head-to-head as we inspected the coin together.

"2004?" Kellan whispered.

Simon boasted. "Yeah! See the bite marks. That's how we know it is the same coin."

Kellan held it to the light. "Holy shit! It's true, I see the bite marks." He grinned. I nodded.

Simon held out his hand, asking for it back as if it were precious to him. Kellan placed it in the palm of his hand. Simon stared at it. "This is a rare Wisconsin quarter. Only a few were minted in 2004," he said. After a moment, putting it back into his pocket, he continued. "Another interesting thing was that the buildings along the coast and deep within the mountain, known as the Heart of Anzulla, seemed ancient, overgrown like a ghost town. At first, we thought nothing of it, but as the centuries crawled by, we began to realize why." Donali puffed his fingers as if it were magic.

Kawa agreed with a smile and a nod. "This is a strange fucking place and time. It's almost as if we exist in a dimension on a changing timeline, outside the reality we came from. We assumed the Anunnaki, Ishtar's kin, lived inside the mountain."

"Right," Simon said. "Ishtar's family was born on another timeline, from another experimental lab, and he had been jumping from reality to reality, destroying Anzulla and leaving nothing but scorched, unfertile wasteland. That's why King Eryn and Ishtar pursued him with Ishtar's time machine."

Kellan leaned closer. "This is it," he whispered. "We're finally getting answers." Ouroboros shot Kellan a warning glance, signaling Simon to continue.

Simon waved his arms animatedly while gazing upward. He was probably imagining what he had seen when they arrived, as he described it to us. "Inside the mountain, enormous red crystals emitted light. A waterfall hundreds of meters high cascaded into a large natural warm water pool. It's so huge inside, you can float on a lazy river through a forest of ancient trees, grasslands, and fields of flowers." This reminded me of Luci's stories. I wanted to know more about their longevity. Was it because of the crystal or something else? I didn't want to interrupt Simon, so I saved my questions for later.

I refocused on Simon's description. "As far as this underground world extended into the earth, the intricate architecture of the facade of the stony city, carved from the rock walls, ran deep into the crust." Simon stretched his arms. "The magnitude was unbelievably breathtaking. Massive columns hundreds of meters high framed doors that had landings perfect for winged ones to land at their doorstep. Slowly, the buildings were repopulated. Life thrived along the coast, where angels and sables lived in the beautiful steepled-roofed Birdman City."

"The hut village?" Kellan asked.

"The destroyed obelisk!" I exclaimed.

"Yes, and the San tribe lived in the jungle beyond the forked rivers. The Birdmen entered the Heart of Anzulla from the coast, while the San accessed it from the jungle's depths," Simon explained.

Kawa continued. "We found evidence of Phoenician presence already here. We brought the scientists, the advanced technology, extended lifespans, and the Omega Project, yet the Birdman and San claimed the mountain and its people were divinely created."

"The kings...and the baby gods," I whispered, awestruck.

Donali interjected. "They called Peter, a Phoenician scientist, Kuku the Birdman God, and Ishtar the Demon God. They were the gods of the mountain. Gugusan told us that his father's father described Ishtar searching for Kuku, as he had always done. Centuries later, we determined that it was because of all-time-jumping, while Apsu was destroying realities by drawing magic from its precious stones and minerals, leaving a trail of barren, desert-like Anzullas behind him. This time and place were constantly adapting and changing."

Simon continued. "After actively pursuing Apsu, we thought they had finally severed the head of the snake, granting us peace for a long time. However, as is often the case with humanity, extensive discussions and discord erupted regarding the Omega Project and men having children with men—not needing females—and producing abominations. But such was the nature of our Phoenician tradition, as

Phoenix City had consisted solely of males since Doomsday."

"When was Doomsday?" I asked Simon skeptically. I exchanged a look with Kellan. We were in a mess. No tunnel maker could fix this. I mouthed a what-the-fuck wordlessly. Kellan tipped his cup, realizing there was only a drop left, then took my cup and emptied it.

Simon's voice drew my attention. "2046 A.D."

Shaking my head, I asked, "How the fuck—"

"We need more drinks," Kellan interrupted, holding our cups so Ouro could refill them.

Simon took a deep breath. "Remember, we are talking about hundreds of years of history, while simultaneously, that same history changed for many people. Look, Phoenix's AI, Lasitor, steered us onto a timeline that was supposedly hidden from Apsu, promising Ishtar that he would help his bloodline live forever. Scientists extracted ancient texts and mathematical equations, which spurred them to recreate the Anunnaki and ultimately a superhuman."

"The golden apple!" Kellan exclaimed. "My father had said something about King Eryn and a golden apple originating from an underground laboratory in South Africa—Now I remember!"

Simon waved his hands in the air. "Wait a second! What do you know about the apple?" Donali and Kawa leaned so close to Kellan that they practically stood on their hands and knees in front of us. Callisto rolled onto his stomach, and he and Ouroboros were having a conversation. I didn't have a clue about the meaning of the apple, but I have seen drawings of apples. It sounded like these men knew what the tiny little apples drawn on the corners of my grandfather's map meant, which also meant that it was in King Solomon's Tomb. It was not part of the deciphering alphabet, and we thought it could mean anything from the original sin to absolutely nothing.

But this was not nothing.

Kellan lifted a flat hand. "Please calm down. I thought it was insignificant."

"Spit it out! We will decide if it is insignificant or not!" Ouro yelled, and Callisto pinned Kellan with an icy blue stare.

"Okay, give me a second," Kellan begged while checking in with me. My eyebrows, like everyone else's, were raised. We waited for him to speak.

"Tell them. I'd also like to know," I whispered.

Kellan nodded. "My father," he began, clearing his throat, "blamed himself for giving the apple to his friend. He thought he should have destroyed it— melted it down, never given it to Ishtar. He was obsessed with leaving a message for the kings and gods, warning them of its creation. But in his research notes—a letter was left to me—he concluded the apple was key to the solution. I only just recalled seeing it on Draxton's map, and now you mention it. That's all I know. It held greater significance," Kellan explained.

Ouro, Callisto, Simon, Donali, and Kawa grunted, slumped back, and scowled. "The solution?" Kawa whispered. Their disappointment was plain to see.

Simon sighed. "The solution? That bloody apple...they killed the AI, Lassitor, for the electronic influences he had spread into the past and future. Those codes on the tablets and the apple led to the establishment of scientific experimentation. The mathematical equations of Ishtar's DNA were blended with those of animals, amphibians, and even reptiles. That was the first generation of children born from those experimental processes, and they were called 'godlike' because they all had some magical power. Traveling back in time and stopping the experimentation would mean self-destruction and the end of this reality. Now, you say it's the solution. And I agree, for hundreds of years, male children were born in a laboratory inside an artificial womb, like almost all children born in Phoenix. But

Callisto and Atlas were babies created from both of their fathers' already spliced DNA. Thus, second-generation offspring exhibit diluted human qualities and contain various prominent DNA from amphibians, reptiles, mammals, and even birds. Who knows what else the scientists did to create King Eryn? He had powers beyond belief." Simon pointed to Callisto. A mewing sound came from the bear.

"Sorry, Callisto, but I have to tell them," Simon said apologetically. The bear grunted and lay down, covering his head with his paws, looking sad.

"Callisto, let them share this with Draxton and Kellan. It's important," Ouro said. Callisto rolled onto his back, exposing his white, furry belly. Whether submitting or playing, I couldn't tell.

"Yes, they are important," Kawa told Callisto. "They're from the future, and if they can get home —with a message with your or Atlas's help, you should help them." I nudged Kellan, giving him a look. He smiled. That was the closest we had come to confirmation of going home since arriving. We sat up, listening intently.

"As I was saying," Simon said. "The boys were the cause of the beginning of all the upheaval. It became clear why Ishtar and Kuku were called the Gods of the Mountains. They created the birdmen, the San." Simon stopped for a sip of his drink.

We waited.

He wiped his mouth with the back of his hand. "I theorize they're the forefathers of what we'll later call the supernatural—each emerging at a different point in our history."

Kawa agreed vigorously. "That's what all of us think, brother."

Simon explained further. "Anyway, when people frowned upon the king's boys for not being humanoid, but something entirely different, we became divided. Some humans wanted to euthanize them. Can you believe it? Innocent children. They even hunted them at one stage!" Simon exclaimed. Callisto cried a weird, howling sound.

"Of course, their fathers wouldn't allow it. The kings said if their children were abominations and the product of faulty DNA manipulation, then everyone was." Simon snapped his fingers. "Just like that, everything changed. After centuries, they suddenly became unhappy with the concept of kings and gods. More and more, King Eryn and Ishtar had to time-travel to stop Apsu. Years of deliberation led to the majority voting to use the time machine to move Phoenix City back to its origin, then after arriving back at the time and place they first jumped from, and after that they had planned to order Lasitor to self-destruct, as well as halting all new births and DNA splicing by killing the Omega Project, originally rolled out to prevent the demise of humans. They figured it was unnatural and unnecessary, because the human species' gene pool was being erased through unnatural selection."

Donali interrupted. "Hence their disappearance, just as the masses of Zelk had arrived."

"It's starting to make sense," I told Kellan.

The bear was now halfway outside the hut. He was on his back, eyes closed, while sunbathing the lower half of his belly with his lower legs splayed open to the sides.

"Once the dust had settled, we thought everything was finally sorted—except a few days later, the sky opened, and thousands of Zelk invaded Anzulla." Simon lifted a hand. "I'll finish, give me a second," he said as he reached for the small barrel to refill everyone's cups.

Having refilled our drinks, he sipped on his, smacked his mouth, and said, "Callisto and Atlas are brothers, the sons of our Kings Eryn and Ivan. They are the true children of Anzulla—our princes. We protected them as much as they fought to protect us. If Callisto came through the door, he would be as old as the day he left. I don't think he is even twenty years old." Simon put his cup down, crossing his two index fingers. I raised a brow at Kellan. This was getting very interesting. It looked like he was asking for time during a soccer match.

Simon finished his drink, swept the hut floor clear in front of him, and upended his cup, repeating the motion several times. The resulting marks looked a bit like the Olympic rings. Kellan and I exchanged puzzled glances, our foreheads furrowed.

"As a dragon, Atlas could see these crossings and openings between the lines. If I had to explain as short and straightforward as possible, I would say it's like ley lines, across time, points where time and realities are crossing. One of those portals identified crossed most points, and we've isolated it. Turned it into—"

"A star door?" I exclaimed excitedly, patting Kellan's knee. "Finally, I am getting my answers!"

"Um, yes...that's why he could send Callisto from one point in time to the other. Only one other person could move behind those veils of time. Ishtar. We think Atlas inherited that Anunnaki ability.

"So, that is how my father ended up in South Africa," Kellan said quietly.

"Yeah, and unfortunately, I've lost my husband like so many others before they even had the chance to escape. See, Atlas was convinced we were supposed to blow up the shield in the sky. He burned everything, and everyone who could attack tried but died. That's why he decided, as a last resort, to send his brother back in time to warn their fathers that we were failing and needed help."

Ouro spoke up. "Then, instead of falling back in time, he fell forward, bringing you, Draxton and Kellan, with him. Atlas retreated, and we think he is hibernating, sleeping, and waiting for their fathers. Callisto thinks so, too, because, like us, they have a mental connection."

"We assumed he covered the mountain with molten rock to hide it. Over time, the magnetization grew stronger, which is a good thing," Simon said, blowing out a tired breath.

I cringed as Kellan cracked his neck. The sound of his vertebrae popping made it seem like he was hurting himself. I looked away, trying to ignore it, but then I remembered a question. "One last thing, could you explain the longevity, please?" I asked politely.

"That's easy," Simon said. "First-generation placental extract. They injected it subcutaneously, in a slow-release gel. Feel!" He leaned closer, placing my hand over his heart. I felt a small, pea-sized lump.

"This is proof of how history is muddled beyond

recognition," I said to Kellan as he felt around for the implantation.

Then, I quoted Plato by standing up and making a big show of it.

"Plato's description of Atlantis. *For it is related in our records how once upon a time your State stayed the course of a mighty host, which, starting from a distant point in the Atlantic Ocean, was insolently advancing to attack the whole of Europe and Asia to boot. For the ocean there was at that time navigable; for in front of the mouth which you Greeks call, as you say, 'the pillars of Heracles, there lay an island which was larger than Libya and Asia together; and it was possible for the travelers of that time to cross from it to the other islands, and from the islands to the whole of the continent over against them which encompasses that veritable ocean. For all that we have here, lying within the mouth of which we speak, is evidently a haven having a narrow entrance; but that yonder is a real ocean, and the land surrounding it may most rightly be called, in the fullest and truest sense, a continent. Now, in this island of Atlantis, there existed a confederation of kings, of marvelous power, which held sway over all the island, and over many other islands also and parts of the continent; and, moreover, of the lands here within the Straits, they ruled over Libya as far as Egypt.*"

I blushed, then, remembering this was for show, I bowed dramatically and took my seat. There was nothing left to say or ask. I was tired of thinking, and hearing this mess made me want to run. "Pour me more wine, please, Ouro." I held my cup up, but Simon quickly filled it for me. Kellan wrapped his arms around my middle and hugged me until he finished with a kiss on my cheek.

"Draxton," Ouroboros called to grab my attention. The smile on my face disappeared as I met his severe glare. "There's no doubt that you're a sharp-witted man. Those words make no sense, yet they sound significant. Are you sure you want Simon to give you that mark? Are you certain you want to enter those buildings filled with the things they call technology, all by yourself?" Ouro's eyes shifted to Kellan. I met Kellan's gaze; he offered me an encouraging pat on my upper leg. I took a deep breath and paused to consider my response. My eyes wandered to Callisto, then further outside as I cleared my mind.

As if I were standing outside and eavesdropping on their conversation, I heard Simon say, "Ouro, that tattoo is meant for one person only. Each design has a subtle variation that can't be detected by the naked eye, only by a scanner. Kellan can't accompany him. Besides, Kellan looks too much like you. Their biometric scanners would flag Kellan before he could enter the building. Draxton is the only option. I hope he has never been scanned and added to the prison's system. It's doubtful, because no one has ever escaped the mines."

I refocused after Simon mentioned the prison. "No, I don't think I was scanned. The only thing they did was slap a collar around my neck, then they pushed me down a chute. I doubt the hover bots scanned my face. I had to kneel and put my forehead on the ground when they approached," I said, and Kellan clucked his tongue while shaking his head. "Yes, I'm going. I'll go inside alone."

"Are you certain?" Ouro asked once more.

"He already said that, didn't he?" Kellan said, lacing his fingers with mine while staring down Ouro. "Thank you, Draxton." Ouro widened his eyes at Kellan and then smiled at me.

Simon shared more valuable intel, and we planned to meet him the next day at Simon's hideout to prepare for our upcoming mission—acquiring a tunnel maker for Ouroboros.

Now, I understood why Donali and Kawa had shaved their heads and who they were. These men were from our future, living in a past that was not their own. They intended to turn me into a lookalike sympathizer, just like them—a Light Continent citizen who could infiltrate and plant a communication device. They still trusted me, and that meant everything to me.

I can't wait to get my tattoo. My grandfather would have been ecstatic if he could see it. I pictured him smiling and saying, "You did well, my boy." He would pat me on the back and shake his head, repeating in disbelief, "Entry. Pass. Trusted. Human."

CHAPTER 26
CALLISTO

AFTER RESCUING DRAXTON AND ESCORTING him to Simon's, I waited outside until Simon, a healer, stabilized him. Kellan came to find me and told me he was going to be transported home, asking me to wait at the boat since he knew I wasn't fond of flying.

That floating contraption with a propeller was falling apart and destined for a grave at the bottom of the ocean. It has a history of crashing, so why would I think it's safe? I didn't wait for another invitation. I was on the boat, claiming my spot for when Simon and his men made their way to the Dark Continent to meet with Ouroboros. While they worked on packing and getting ready to set sail, I stayed on the ship and didn't leave until we reached the Dark Continent. In the meantime, Snow had flown the airplane back home while Kellan took care of Draxton.

When we arrived at the village, I jumped off the ship and ran home to check if Kellan and Draxton were safe. Draxton was sleeping, and Kellan kept a watchful eye on him, promising me a hammer to the head if I made a noise and woke Draxton up. The whole village was warned, so I didn't take the threat too personally.

I was not a dog, but they treated me like one—and I went along with it. I exhaled slowly, my nose twitching at the aroma of roasted piglets lingering in the air. As a reward for all my hard work in saving Draxton, Sopora had been kind enough to feed me a couple, and my stomach was finally full for the first time in weeks.

"Hmmm." I let out a low rumble of dissatisfaction as I lay on my back, legs splayed open, head tilted, mouth agape, basking my balls in the dying heat of the small fire in the fireplace. I growled again languorously and opened my eyes, staring at the audacity of the dying fire, and shook my head at the orange-brown clay ceiling of the hut. The coals were dead. They shifted from fiery red to icy gray too fast. How dare they? I rolled my hefty body off my dog bed, pushed myself up to my paws, and climbed back onto the furs. Curling my front paws under my chin, I contemplated. My eyes fluttered shut, and I continued to relax.

The next morning, Draxton had woken up. I'd waited for them outside to finish their human recuperating and bonding rituals. They made a lot of noise, and I could tell they were having a great time. Kellan was thrilled to be reunited with Draxton, which brought me joy—and relief. I had felt a bit anxious at one point, being threatened with a hammer and all, but in the end, Draxton was alive and yodeling all kinds of notes. Hearing them produce ecstatic, inhuman sounds, followed by laughter and then more grunting, indicated that I had done a great job. It went on and on. They deserved to enjoy the little time they had left before heading to the Light Continent.

When they emerged from the hut, Draxton told me he was grateful to me for watching over him and bringing him back to Kellan. Then, we'd made our way to Snow's, where Ouro, Simon, and his men waited for us. As usual, they were festive yet productive. New plans were made, and the excitement was winding down, thanks to Kellan and Draxton taking their time getting reacquainted. We were all glad to hear that at least one birdman survived, and that Luci was the one who was alive. The news about the

Loursveto juice was old, but we didn't want to rain on Draxton's parade, so Ouro and I thanked him amicably.

"When we wake Atlas, we must be prepared for war!" Ouro had told me. I knew what war looked like, and I agreed with Ouroboros. If my brother woke up, we needed a plan and warriors. We couldn't let him take off and burn everything to ash again.

After the meeting, Kellan pleaded with me, his fingers curling in the air. "Let Draxton and me handle this together. You stay here with Sopora." Honestly, I'd much rather remain here with Ouro and explore the mountains instead, so to appease him, I feigned unhappiness for a moment. They are going inside the buildings on that scorching continent to meet with another informant, Zaidon Malherbe, who is Joseph Malherbe's son—the informant who was executed just days ago. So, staying here was no burden. Not at all.

The plan was underway. After that, Simon and his men had loaded up their boat, which was once again heavy with meat and vegetables to trade on the black market of Spire City. Kellan, Draxton, and Snow got back into that airplane the next morning to find Ouro a tunnel maker.

As I drifted off to sleep, I smiled to myself. I was

a badass, executing a flawless daring rescue mission. I was sure Atlas would be proud of me. As sleep claimed me, I hoped once more, with their help, that Atlas and I would be reunited. I missed my brother, and I longed for his wings wrapping around me and his warm, rumbling voice whispering in my ear. I couldn't wait for it to become real.

AND THEN I DREAMED...

Kneeling before me, Atlas nuzzled my snout and spoke to me, mind to mind. *"Callisto, look at me!"* His rumbling voice vibrated through my skull as he whispered urgently, desperation evident, with tears streaming from his flaming blue eyes. Every muscle in my body trembled as I gazed into them. They used to sparkle with mischief and life, but now they were filled with anguish, desperation, and terror— total agony.

Lowering his massive head, tendrils of smoke escaped from his nostrils, which were so large that I swear I could fit into one of them. I was rarely that small when I was with my brother, but I had to shrink myself to fit through the opening.

I couldn't fight it or pretend that everything was all right. Not when Atlas, the strongest and bravest among us, was giving up right before my eyes. Once shining iridescent blue-black, his wings were now matted with ash and dirt. His usually immaculate scales were chipped and dented, and his once-proud horns were dull and cracked. He was a shadow of his former self, all because of the war.

"*Callisto, please,*" Atlas begged, his voice raspy from spewing fire. "*You must go. Only you can.*"

I wanted to look away, to ignore his desperation and pretend I didn't see the devastation around me. But I couldn't. I had to be strong for him, for all of us. I needed to find a way to fix this, to make things right again.

With a deep breath, I leaned forward and rested my forehead against Atlas's, closing my eyes and reaching out to him through our mental connection. I would find a way to save our burning world.

My white mane was tangled with blood, and the familiar glow that used to surround it was replaced by the stench of death. My body felt hot and cold at the same time, the adrenaline from the lost battle still coursing through my veins. Embers danced around my face as I gave a crooked smile, revealing my jagged teeth dripping with blood. We'd tried our best, but ultimately, we'd failed. Now, I was our last hope.

Atlas understood me. My older brother, my best friend, protected me from the air and fought by my side through countless battles. But I could see the worry in his eyes as he looked at me. I knew what he was going to ask. I didn't want to do it, didn't want to leave him behind, but I couldn't deny his request. I tipped my chin up and down, agreeing while snorting a this-is-so-unfair way, as he gave me a knowing nod.

"*Good,*" he said, gesturing toward the door. I lifted my paw to take a step but then froze, unable to cross the threshold into the chamber beyond. My heart ached with the weight of the decision I had to make, and I couldn't help but feel torn between my loyalty to Atlas and my fear of the unknown ahead. I waved my paw at him. Atlas, a wise and gentle dragon with blue eyes that mirrored mine, urged me to enter. "*It is the only way,*" he said with conviction, yet tinged with sadness.

I had followed him through this treacherous war, trusting his guidance and wisdom. But now, as we stood outside the entrance to this time portal, apprehension and doubt crept inside me. This was indeed the only way, even if I didn't know what would become of us once I crossed that threshold.

I looked back at Atlas, searching his steady gaze. He nodded reassuringly, but I could see the pain. My last heroic act would affect him and everyone who was still alive and breathing.

Taking a deep breath, I stepped forward into the unknown.

I turned and grunted at Atlas, *"Are you sure this is the way? Do you really want me to go? If you do, I won't let you down."* I winced and let out a high-pitched, bear-like bark.

His enormous legs trembled under the strain. He was utterly exhausted, yet he still summoned the last of his magic for the portal. I was about to time travel, but I didn't know how to go where he desired.

My heart shattered as I stared at him. *"I love you, brother,"* I huffed. *"I'm going to do my best to make you proud."* I growled, lifting my other paw and sitting on my hind legs as I waved at him.

I was buying time. He curled in on himself, rolling onto his side. His belly was cut open. His innards were showing. Blood, which should have been inside him, was now running down his black-scaled hind legs. It flowed over his claws and onto the chamber floor. *He needed time to rest and heal.* I hurriedly turned and slipped through as the loud cluck-cluck noises followed. The lightning sounded like gears turning, locking me inside. I couldn't see his tears, but I heard his cries in my mind.

I lay down, waiting for the world to spin and disappear beneath me. Unable to wave, I poured out my love, promising I wouldn't fail him. Atlas soothed my mind with gentle touches, and I closed my eyes, ready to plunge into the past and warn our fathers of the approaching invasion.

He purred his thanks, as usual, but I sensed his utter exhaustion. I prayed sleep would bring healing, not death.

"*I'll be okay,*" I whispered, paws clamped over my ears as the clucking intensified. The floor rippled beneath me, the chamber filled with wind, the ground vibrating. Then, like a stone dropping into still water, I sank into the vortex, a warm, melting sensation. Light flashed and swirled. Atlas's pained grunts faded, and I growled, sensing the danger, but the wind swallowed my cry.

I felt weightless and powerless. Time pulled me along. I was falling. Atlas might die alone. My heart shattered. My tears dried. I roared.

I fell far from Atlas. My large, lumpy bear body spun uncontrollably. I swam and treaded through the air. "*I will tell them and help them!*" I roared. Thunder, wind, and lightning drowned me out. Gravity pulled me, and then I descended back to Anzulla.

AFTERWORD

resemblance to actual persons, living or dead, events, or locales is entirely coincidental.

ABOUT THE AUTHOR

"I found it surprisingly beautiful. In a brutal, horribly uncomfortable sort of way." —Tyrion Lannister to Janos Slynt.

I am a Canadian speculative Male/Male Sci-Fi Fantasy and Paranormal Romance writer. I currently reside in the Rocky Mountains of beautiful British Columbia, Canada.

My writing explores who we are, where we come from, and where we are going as a human race on Earth.

I like to weave and bubblegum questions and subjects by creating new, exciting worlds and characters. My stories are unpredictable, twisted with a dash of humor, and centered on gay characters.

You will question your existence among these worlds and wish you could escape to these places filled with foul-mouthed heroes who struggle and strive to save humankind.

I hope you've discovered something that excites and intrigues you. Please share your thoughts by leaving a review or visit www.kashelchar.com to contact me or learn about my latest works.

facebook.com/KashelCharAuthor
instagram.com/kashelchar

www.ingramcontent.com/pod-product-compliance
Lightning Source LLC
Chambersburg PA
CBHW031100030726
47496CB00002BA/308